U0165851

圖解
商業英文單字片語

◎ 李冠潔 著 ◎

書泉出版社 印行

Preface 序

▶ 在國際化程度愈加深的時侯，英文就愈顯得更重要，尤其是商業英文，更是進入福利好的外商公司，或是本地公司面試應徵錄取決戰關鍵以及升級主管必備工具。

▶ 有鑑於此，本書第一篇，作者將商業各種情境用到的主題分門別類，將相關單字通通歸在一起，如此，有助於讀者瞭解相關主題之單字片語以及相關搭配。

▶ 本書第二篇，則是商業場合常用必備的單字以及重要的詞類變化，比如deliver 和delivery，前者是動詞，而後者是名詞。兩個單字要一起學，這樣才能短時間倍增單字量。

▶ 本書第三篇，是商業場合常用必備的同義單字以及反義單字，比如allow和permit是同義單字，可以交換使用。而inferior和superior 則是反義單字。如此要仔細區別，才不會犯錯哦！

▶ 本書第四篇是形似篇，讀者務必小心使用，「錯把馮京當馬涼」或是「老鼠老虎傻傻分不清楚」，那可就不妙了。

▶ 本書第五篇是片語篇，作者將商場最實用的片語整理在一起，熟讀這些片語，活用於商場，才能立於不敗之地。

▶ 本書篇章之完整，單字片語蒐集之完整，有助於讀者在最短時間內吸收最實用最精準的英文商業用法。

Contents 目錄

聯想主題篇

第 1 篇

⊙ 聯想主題／商業生意

商業及其衍生

business ['bɪznɪs] n 商業；生意

I like doing **business** with that new firm because their deals are fair and square.
我喜歡和那家新公司做生意，因為他們提供的交易光明磊落。(do business with 和…做生意)

Business Model 商業模式

This will be our new **business model** for next year.
這是我們明年的新商業模式。

Business Weekly 商業週刊

This week's issue of **Business Weekly** analyzes current economic trend.
這期的商業週刊分析了目前的經濟走勢。

International Business Machine 國際商用機器公司

The **International Business Machine** is now one of the top corporations in the world.
國際商用機器公司現在是頂尖世界級企業之一。

商人生意人

businessman ['bɪznɪsmən] n 商業家；商人

How Jack became a successful **businessman** had much to do with his parents.
傑克能成為一個成功的商人，與他的父母大有關係。

businesswoman ['bɪznɪs,wumən] n 女商人

She's an outstanding **businesswoman** who always has innovative ideas.
她是個總是有創新點子的女實業家。

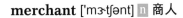

merchant ['mɝtʃənt] n 商人

This meeting gathers watch **merchants** from all over the world.
這個會議聚集了來自世界各地的手錶商。

dealer ['dilɚ] n 商人；業者

We asked the **dealer** to write down the agreement in black and white.
我們要求業者白紙黑字把協議寫下來。(in black and white 白紙黑字)

businessman

businesswoman

contract

shake hands

批發和零售

wholesale ['hol,sel] n 批發；v 批發

We **wholesale** the bags at $15 each.
我們以每件十五美元的價格批發出售這些包包。

● 聯想主題／商業生意

retail ['ritel] n 零售

We sell our products to **retail** stores.
我們將產品賣給零售商店。

retailer ['ritelɚ] n 零售商

The **retailer** finished the transaction in good time.
那位零售商及時地完成了交易。**(in good time 及時地)**

sale [sel] n 出售；銷售額

Sales are usually at their highest in spring.
通常銷售量會在春天達到最高。

sales quota 銷售配額

Bob has no idea on how to achieve his **sales quota**.
鮑伯對於如何達到銷售配額一籌莫展。

direct sale 直銷

The **direct sale** market is growing and expanding.
直銷市場正在成長和擴張。

wholesale

retail

貿易出口進口

貿易及其衍生

trade [tred] n 貿易；v 做買賣

Louis loves to trade ancient artifacts.
路易絲喜歡買賣古文物。

trading ['tredɪŋ] n 貿易

Our trading with American electronic company will start in June.
我們和美國電子公司的貿易將在六月開始。

trading company ['tredɪŋ] ['kʌmpənɪ] 貿易公司

He runs a trading company in California.
他在加州開了間貿易公司。

international trade [ˌɪntɚ'næʃənl] [tred] 國際貿易

We hope to increase international trade with Germany by 5%.
我們希望和德國的國際貿易增加百分之五。

trade secret [tred] ['sikrɪt] 商業祕密

George got fired because he let on trade secrets.
喬治被解雇是因為他洩露了商業祕密。(let on 洩露)

出口進口

export [ɪks'port] n 出口；v 出口；輸出

Taiwan exports various kinds of tea to Japan.
臺灣出口各式各樣的茶到日本。

◉ 聯想主題／貿易出口進口

container [kən'tenɚ] n 貨櫃；集裝箱

Some **containers** are still undergoing custom clearance.
有些貨櫃還在清關中。

harbor ['hɑrbɚ] n 海港

These cars are sent from the **harbor** to our exhibition center.
這些車是從港口運到我們的展示中心。

ship [ʃɪp] n 船；v 用船運

The **ships** from India with spices are still on the way.
從印度載著香料的船還在路途中。

import [ɪm'port] n 進口；v 進口

Some of the machines are **imported** from Germany, the others from Japan.
一部分機器由德國進口，其餘的來自日本。

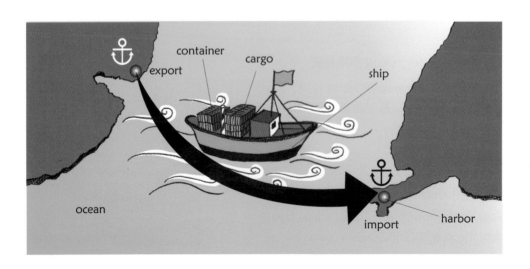

商業及其衍生

commerce ['kɑmɝs] n 商業；貿易

Today, commerce activity can also be Internet based.
現今，商業活動也可以以網路化為基礎。

commercial [kə'mɝʃəl] adj 商業的

These are commercial vehicles; therefore the mileage is much higher.
這些是商業用車所以里程數高出許多。

commercial area [kə'mɝʃəl] ['ɛrɪə] 商業區

She owns two clothing stores at the commercial area.
她在商業區擁有兩家服飾店。

commercial ad. [kə'mɝʃəl] [æd] 商業廣告

Commercial ad. has helped to increase cell phone sale significantly.
商業廣告大幅增加了手機的銷量。

交通和運輸

transport [træns'pɔrt] v 運輸

The logistic company will transport our goods to the mall.
物流公司會把我們的貨運至購物中心。

transportation [ˌtrænspɚ'teʃən] n 交通

Cars are one of the basic means of transportation.
汽車是基本交通工具之一。

● 聯想主題／交通和運輸

vehicle ['viɪkl̩] n 交通工具

Most **vehicles** yield to pedestrians.
大多數車輛都會讓路給行人。**(yield to 讓步)**

交通和運輸

航運和提單

shipping ['ʃɪpɪŋ] n 航運

The buyers will be responsible for paying the **shipping** costs.
買家將負責負擔運費。

shipment ['ʃɪpmənt] n 裝貨；裝載的貨物

The **shipment** of furniture has delayed for 3 days.
家具的運送已經延遲了三天。

B/L : bill of landing 提單

Remember to check the **B/L** carefully while picking up the goods.
記得在領貨的時候核對提單。

貨物和貨船

cargo ['kargo] **n** 貨物

Please load the **cargo** carefully as the contents are fragile.
請小心裝載貨櫃，因為裡面有易碎的內容物。

cargo ship ['kargo] [ʃɪp] **n** 貨船

This **cargo ship** was damaged from crashing the icebergs.
這艘貨櫃船因為和冰山撞擊而受損。

ship [ʃɪp] **n** 船；艦

The **ships** will always dock at the pier during high tide.
漲潮時，船隻總會停靠在碼頭邊。(high tide 高潮；漲潮)

shipwreck ['ʃɪp,rɛk] **n** 海難

Linda survived the terrible **shipwreck**.
琳達在可怕的沉船事件中活了下來。

交通和運輸

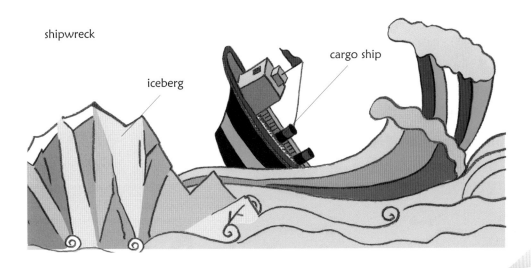

shipwreck

iceberg

cargo ship

財務和金融

finance [faɪ'næns] n 財政；金融

I am the one who's in charge of the store's **finance**.
我是這間店的財務負責人。

⌄
⌄

financial [faɪ'nænʃəl] adj 金融的

The annual **financial** report is being checked.
年度財經報告正在被審閱。

⌄
⌄

financial statement [faɪ'nænʃəl] ['stetmənt] 財務報表

This will do for now. I will see your **financial statement** later.
目前這樣就可以了，我晚點再看你的財務報告。

⌄
⌄

financial status [faɪ'nænʃəl] ['stetəs] 財務狀況

In view of your **financial status**, we cannot grant you the loan.
由您的財務狀態看來，我們不能夠批准這筆貸款。

⌄
⌄

financial crisis [faɪ'nænʃəl] ['kraɪsɪs] 金融危機

The managers have all been on the alert for possible **financial crisis**.
經理們都在保持警惕，以防發生金融危機。

經濟及其衍生

economy [ɪ'kɑnəmɪ] n 經濟；節約

The war greatly damaged the **economy**.
戰爭重創經濟。

⌄
⌄

economic [ˌikəˈnɑmɪk] adj 經濟的

After years of recession, economic growth seems harder and harder.
在好幾年的不景氣後，經濟成長看似越來越困難。

economic crisis [ˌikəˈnɑmɪk] [ˈkraɪsɪs] 經濟危機

This company was still in good condition after the economic crisis.
經濟危機過後，這家公司依然保持良好的狀態。

economic depression [ˌikəˈnɑmɪk] [dɪˈprɛʃən] 經濟蕭條

We are proud of the fact that our company survived the economic depression.
我們對於公司能夠撐過經濟蕭條時期而自豪。

economic development [ˌikəˈnɑmɪk] [dɪˈvɛləpmənt] 經濟發展

Children's pocket money increased in accordance with the economic development.
孩子們的零用錢隨著經濟發展而提高了。

財務經濟

發展及其衍生

develop [dɪˈvɛləp] v 發展；生長

It will take years to develop a commercial area.
建設一個商業區將會花好幾年的時間。

developing [dɪˈvɛləpɪŋ] adj 發展中的

The developing market of green energy technology increases employment opportunity.
綠能科技的市場發展增加了就業機會。

◎ 聯想主題／財務經濟

developing country [dɪ'vɛləpɪŋ] ['kʌntrɪ] 發展中國家

It was agreed that the debt of some developing countries could be written off.
一些發展中國家的債務被同意得到消除。(write off 取消；勾銷)

developed [dɪ'vɛləpt] adj 發達的

This well-developed company is in the world's 10 biggest companies.
這間發展良好的公司是全世界前十名最大的公司。

developed country [dɪ'vɛləpt] ['kʌntrɪ] 已開發國家

Our object is to catch up with developed countries by next year.
我們的目標是於明年達到已開發國家的水準。(catch up with 趕上；追趕)

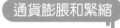

development [dɪ'vɛləpmənt] n 發展

The development in Internet shopping impacted our sales in physical shops.
網路購物的發展影響了我們實體店面的銷售。

通貨膨脹和緊縮

inflation [ɪn'fleʃən] n 通貨膨脹

We cannot stop inflation. In other words, prices will keep going up.
我們不能阻止通貨膨脹，換句話說，物價還會繼續上漲。

deflation [dɪ'fleʃən] n 通貨緊縮

We are experiencing deflation in the selling price of fruits.
我們正在經歷水果售價的通貨緊縮。

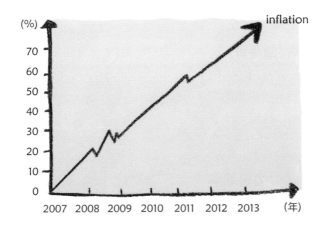

公司企業和聯盟

company ['kʌmpənɪ] n 公司；同伴

Our **company** consists of 200 members.
我們公司由兩百名員工組成。(consist of 組成)

firm [fɝm] n 公司

Due to financial crisis, many **firms** were bankrupted.
由於金融危機，許多公司破產了。

enterprise ['ɛntɚˌpraɪz] n 企業

The ranking of the top 500 **enterprises** of the world is changing all the time.
世界五百強企業的排名一直都在變化。(all the time 一直)

group [grup] n 集團；團隊

I was hoping you would join our **group**.
我希望你可以加入我們的團隊。

財務經濟 ⇣ 公司企業組織

聯想主題／公司企業組織

association [ə,sosɪ'eʃən] n 聯盟

The economic **association** published a paper analyzing economic policy.
經濟學會發表了一篇分析經濟政策的文章。

總部和分部

headquarters ['hɛd'kwɔrtɚz] n 總部

Most companies locate their **headquarters** at the capital city.
大多數的公司都把總部設在首都。

main office [men] ['ɔfɪs] 總公司

You need to go to the **main office** to get your documents.
你需要到總公司去取資料。

branch [bræntʃ] n 分部

You can deposit the check at any of the bank's **branches**.
你可以在任何銀行分行存入支票。

subdivision [sʌbdə'vɪʒən] n 支部

Every **subdivision** under the department of commerce has about 50 staff.
商務部底下的每個單位有大約五十名員工。

division [də'vɪʒən] n 部門

This design **division** is newly created to expand the market.
這個設計部門是為了擴展市場而新設立的。

bureau ['bjuro] n 局

The Bureau of Trade implements a new consumer protection law.
貿易局實行了一條新的消費者保護法。

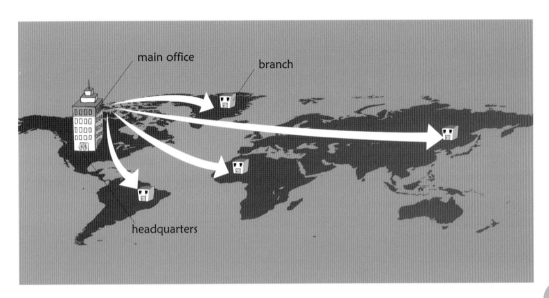

main office

branch

headquarters

建立倒塌

establish [ə'stæblɪʃ] v 建立

The government established a new policy to decrease tariff.
政府制定了減低關稅的新政策。

establishment [ɪs'tæblɪʃmənt] n 確定

Establishment of partnership with foreign companies is our next goal.
與外國公司建立合作關係是我們的下一個目標。

公司企業組織

found [faʊnd] v 建立

The consumer association was **founded** 40 years ago.
消費者協會是在四十年前成立的。

⇊
⇊

foundation [faʊn'deʃən] n 基礎

Heavy metal is the **foundation** of industrialization.
重金屬是工業化的基礎。(the foundation of …的基礎)

⇊
⇊

collapse [kə'læps] v 倒塌；n 倒塌

The financial **collapse** in Greece affects the rest of Europe.
希臘經濟崩盤影響了其他歐洲國家。

工廠和製造商

factory ['fæktərɪ] n 工廠

Great waste is the cause of the **factory's** bankruptcy.
巨大資源浪費是導致這家工廠破產的原因。

⇊

manufacture [ˌmænjə'fæktʃɚ] v 製造

This company **manufactures** cars, vans, trucks and so forth.
這家公司生產轎車、小貨車和卡車等等。(and so forth等等)

材料和生產

material [mə'tɪrɪəl] n 原料；adj 物質的

We have stored a large quantity of information here, ranging from **materials** to clients.
我們這裡儲存大量資訊，涵蓋範圍由產品原料至客戶資料。

⇊
⇊

公司企業組織 工廠生產

raw material [rɔ] [məˈtɪrɪəl] 原材料；原料

Raw material rises in price by 2%.
原物料價格上漲百分之二。

produce [prəˈdjus] v 生產

Aside from cars, the factory also produces bicycles.
除了汽車以外，這間工廠還生產腳踏車。

product [ˈprɑdəkt] n 產品

The client is far from being satisfied with the product.
顧客對產品很不滿意。(be satisfied with滿意)

production [prəˈdʌkʃən] n 生產；產量

Please ensure the quality of clothing production.
請確保服裝生產的品質。

production line [prəˈdʌkʃən] [laɪn] 生產線

One of the workers at the production line made a mistake.
其中一個在生產線的工人犯了錯。(make a mistake犯錯)

assembly line [əˈsɛmblɪ] [laɪn] 裝配線

Mechanization at the assembly line reduces production time.
裝配線的機械化減少了生產時間。

產品和商品

product ['prɑdəkt] n 產品

This is our number one selling **product**.
這是我們銷售第一的產品。

⌄
⌄

goods [gʊdz] n 商品

David threatened to switch to another delivery company if **goods** are delayed again.
大衛威脅說如果送貨再次延遲，就要更換快遞公司。

⌄
⌄

commodity [kə'mɑdətɪ] n 日用品

You can minimize trading costs by selling the **commodities** directly.
你可以通過直接銷售商品來減少銷售成本。

⌄
⌄

warehouse ['wɛr,haʊs] n 倉庫

Walls were built around the **warehouse** in case of theft.
倉庫周圍建起了高牆以防盜竊。

warehouse

product

truck

品質數量

quality ['kwɑlətɪ] n 品質

To customers, quality and price are the most important of all things.
對於顧客來說，品質和價格是最重要的。

quantity ['kwɑntətɪ] n 數量

The output quantity has increased by twenty percent since David became our CEO.
自從大衛成為我們的總裁後，公司產量提高了百分之二十。

服務和保證

serve [sɝv] v 服務；為…服務

We look forward to another chance to serve you.
我們期待再次為您服務。

service ['sɝvɪs] n 服務

John is always at his boss' service.
約翰隨時準備聽從老闆吩咐。(at one's service聽候某人吩咐)

promise ['prɑmɪs] v 許諾；n 保證

The seller promised to answer for the computer he sells.
銷售員承諾會對賣出的電腦負責。(answer for負責)

guarantee [ˌgærən'ti] v 保證；n 保證書；保證

We offer life time guarantee for all the air conditioners.
所有的冷氣我們都有提供終生保固。

工廠生產

服務和抱怨

warrant ['wɔrənt] v 擔保

I warrant you the packaging of products will be done soon.
我向你保證產品的包裝很快就會完成。

warranty ['wɔrəntɪ] n 擔保；授權

You can receive free service within warranty period.
你可以在保固期內得到免費的服務。

抱怨和退款

complain [kəm'plen] v 抱怨；發牢騷

He complains all the time.
他一直在抱怨。

refund [rɪ'fʌnd] v 退款；n 退還

You did not deliver the goods on time, so I am asking for a refund.
你們並沒有按時送貨，因此我要求你們退款。(ask for a refund要求退款)

pay back [pe] [bæk] 償還；報答

Surely enough, Mary will ask Jane to pay back the money she lent her.
瑪麗無疑地會叫珍還錢。

領導帶領

lead [lid] v 引導；領路

Her unhappiness led to depression.
她的痛苦導致了憂鬱症發作。(lead to導致)

leader ['lidɚ] n 領導

President Lincoln will never be forgotten as a great leader.
作為一名偉大的領袖，林肯總統將永不被遺忘。

leadership ['lidɚʃɪp] n 領導能力

We are looking for someone with strong leadership.
我們正在尋找一位領導能力強的人。

mislead [mɪs'lid] v 誤導

This advertisement misleads consumers on the effect of the cleanser.
這廣告誤導了消費者關於洗面乳的功效。

misleading [mɪs'lidɪŋ] adj 誤導的

The grocery store removed all the misleading price tags.
這家雜貨店把所有令人誤解的價格標籤都拿掉了。

leading ['lidɪŋ] adj 領導的

The leading supplier of coffee beans is joining the conference.
咖啡豆的領先供應商會參加討論會。

conduct [kən'dʌkt] v 引導；帶領

The research should be conducted in line with the professor's instructions.
研究應該根據教授的指示進行。(in line with 符合)

conductor [kən'dʌktɚ] n 管理者；領導者

I am meeting the conductor of this project tomorrow.
我明天會和這個企劃的領導者見面。

⊙ 聯想主題／領導管理

控制和管理

control [kən'trol] Ⅴ 控制；ｎ 控制

Some people believe that this world is under God's **control**.
有些人認為這個世界由上帝掌控。

handle ['hændl] Ⅴ 處理

This case is too hard for a trainee to **handle**.
這個案子對實習生來說太難處理了。

administer [əd'mɪnəstɚ] Ⅴ 管理

She learned to **administer** a corporation within a short time.
她在短時間內就學會管理一家公司。

『control』必備片語

under control 處於控制之下

It was easy for the military officer to keep the battles **under control**.
對於軍官而言，要控制戰役的局勢很容易。

out of control 失去控制

The fire was **out of control** when the firemen arrived.
消防隊員抵達時，火勢完全不受控制。

in control of 掌控著；控制著

While his parents were out, Tom was **in control of** his siblings.
當父母出門時，弟妹都由湯姆掌管。

quality control 品質控管

Poor **quality control** is the main drawback of your factory; it holds back your production.
你們工廠的主要弱點是品質控管不夠嚴格，這降低了你們的產量。

運轉調整

run [rʌn] **v** 跑；運行

She **runs** Chinese restaurants in many Asian countries.
她在好幾個亞洲國家都有經營中國餐館。

operate ['ɑpə,ret] **v** 運作

The jewelry store is **operated** by a family.
那家珠寶店是由一家族所經營的。

operation [,ɑpə'reʃən] **v** 操作；手術

He overheard there's something wrong with the company's **operation**.
他偷聽到公司在運作上有些問題。(something wrong with 有問題)

regulate ['rɛgjə,let] **v** 管理

The scale of mining is strictly **regulated** by the government.
政府嚴格管控採礦的規模。

regulation [,rɛgjə'leʃən] **n** 規定

The director repeated the company's **regulations** over and over again.
主管一遍又一遍的重申公司規章。(over and over again 一次又一次)

『run』必備片語

run away 跑開

Frank attached a rope to his dog's collar in case it **ran away**.
弗蘭克在狗的項圈上繫了一根繩子，以防牠逃走。

run over 撞倒輾過；快速瀏覽

Although Dan was very careful, he still **ran over** the stray dog.
雖然丹很小心駕駛，還是輾到了那條流浪狗。

run through 穿越

The Yangtze River **runs through** China from west to east.
長江自西向東穿越中國。

run errands 跑腿

Tom always **runs errands** for his colleagues.
湯姆總是為他的同事們跑腿。

run wild 恣意妄為

Jack allowed his children to **run wild**.
傑克任憑孩子們撒野。

run into debt 負債

Lily was not careful with her spending habits and **ran into debt**.
莉莉沒有注意自己花錢的習慣，結果負債了。

run a risk 冒險

He had to **run a risk** of making that investment.
他必須冒險進行投資。

driver

run over

wheel

檢查監督

check [tʃɛk] Ⅴ 檢查；ⁿ 檢查

The worker was asked to double **check** his work every day.
工人被要求每天仔細檢查自己的工作內容。

verify ['vɛrə,faɪ] Ⅴ 證明

Remember to **verify** your shipping address before checking out.
記得在結帳前確認你的郵寄地址。

supervise ['supɚ,vaɪz] Ⅴ 監督

His job is to **supervise** the quality of toy production.
他的工作是監督玩具生產的品質。

oversee ['ovɚ'si] v 監視

He **oversees** the resort's running and development.
他監督渡假村的營運和發展。

『check』必備片語

in check 檢查中

He was asked to stay at the counter when his baggage was **in check**.
行李檢查期間他被要求留在櫃檯。

check in 辦理登記手續；簽到

You have to **check in** before you enter college.
進入大學之前你必須先登記。

check out 結帳離去；辦妥手續離去

They **checked out** ten minutes ago.
他們十分鐘前就結帳離開了。

cash the check 兌現支票

On **cashing the check**, John was told that it was a fake one.
去兌現支票的時候，約翰被告知那是一張假支票。

keep a close check on 密切注意

The supervisor would like to **keep a close check on** the company's expenditure.
管理者打算密切關注公司的開支。

經銷和授權

distribute [dɪ'strɪbjut] Ⅴ 分配；分發

Flyers are **distributed** to make the event known to the public.
分發傳單是為了讓大眾知道這個活動。

distribute

potential customer

flyer

distributor [dɪ'strɪbjətɚ] ｎ 分配者

We are the only **distributor** of incense in this area.
我們是這一帶唯一的薰香批發商。

distribution [,dɪstrə'bjuʃən] ｎ 分配

Unequal **distribution** of wealth is commonly seen around the world.
財富的分配不均在全世界都是常見的。

聯想主題／經銷和銷售

distribution center [ˌdɪstrə'bjuʃən] ['sɛntɚ] 配送中心

The closest distribution center is 5 miles away.
最近的配送中心在五英哩外。

authorization [ˌɔθərə'zeʃən] n 授權

What documents are needed to apply for employment authorization?
申請工作許可需要什麼資料呢？

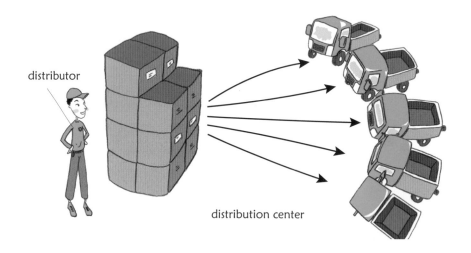

distributor

distribution center

市場及其衍生

market ['mɑrkɪt] n 市場

The first thing we should do after we enter a new market is to build up a good reputation.
進入新的市場之後，我們應該做的第一件事情是建立良好的聲譽。

market share ['mɑrkɪt] [ʃɛr] 市場占有率

Our market share in biotechnology industry is about 4%.
我們在生物科技產業的市場占有率是百分之四。

marketing ['mɑrkɪtiŋ] n 銷售

The **marketing** manager is very experienced in apparel market.
這位行銷經理對服裝市場很有經驗。

market capitalization ['mɑrkɪt] [ˌkæpətlə'zeʃən] 市值

Here's a list of companies ranked by their **market capitalization**.
這是一張以公司市值來排名的清單。

circulate ['sɝkjəˌlet] v 使傳播；發行

The rumor of the well-known company's bankruptcy **circulates** quickly.
那家知名公司倒閉的謠言傳播的很快。

circulation [ˌsɝkjə'leʃən] n 傳播；流傳

Circulation of forged notes has dropped tremendously.
偽鈔的流通已大幅減少。

銷售買賣

sale [sel] n 銷售；行銷

There is a villa around the corner for **sale**.
前面拐角處有一幢別墅要出售。(for sale 待售)

sell [sɛl] v 銷售

The ticket to the football game is **sold** out.
足球比賽的票已售完。(be sold out 售完)

● 聯想主題／經銷和銷售

bargain ['bɑrgɪn] n 買賣；便宜貨

The company hoped to strike a **bargain** during the negotiation.
公司希望在談判時達成協議。(strike a bargain達成協議)

buy [baɪ] v 買

We have been **buying** raw materials from China.
我們一直以來都向中國購買原物料。

receipt [rɪ'sit] n 收據

A **receipt** will be mailed to you along with the goods.
收據會和貨品一起寄給你。

invoice ['ɪnvɔɪs] n 發票

You will need the **invoice** for an exchange.
你需要發票才能換貨。

銷售點

shop [ʃɑp] n 商店

Our duty-free **shop** at the airport sells cosmetics.
我們在機場的免稅商店專賣化妝品。(duty-free shop免稅商店)

store [stor] v 貯存；n 商店

Aso Shoes is a well-known chain **store** in Taiwan.
阿瘦皮鞋是臺灣有名的連鎖商店。(well-known有名的)

jewelry store ['dʒuəlrɪ] [stor] 珠寶店

The three burglars ran out from the jewelry store carrying stolen goods.
三名盜賊帶著贓物從珠寶店跑出來。

drugstore ['drʌg,stor] n 雜貨店；藥局

Now contact lenses can be bought from drugstores.
現在隱形眼鏡可以在藥局買到了。(contact lenses隱形眼鏡)

jewelry store

necklace

diamond

經銷和銷售

買主和賣主

買主客戶和消費者

customer ['kʌstəmə] n 顧客

This customer is hard to deal with; you'd better not argue with her.
這個顧客很難對付，你最好不要和她理論。

consumer [kən'sjumə] n 消費者

Designs of products are changed to cater consumers' preferences.
改變產品的設計來迎合消費者的喜好。

◎ 聯想主題／買主和賣主

client ['klaɪənt] n 委託人

Our company used to have a lot of **clients**, but not anymore now.
以前我們公司有很多的客戶，但現在沒有了。

buyer ['baɪɚ] n 購買者

Buyers' personal information should not be disclosed to third party.
買家的個人資料不應該公開給第三方。

purchaser ['pɝtʃəsɚ] n 買主

Discounts are only offered to the first 15 **purchasers**.
折扣只提供給前十五名購買者。

purchase ['pɝtʃəs] v 購買

Although the car looks old, it had just been **purchased** from the retailer.
雖然車子看起來舊舊的，但是它是剛從零售商那裡買來的。

賣主和推銷員

seller ['sɛlɚ] n 銷售者

I only buy things from **sellers** with good reputation.
我只向信譽好的賣家買東西。

merchant ['mɝtʃənt] n 商人

We have also invited jewelry **merchants** to the conference.
我們也邀請了珠寶商來參加會議。

vendor ['vɛndɚ] n 小販

This vendor sells all kinds of antiques.
這個小販賣各式各樣的古董。

street vendor [strit] ['vɛndɚ] 攤販

Street vendors attract customers with colorful food carts.
路邊攤利用色彩豐富的餐車吸引顧客。

salesman ['selzmən] n 推銷員

I heard that the new company is hard up for salesmen.
我聽說那間新公司暫缺銷售員。(be hard up for缺…)

saleswoman ['selz,wumən] n 女店員

This saleswoman achieved the greatest sales performance in the store.
這名女銷售員達到了店內的最高銷售成績。

salesperson ['selz,pɚsn] n 店員

A good salesperson knows the best choices for customers.
好的銷售員知道最適合顧客的選擇。

sales representative [selz] [rɛprɪ'zɛntətɪv] 銷售代表

There's a sales representative visiting our company this afternoon.
今天下午會有個銷售代表來拜訪我們公司。

● 聯想主題／買主和賣主

street vendor
seller

consumer
customer

買主和賣主

付款和佣金

pay [pe] v 支付

She left the store after she **paid** for the mobile.
她支付手機費後便離開了店家。(pay for支付)

payment ['pemənt] n 付款

We accept **payments** by cash, debit card or credit card.
我們接受現金、轉帳卡或者信用卡付款。

commission [kə'mɪʃən] n 佣金

Sales **commission** for every product here is 5%.
這裡每樣商品的銷售佣金是百分之五。

老闆和高階主管

boss [bɔs] n 老闆

I have a permission from boss to take a day off.
我得到老闆的允許可以放一天假。

president ['prɛzədənt] n 主席；董事長

The president of company liked to make his employees feel like they were part of a big family rather than just workers.
公司的董事長喜歡讓員工感覺他們是大家庭的一部分，而不僅僅是工作者。

general manager ['dʒɛnərəl] ['mænɪdʒɚ] 總經理

The general manager is on a business trip tomorrow.
總經理明天要出差。

CEO **Chief Executive Officer** 執行長(= CEO)

The CEO sets a direction on which market to enter and expand.
執行長設定新方向，擬定該進入、擴充哪個市場。

CFO **Chief Financial Officer** 財務長(= CFO)

The CFO holds a full record of company's earnings and expenses.
財務長握有公司收入和支出的完整紀錄。

經理主管

manager ['mænɪdʒɚ] n 經理

The manager is impressed with our efficiency in completing tasks.
經理對我們完成工作的效率印象深刻。

manage ['mænɪdʒ] v 管理

Business operators should know how to **manage** risks.
經商者應該要知道如何管理風險。

managerial [ˌmænə'dʒɪrɪəl] adj 管理人的

Staff from higher **managerial** levels are the main decision makers.
比較高管理階層的職員是主要的決策者。

management ['mænɪdʒmənt] n 管理

Due to poor **management**, the factory is on the brink of bankruptcy.
由於經營不善，該工廠瀕臨破產。

人員職員和雇主

personnel [ˌpɝsn'ɛl] n 人員

She is in charge of **personnel** in that company.
她在那家公司負責人事管理。**(in charge of 負責；主管)**

clerk [klɝk] n 職員

Counter **clerks** can help you with checking out the items.
櫃檯人員可以幫你將商品結帳。

employee [ˌɛmplɔɪ'i] n 受雇者

George is good at inspiring his **employees**.
喬治很善於激勵他的員工。

employer [ɪm'plɔɪə˞] n 雇主

Employers are responsible of providing safe working environment.
雇主有責任提供安全的工作環境。

『employment』和『unemployment』

employment [ɪm'plɔɪmənt] n 雇用；受雇

A large office requires the employment of many people.
一個大公司需要雇用很多人員。

be out of employment 失業

Many were out of employment during the Great Depression.
許多人在大蕭條時期都失業了。

fall out of employment 失業

In that country, many workers fall out of employment every month.
在那個國家，每個月都有很多工人失業。

unemployment [ˌʌnɪm'plɔɪmənt] n 失業；失業狀態

Many people will face unemployment if the factory closes down.
那間工廠如果關閉，很多人要面臨失業。

unemployment rate 失業率

The unemployment rate will rise to a double-digit in time.
再過一陣子，失業率將攀升至二位數。

應徵面試

resume [ˌrɛzjuˈme] n 履歷

I have included all related working experiences in my **resume**.
我把所有相關的工作經驗都寫進我的履歷表了。

applicant [ˈæpləkənt] n 申請人

All of the job **applicants** were present for the interview.
所有的求職者都出席了面試。

appointment [əˈpɔɪntmənt] n 約會；約定

I had an **appointment** with Manager Li.
我和李經理約好了。

interview [ˈɪntəˌvju] v 面談

I felt bad when the **interview** was over.
我在面試結束後感覺很糟。

interviewee [ˌɪntəvjuˈi] n 被接見人

Most of the **interviewees** this time are fresh graduates.
這次大部分的面試者都是社會新鮮人。

interviewer [ˈɪntəvjuə] n 接見者

Be yourself when you are facing the **interviewers**.
面對面試官時要保持自然。

recruit [rɪˈkrut] v 雇用

We have **recruited** 10 staff from abroad.
我們雇用十名海外員工。

interviewer

resume

applicant
interviewee

interview

雇用任用

admit [əd'mɪt] v 承認；准許進入

You will need a visa to be **admitted** into the United States.
你需要簽證才能進入美國。

an admission notice 入場通知

I have received **an admission notice** from the business school.
我收到了商學院的錄取通知書。

a job acceptance letter 工作接受信

She sent out **a job acceptance letter** by email.
她以電子郵件發送出工作接受信。

hire [haɪr] v 租借；雇用

Mr. Robert decided to **hire** a bodyguard when he went to Africa for business.
當羅伯特先生去非洲做生意時，他決定雇用一名保鑣。

聯想主題／面試雇用

employ [ɪmˈplɔɪ] v 雇用

The foreign company **employs** more than 1000 workers.
這家外商公司雇用了超過一千名員工。

newcomer [ˈnjuˈkʌmɚ] n 新來的人

Newcomers are encouraged to give creative ideas.
新人被鼓勵提供有創意的點子。

薪水薪資

wage [wedʒ] n 薪水

Wages are paid on the 5th of every month.
薪水在每個月五日支付。

salary [ˈsælərɪ] n 工資

John's **salary** was inconsistent with his expectation.
工資和約翰的期望相距甚遠。

get paid 獲得報酬

The employees ought to **get paid** for working overtime.
員工們超時工作應該領取薪水。

well-paid 高報酬

John loves his job although it's neither easy nor **well-paid**.
約翰熱愛他的工作，雖然他的工作既不輕鬆，報酬也不高。

面試雇用

income ['ɪn,kʌm] n 收入

I have no income for 6 months.
我已經六個月沒有收入了。

income tax ['ɪn,kʌm] [tæks] 所得稅

I have to pay income tax for my overseas earnings, too.
我也需要為我海外的收入付所得稅。

解雇開除

fire [faɪr] n 火；v 開除

Peter was always absent minded, so the boss fired him at last.
彼得總是心不在焉，因此最後老闆解雇了他。

dismiss [dɪs'mɪs] v 解雇；開除

The dismissed clerk wandered somewhere about the firm.
被解雇的職員在公司附近轉來轉去。

dismissal [dɪs'mɪsḷ] n 解散

After the dismissal of some workers, our workload has increased.
在解雇了一些員工後，我們的工作量變多了。

lay off 解雇

Going out of business, Jim' company is about to lay off some employees.
面臨倒閉，吉姆的公司打算解雇部分員工。

● 聯想主題／解雇離職

離職辭職

quit [kwɪt] Ⅴ 放棄；離開；退出

He will **quit** his job soon to make way for the younger generation.
他不久將要辭職，好讓位給新一代。

resign [rɪ'zaɪn] Ⅴ 辭職

It is said that Mr. Brown is going to **resign** within a week.
聽說布朗先生將在一週內辭職。

resignation [ˌrɛzɪg'neʃən] � 辭職

We need to find a substitution after the accountant's **resignation**.
我們需要找人代替辭職的會計師。

a two-week notice 為期兩週的通知

You need to give **a two-week notice** before resignation.
你需要在辭職前兩週提出通知。

退休

retirement [rɪ'taɪrmənt] Ⅺ 退休

Ann no longer cares about what goes around in the company after her **retirement**.
安在退休之後便不再關心公司的事了。

retire [rɪ'taɪr] Ⅴ 退休

He **retired** after working 30 years for the company.
他在為公司工作三十年後退休了。

解雇離職

tire [taɪr] v 使疲倦

A week's participation in the exhibition tired him.
參加一整個星期的展覽會讓他感到很疲倦。

tired [taɪrd] adj 疲倦的；厭煩的

The manager is tired of correcting the newcomer's mistakes.
經理對改正新人的錯誤感到厭煩了。

工作及其衍生

jobless ['dʒɑblɪs] adj 失業的

The government offers trainings for jobless people.
政府為失業人士提供訓練。

job [dʒɑb] n 工作

Having failed to get the job made me sad for the whole week.
沒有得到這份工作使我傷心了一整個星期。

work [wɝk] n 工作；v 工作

Tom walked back and forth in the room, thinking about his work.
湯姆在屋裡來回走動，思考著工作上的事情。(think about 思考)

workshop ['wɝk,ʃɑp] n 工廠

We plan to arrange a handcraft workshop to attract crowds.
我們計畫安排一個手工藝工作坊來吸引人群。

○ 聯想主題／工作和任務

工作相關搭配用法

job creation [dʒɑb] [krɪ'eʃən] 創造就業機會

The government is working on **job creation**.
政府正致力於創造工作機會。

❤

job description [dʒɑb] [dɪ'skrɪpʃən] 工作描述

A good **job description** will find a company right candidates.
好的職務說明會為公司找到對的求職者。

❤

job hunter [dʒɑb] ['hʌntɚ] 求職者

This workshop helps **job hunters** who struggle to find a job.
這個工作坊幫助那些努力找工作的求職者。

任務和責任

task [tæsk] n 任務

Although the work here is done, we have to carry on another **task**.
雖然這裡的工作已經結束，我們還是得繼續進行下一項任務。

❤

duty ['djutɪ] n 責任

Stop complaining about him, he was just doing his **duty**.
不要再抱怨他了，他不過是在履行他的職責。(complain about 抱怨)

responsibility [rɪ,spɑnsə'bɪlətɪ] n 責任

He took the **responsibility** for the car crash.
他為撞車事件負起了責任。(take the responsibility 負責；承擔責任)

❤

工作和任務

044

responsible [rɪ'spɑnsəbl] `adj` **負責的**

I am **responsible** for processing orders placed by customers.
我負責處理客戶下的訂單。

be responsible for 對…負責

In my judgment, the director should **be responsible for** the accident.
依我看，主管應該對這起事故負責。

辦公室相關搭配用法

office ['ɔfɪs] `n` **辦公**

She walked into the **office**, smiling.
她笑著走進了辦公室。(walk into 走進)

office building ['ɔfɪs] ['bɪldɪŋ] **辦公大樓**

Our company is located at this **office building**.
我們的公司位於這棟辦公大樓裡。

office hours ['ɔfɪs] [aʊrz] **辦公時間**

You may call this number for assistance during **office hours**.
你可以在辦公時間打這個號碼尋求協助。

office equipment ['ɔfɪs] [ɪ'kwɪpmənt] **辦公設備**

We need a replacement for the **office equipment**.
我們需要更換辦公室設備。

工作和任務

辦公室

office party [ˈɔfɪs] [ˈpɑrtɪ] 辦公室舞會

We are holding an office party next week.
我們下個星期會舉辦辦公室聚會。

辦公室設備用品

cubicle [ˈkjubɪkl̩] n 小隔間

She's sitting at the cubicle right next to the window.
她就坐在窗戶旁邊的小隔間。

partition [pɑrˈtɪʃən] n 隔板；v 隔成

The large room is usually partitioned into two meeting rooms.
大房間通常被隔成兩間會議室。

stationery [ˈsteʃənˌɛrɪ] n 文具

Please buy office stationery from the wholesaler.
請向批發商購買辦公室的文具。

telephone [ˈtɛləˌfon] n 電話

The telephone rang when I was on the point of leaving.
我正要離開的時候，電話就響了。(on the point of 正要…的時候)

fax [fæks] n 傳真機

You may give us your feedback via email or fax.
你可以以電子郵件或傳真的方式給我們你的意見。

xerox ['zɪrɑks] n 靜電影印機

The office needs several more **Xerox** machines.
辦公室裡需要多幾台影印機。

辦公室同事

coworker ['ko,wɝkɚ] n 同事

I have a **coworker** who always screws things up.
我有個常把事情搞砸的同事。

colleague ['kɑlig] n 同事

Some **colleagues** are thinking of quitting for another company.
一些同事想跳槽到另一家公司。

staff [stæf] n 職員

The firm cut down on **staff** so as to reduce cost.
公司為了降低成本而裁員。(cut down 砍掉)

partner ['pɑrtnɚ] n 夥伴

Nobody knows which company will be chosen as Intel's **partner**.
沒有人知道英代爾會挑選哪家公司來當合作夥伴。

辦公室檔案資料整理

memorandum [,mɛmə'rændəm] n 備忘錄

A **memorandum** of the meeting was made to the manager.
做了一份會議的備忘錄給經理。

辦公室

◉ 聯想主題／辦公室

memo ['mɛmo] n 備忘錄

Please read the **memo** of agreement again before signing.
請在簽名前再讀過這份合約備忘錄。

document ['dɑkjəmənt] n 文件

These **documents** should be filed according to their categories.
這些文件應該要照各自的類別歸檔。

portfolio [port'folɪˌo] n 資料夾

Give me a product **portfolio** with the latest market share.
給我含有最新市場占有率的產品目錄。

in-tray [ɪntre] n 收文盤

The **in-tray** on boss's desk is already full.
老闆桌上的收文盤已經滿了。

out-tray ['auttre] n 發文盤

Letters to be mailed out will be placed in **out-tray**.
要寄出去的信件會放在發文盤。

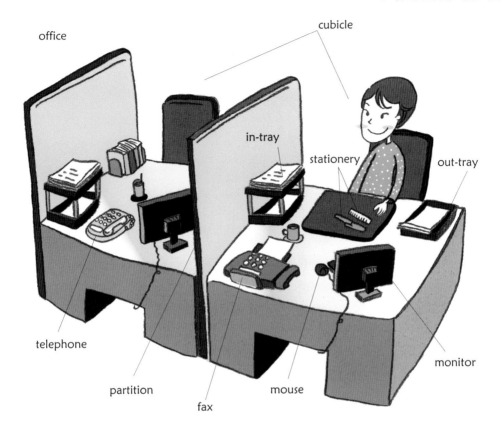

office
cubicle
in-tray
stationery
out-tray
telephone
partition
fax
mouse
monitor

辦公室常見片語

call in sick 打電話請病假

He called in sick today.
今天他打電話請病假。

absence of mind 心不在焉

Jessica's absence of mind during the meeting angered the boss.
潔西嘉開會時心不在焉的樣子讓老闆很生氣。

辦公室

◉ 聯想主題／會議和約會

hang up 掛斷電話

How long have you been talking over the phone before you hang up?
在掛斷電話前，你講了多久電話？

⌄
⌄

be late for work 上班遲到

Because of the storm, more than half of employees in the office were late for work.
辦公室裡有一半以上的職員因為暴風雨遲到了。

約會及其衍生

appointment [ə'pɔɪntmənt] n 約會；任命；職位

Did you make an appointment to meet with our boss?
你有和我們老闆預約見面嗎？

⌄
⌄

appoint [ə'pɔɪnt] v 約定；任命

Tom has been appointed on behalf of our company to sign the contract with you.
湯姆是由我們這邊指定，代表本公司來和您簽署合約的人。(on behalf of 代表)

會議及其衍生

meeting ['mitɪŋ] n 會議

To decide what to sell on TV next week, the sales manager held a meeting.
為了決定下週將在電視上販賣的產品，銷售經理們開了個會。(hold a meeting 舉行會議)

⌄
⌄

meet [mit] v 遇見；符合

Your samples did not meet our demands; therefore we will not place an order.
您的樣品不符合我們的需求，因此我們不會下訂單。(meet one's demands 符合…的需求)

會議討論會

conference [ˈkɑnfərəns] n 會議

The content of this conference should be kept in secret.
這場會議的內容應該保密。(in secret 保密)

conference agenda [ˈkɑnfərəns] [əˈdʒɛndə] 會議議程

Please refer to the conference agenda for an outline of the conference.
會議的大綱請參考大會議程表。

press conference [prɛs] [ˈkɑnfərəns] 記者招待會

We were held up by the traffic jam for four hours and missed the press conference.
我們因為塞車延誤了四個小時，錯過了記者會。(hold up使停頓)

press conference

journalist

reporter

◉ 聯想主題／會議和約會

present ['prɛznt] adj 出席的；在場的；n 目前

Don't miss the last plane today if you want to be **present** at tomorrow's international conference.
如果你想出席明天的國際會議，就不要錯過今日最後一班飛機。

presence ['prɛzns] n 出席

The child practiced very hard in the **presence** of his parents.
孩子在父母親的面前刻苦地練習著。(in the presence of 在…的面前)

attend [ə'tɛnd] v 參加

The meeting will be put off until all the board members are able to **attend**.
會議將延遲至所有董事會成員都能夠出席為止。(put off 推遲；延期)

absence ['æbsns] n 缺席

Due to the **absence** of several board members, the conference has been put back to next week.
由於數名董事會成員缺席，會議被推遲至下週舉行。(board members 董事會成員)
When people are worried about something, they usually suffer from an **absence** of mind during work.
當人們為某件事情擔憂的時候，工作時往往會心不在焉。(an absence of mind 心不在焉)

absent ['æbsnt] adj 缺席的

The class monitor was in charge of the class when the teacher was **absent**.
老師不在時，由班長負責管理班級。(in charge of 主管；負責)

attend a meeting

present

a conference hall

absent

跟會議有關的片語

attend a meeting 參加會議

Instead of going to the party, I would like to **attend** the important **meeting**.
與其去派對，我更想去參加那場重要會議。

present ... in a new light 提出不同看法

Allen **presented** things **in a new light**.
艾倫提出了不同的看法。

by way of PowerPoint presentation 運用投影片的方式呈現

I am going to explain this case **by way of PowerPoint presentation**.
我將以運用投影片的方式為大家解釋這項企劃案。

put off 延後；推遲(= delay, postpone)

The employees were very tired and decided to **put off** the meeting.
員工們非常疲倦，決定推遲會議。

展覽及其衍生

exhibit [ɪg'zɪbɪt] v 展示；n 展示品

Visitors were told to keep their hands off **exhibits**.
參觀者被告知不得觸摸展覽品。(keep one's hands off 不得碰觸)

exhibition [ˌɛksə'bɪʃən] n 展覽

Most travel agencies offer discounts at the travel **exhibition**.
大多數的旅行社在旅遊展會提供折扣。(travel exhibition旅遊展)

display [dɪ'sple] v 展示；陳列；n 展示

This artwork is only for **display**, not for sale.
這件藝術品只供展示，不販售。

illustrate ['ɪləstret] v （用圖）說明

She uses charts and pictures to **illustrate** her project.
她利用圖表和圖片來講解她的企劃。

illustration [ɪˌlʌs'treʃən] n 圖示

The user guide makes use of simple **illustrations**.
這本使用者說明書利用簡單的圖解。

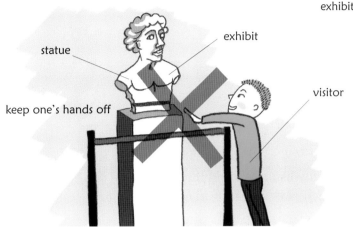

exhibition

exhibit

statue

visitor

keep one's hands off

示範及其衍生

demonstrate ['dɛmən,stret] v 證明；顯示

The salesman demonstrated his excellent customer service skills.
這名銷售員展現了他優秀的顧客服務技巧。

demonstration [,dɛmən'streʃən] n 論證；示範

We decided to buy the camera after the salesperson's demonstration.
在銷售員示範過後，我們決定買那部相機。

show [ʃo] v 顯示；陳列；露面

We had better show our determination before the employees.
我們最好在員工面前展現我們的決心。

◎ 聯想主題／展覽示範、專業人士

跟『show』有關的片語

show up 出現；出席

She wondered if the man would **show up** or not.
她想知道那個男人會不會出現。

show off 愛現；炫耀

Senior workers usually like to **show off** their abilities.
資歷較深的工作者一般喜歡炫耀自己的能力。

博覽會和集市

exposition [ˌɛkspə'zɪʃən] n 闡述；說明

She wrote a short **exposition** on global economic trend.
她寫了一篇關於國際經濟走勢的說明短文。

expose [ɪk'spoz] v 使暴露

A lot of factory workers are **exposed** to toxic chemicals.
很多工廠的工人都暴露在有毒的化學物質中。

fair [fɛr] n 集市

There's a book **fair** held on this Sunday.
這週日有舉辦書展。

會計師及其衍生

accountant [ə'kauntənt] n 會計師

As an **accountant**, Linda deals with forms and charts all the time.
作為一名會計師，琳達總是在處理表格和圖表。

accounting [ə'kaʊntɪŋ] [n] 會計

We need someone from the **accounting** profession to give us advice.
我們需要從事會計專業的人給我們建議。

account [ə'kaʊnt] [n] 帳目；帳戶

Funds will be transferred to your bank **account** shortly.
款項不久後將會轉進你的銀行帳戶。

律師及其衍生

attorney [ə'tɜ·nɪ] [n] 律師

If you would like to ask questions, please contact my **attorney**.
如果你想問問題的話，請聯繫我的律師。

lawyer ['lɔjə·] [n] 律師

After Molly graduated from the university, she became a **lawyer**.
莫莉大學畢業後，成為了一名律師。

law [lɔ] [n] 法律

By **law**, you cannot sell medical products online.
依照法律，你不能在網路上販賣醫藥用品。

lawful ['lɔfəl] [adj] 合法的

It is **lawful** to own guns in certain states in the U.S.
在美國某些州持有槍械是合法的。

● 聯想主題／專業人士

unlawful [ʌnˈlɔfəl] adj 不合法的

It is unlawful for employers to underpay their workers.
雇主少付工資給員工是不合法的。

legal [ˈligl̩] adj 合法的

Citizens above 20 have the legal right to vote.
二十歲以上的公民擁有投票的合法權利。

illegal [ɪˈligl̩] adj 非法的

It is illegal to trade drugs and guns.
毒品和槍械交易是違法的。

工程師及其衍生

engineer [ˌɛndʒəˈnɪr] n 工程師

The engineer answered the question in reference to the data.
工程師參照資料回答了問題。(in reference to關於)

engineering [ˌɛndʒəˈnɪrɪŋ] n 工程

One of our new recruits majored in engineering.
我們其中一位新職員主修工程學。

程式設計師及其衍生

programmer [ˈprogræməˌ] n 程式設計師

He works as a computer programmer in a video games company.
他在電動遊戲公司裡當電腦工程師。

program ['progræm] n 程式

The company arranged further education in computer **program** for workers.
公司為員工安排進修電腦程式。

TV program ['ti'vi] ['progræm] 電視節目

A **TV program** will be designed to boost washing machine sales.
一套用來推銷洗衣機電視節目將被規劃出來。

作家作者及其衍生

writer ['raɪtɚ] n 作者；作家

The **writer** is planning to write a book about life in the United States.
作家正在計畫寫一本關於在美國生活的書。

author ['ɔθɚ] n 作家

Jimmy is a famous **author**.
幾米是著名的作家。

freelance ['fri'læns] n 自由作家

In addition to being a teacher, he's also a **freelance** writer.
除了是教師，他也是一名自由作家。

大眾傳播媒體及其衍生

medium ['midɪəm] n 媒體；中間

Symbols are the first created **medium** of communication.
符號是最先被創造出來的溝通媒介。

● 聯想主題／大眾傳播媒體

media ['midɪə] [n] **媒體**

Media reporting could sometimes be exaggerating.
媒體報導有時會誇張些。

mass media [mæs] ['midɪə] **大眾傳媒**

The mass media plays a role in influencing people's values.
媒體扮演著影響人們價值觀的角色。

mass communication [mæs] [kə,mjunə'keʃən] **大眾傳播**

She has a degree in mass communication.
她有大眾傳播的學位。

communication [kə,mjunə'keʃən] [n] **交流**

English is an important means of communication in today's international conferences.
英語在現代國際會議當中是一種重要的溝通媒介。

新聞媒體及其衍生

television ['tɛlə,vɪʒən] [n] **電視**

He was invited to attend a television show.
他被邀請上電視節目。

newspaper ['njuz,pepɚ] [n] **報紙**

The newspaper just published an article about the risk of eating fast food.
報紙上剛發布了一則有關吃速食之危險性的報導。(fast food 速食)

magazine [ˌmægəˈzin] n 雜誌

You should subscribe to one or more weekly **magazines** such as Time or Newsweek.
你應該訂閱一種以上的週刊，例如《時代雜誌》或《新聞週刊》。(subscribe to 訂閱)

broadcast [ˈbrɔdˌkæst] n 廣播

Employees who want to improve their English should listen to English **broadcasts** every day.
想要提高英語水準的員工應該每天收聽英文廣播。(English broadcast 英文廣播)

新聞報導

news report [njuz] [rɪˈport] 新聞報導

The department store's grand opening was on the **news report**.
那家百貨公司的開幕式出現在新聞報導裡。

news release [njuz] [rɪˈlis] 新聞稿

This **news release** announced the company's news conference.
這篇新聞稿宣布了公司的記者招待會。

news conference [njuz] [ˈkɑnfərəns] 新聞發布會；記者招待會

We will clarify our financial condition at the **news conference**.
我們將會在記者招待會上澄清我們的財務狀況。

reporter [rɪˈportɚ] n 記者

There are many **reporters** waiting to interview the minister of finance.
有很多記者等著訪問財政部長。

journalist ['dʒɜ·nəlɪst] n 新聞工作者

As a journalist, she hardly has time for vacation.
身為一個新聞工作者，她幾乎沒有假期。

廣告及其衍生

advertise ['ædvɚ,taɪz] v 廣告；打廣告

We plan to advertise our products on TV.
我們打算在電視上為產品打廣告。

↓

advertisement [,ædvɚ'taɪzmənt] n 廣告

The advertisement cost a lot, but it also had great effects on sales.
廣告固然昂貴，但在銷售方面的效果很大。

↓↓

advertising agent ['ædvɚ,taɪzɪŋ] ['edʒənt] 廣告代理商

The advertising agent helps to create advertising and slogan.
廣告代理人會幫忙創作廣告和標語。

宣傳促銷

publicity [pʌb'lɪsətɪ] n 宣傳；名聲

Flyers are distributed to the public to maximize publicity.
分發傳單給公眾來達到最大的宣傳效果。

↓

propaganda [,prɑpə'gændə] n 宣傳

Political propaganda can be in forms like slogans and cartoons.
政治宣傳可以是標語或漫畫的形式。

↓↓

大眾傳播媒體 ▶ 廣告宣傳

promote [prə'mot] v 晉升

Congratulations came to William as he got **promoted**.
當威廉晉升時，收到很多祝賀。(get promoted 晉升；升職)

promotion [prə'moʃən] n 促銷；晉升

During the **promotion** period, all items are 20% off.
促銷期間所有的產品都打八折。

promote / promotion

C.E.O.

manager

clerk

宣布發布

announce [ə'nauns] v 宣布

When Harry went on the stage to **announce** the delay, people began to boo.
當哈利上台宣布表演將延遲時，人們開始發出噓聲。

inform [ɪn'fɔrm] v 通知

Please **inform** me who's going to the business trip.
請告知我是誰會去出差。

聯想主題／廣告宣傳、科技技術

information [ˌɪnfəˈmeʃən] n 信息；消息

I received the **information** about manager's promotion.
我收到經理要升職的消息。

科技和科學

technology [tɛkˈnɑlədʒɪ] n 技術

High **technology** will be required in this project.
這項工程將需要高科技的支援。

technological [tɛknəˈlɑdʒɪkļ] adj 技術的

I need **technological** assistance to reinstall this computer.
我需要技術上的協助，重新安裝這部電腦。

scientific [ˌsaɪənˈtɪfɪk] adj 科學的

Scientific evidence is needed to prove the product's effect.
為了證明產品的效用，科學證據是必要的。

science [ˈsaɪəns] n 科學

Madame Curie committed her body and soul to **science**.
居里夫人將自己的全部都貢獻給了科學。

scientist [ˈsaɪəntɪst] n 科學家

Scientists are working to detect creatures on Mars.
科學家們正在工作，偵測火星上的生物。

『technology』相關搭配

technology trend [tɛk'nɑlədʒɪ] [trɛnd] 技術趨向

Touch computing is one of the top 10 technology trends.
觸控介面是十大科技趨勢之一。

technology management [tɛk'nɑlədʒɪ] ['mænɪdʒmənt] 技術管理

Technology management is the designing and managing of technological products.
科技管理是科技產品的設計和管理。

technology analysis [tɛk'nɑlədʒɪ] [ə'næləsɪs] 技術分析

Implement best suited technology for the company with technology analysis.
利用技術分析施行最適用於公司的技術。

information technology [ˌɪnfə'meʃən] [tɛk'nɑlədʒɪ] 資訊技術

Information technology expedites communication among people around the world.
資訊科技促進了世界各地人們的交流。

high technology [haɪ] [tɛk'nɑlədʒɪ] 高科技

Interactive smart phones are the product of high technology.
互動式的智慧型手機是高科技的產物。

『technological』相關搭配

technological forecasting [tɛknə'lɑdʒɪk!] ['for,kæstɪŋ] 技術預測

Technological forecasting predicts Mars will be a human colonization.
科技預測預測火星將成為人類的殖民地。

technological revolution [tɛknəˈladʒɪkl] [ˌrɛvəˈluʃən] 科技革命

Wireless communication is one of the achievements of technological revolution.
無線通訊是科技革命的成果之一。

⇩

technological and economic development of economy 經濟上的科技和經濟的發展

Technological and economic development of economy improve standard of living.
經濟上的科技和經濟發展提高了生活水準。

『technologically』相關搭配

technologically impossible [ˌtɛknəˈladʒɪklɪ] [ɪmˈpasəbl] 技術上不可能

What is technologically impossible now might one day be achieved.
現在技術上不可能達到的事有一天可能會被達成。

⇩

technologically efficient [ˌtɛknəˈladʒɪklɪ] [ɪˈfɪʃənt] 技術效率

We need a technologically efficient machine to reduce material waste.
我們需要一台具有技術效率的機器來減少原料的浪費。

⇩

technologically advanced [ˌtɛknəˈladʒɪklɪ] [ədˈvænst] 技術先進

Japan is a technologically advanced country in Asia.
日本是亞洲區裡一個技術先進的國家。

發明和發明家

invent [ɪnˈvɛnt] Ⅴ 發明

The newly invented laptop is very light.
這個最新研發的筆記型電腦極為輕巧。

⇩

科技技術
發明創造

inventor [ɪnˈvɛntɚ] n 發明家

Edison is the inventor of light bulb.
愛迪生是燈泡的發明者。

invention [ɪnˈvɛnʃən] n 發明；發明物

Through hard work, Edison brought about many great inventions.
通過努力不懈，愛迪生帶來了許多偉大的發明。

inventory [ˈɪnvənˌtɔrɪ] n 存貨；存貨清單

We still have enough goods in stock according to the inventory.
根據存貨清單，我們還有足夠的庫存。

Edison

light bulb
invention

inventor

創造

create [krɪˈet] v 創造

This company was created by Terry.
這家公司是由特瑞創造的。

發明創造

◉ 聯想主題／發明創造

creator [krɪˈetɚ] n 創造者

The **creator** of this brand won the international design award.
這個品牌的創作人贏得了國際設計獎。

creative [krɪˈetɪv] adj 創造的；創意的

Only **creative** titles can attract potential buyers.
只有具有創意的標題才能吸引潛在的顧客。

creation [krɪˈeʃən] n 創造

The **creation** of this new computer software took a year.
新電腦軟體的開發花費了一年。

專利

patent [ˈpætn̩t] n 專利

You should apply for a **patent** for your innovative technology as soon as possible.
你應該儘快為你創新的科學技術申請專利。

register [ˈrɛdʒɪstɚ] n 登記

Please **register** yourself at the counter for a record.
請在櫃檯登記作為紀錄。

license [ˈlaɪsn̩s] n 許可

My uncle has not gotten his business **license** yet.
我叔叔尚未取得商業執照。(business license 商業執照)

duration [djʊˈreʃən] n 持續；持續期間

The **duration** of this carnival is a week.
嘉年華會為期一個星期。

expire [ɪkˈspaɪr] v 期滿

This jam contains no preservative and will **expire** in a week.
這瓶果醬不含防腐劑，一個星期內就會過期。

機器及其衍生

machine [məˈʃin] n 機器

The engineer came to the conclusion that the **machine** cannot be repaired.
工程師得出了結論，這台機器無法維修。

machine code [məˈʃin] [kod] 電腦語言

A correct **machine code** is needed to operate the machine.
要能操作這機器需要正確的機器碼。

machinery [məˈʃinərɪ] n 機械

There is a defect in this model of **machinery**.
這個型號的機械有個瑕疵。

mechanism [ˈmɛkə͵nɪzəm] n 機械裝置

What is the **mechanism** of this new gearbox?
這款新的變速箱的機制是什麼？

◎ 聯想主題／機器設備

mechanic [mə'kænɪk] n 機械工

Please contact the **mechanic** to repair the machinery.
請聯絡機械師修理機械。

引擎和發電機

engine ['ɛndʒən] n 引擎

My **engine** won't start.
我的引擎無法啟動。

generator ['dʒɛnə,retə-] n 發電機

We need a **generator** in case of power failure.
我們需要一台發電機以防停電。

generate ['dʒɛnə,ret] v 產生

The new business plan helps us **generate** higher revenue.
新的商業計畫幫我們製造更高的收益。

robot ['robət] n 機器人

The robot needs improving.
這個機器人需要改進。

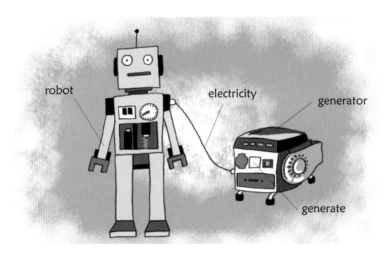

robot

electricity

generator

generate

設備

equip [ɪ'kwɪp] v 裝備

In case of fire, every workshop was equipped with fire extinguisher.
為了防備火災，每個工作坊都配備了滅火器。

equipment [ɪ'kwɪpmənt] n 設備

The factory's turnover doubled after the new equipment had been brought in.
引進新設備以後，工廠的營業額翻了一倍。

● 聯想主題／機器設備

apparatus [ˌæpəˈretəs] n 器械

Our company is investing in medical **apparatus**.
我們的公司正在投資醫療器材。

『electric』和『electrical』

electric [ɪˈlɛktrɪk] adj 電的

Electric cars are still not widely used.
電動車的使用仍然不普及。

electric blanket [ɪˈlɛktrɪk] [ˈblæŋkɪt] 電熱毯

Due to a warmer winter, **electric blanket** sells poorly.
因為暖冬的關係，電毯的銷量很不好。

electric guitar [ɪˈlɛktrɪk] [gɪˈtɑr] 電吉他

This **electric guitar** is a limited edition made in Italy.
這把限量版電吉他是在義大利製造的。

electrical [ɪˈlɛktrɪkl̩] adj 與電有關的

Please check the safety of these **electrical** equipments.
請檢查這些電器設備的安全性。

electrical appliance [ɪˈlɛktrɪkl̩] [əˈplaɪəns] 電器

Our store can fix any **electrical appliances** for you.
我們的店可以為你修理任何電器用品。

electrical engineer [ɪ'lɛktrɪkl] [ˌɛndʒə'nɪr] 電氣工程師

An electrical engineer is hired to maintain electronic systems.
雇用了一名電子工程師維護電子系統。

各種不同的電腦

computer [kəm'pjutɚ] n 電腦

My computer needs repairing.
我的電腦需要修理。

desktop ['dɛsktɑp] n 桌上型電腦

Desktop computers are sold in every computer store in town.
鎮上任何一家電腦店都有販賣桌上型電腦。

notebook ['not,bʊk] n 筆記型電腦

The boss equipped everyone with a notebook.
老闆配給每人一台筆記型電腦。

laptop ['læptɑp] n 膝上型電腦；筆記型電腦

This laptop is famous for its Dolby sound effect.
這台筆記型電腦的杜比音效很有名。

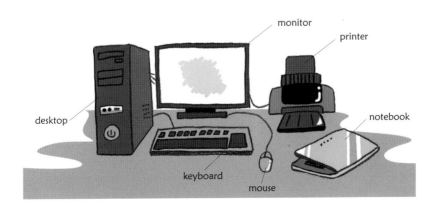

電腦

073

軟體硬體

software ['sɔft,wɛr] n 軟體

You will not regret buying the software! It can help you sort out your expenditures.
你不會後悔購買了這套軟體，它能幫助您整理您的支出項目。

hardware ['hɑrd,wɛr] n 硬體

High temperature and humidity can damage computer hardware.
高溫和溼度會毀損電腦硬體。

monitor ['mɑnətɚ] n 監視器；螢幕

The monitor suddenly blacked out and wouldn't respond.
螢幕突然黑掉而且沒有反應。

keyboard ['ki,bord] n 鍵盤

She typed slowly with the computer keyboard.
她緩慢地在電腦鍵盤上打字。

printer ['prɪntɚ] n 印表機

The printer jammed while I was printing documents.
印表機在我列印文件的時候卡住了。

網路及上網

Internet ['ɪntɚ,nɛt] n 網路

In the Internet age, we communicate through emails.
在網路時代，我們用電子郵件溝通。

get on the Internet 連接網路

I can get on the Internet with my smartphone.
我可以用我的智慧型手機上網。

surf the net 飆網

You may surf the net during free time.
有空的時候你可以上網瀏覽。

get wireless Internet 連接無線網路

Most international airports have gotten wireless Internet.
大部分的國際機場都有無線網路。

瀏覽搜尋

browse [brauz] v 瀏覽

You may browse the menu first before making an order.
在點菜前你可以先翻閱一下菜單。

browser ['brauzɚ] n 瀏覽器

My browser is set to block pop-up windows.
我的瀏覽器被設定為阻擋視窗彈出。

homepage ['hom,pedʒ] n 首頁

I set my blog as my homepage.
我把我的部落格設定成首頁。

聯想主題／網路

search [sɝtʃ] v 搜索

I am **searching** for online stores that sell coffee beans.
我正在搜尋有賣咖啡豆的網路商店。

search engine [sɝtʃ] ['ɛndʒən] 搜尋引擎

So far Google is the mostly widely used **search engine**.
到目前為止，谷歌是最被廣泛使用的搜尋引擎。

網路

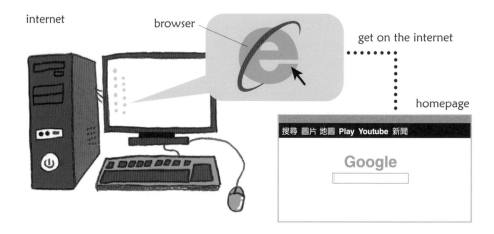

internet

browser

get on the internet

homepage

搜尋 圖片 地圖 **Play** **Youtube** 新聞

Google

電子郵件及其操作方式

email ['imel] n 電子郵件；v 寄電子郵件（= e-mail）

I will be **emailing** you my resume in the morning.
我會在早上用電子郵件把我的履歷發給你。

send [sɛnd] v 發送；寄送

Job applications have been **sent** to several corporations.
已發送工作申請給好幾家企業。

reply [rɪ'plaɪ] v 回覆

She always **replies** emails within a short time.
她總是在很短的時間內回覆電子郵件。

forward ['fɔrwɚd] v 轉寄

I have **forwarded** the email to my colleague.
我已將電子郵件轉寄給我的同事了。

spam [spæm] n 垃圾郵件

It is annoying to receive **spam** mails.
收到垃圾郵件真是煩人。

delete [dɪ'lit] v 刪除

The boss told the secretary to **delete** the files from the old computers.
老闆告訴祕書把舊電腦裡的資料刪除掉。

網路

email

● 聯想主題／出版印刷

出版印刷

publish ['pʌblɪʃ] [v] 出版；發行

Articles must be checked up carefully before being **published**.
出版之前，文章必須經過仔細檢查。(check up 檢查)

publisher ['pʌblɪʃ⋺-] [n] 出版者

I am working for a magazine **publisher**.
我為一家雜誌出版社工作。

publication [ˌpʌblɪ'keʃən] [n] 出版

Medical journals have to be peer-reviewed before **publication**.
醫學刊物在出版前必須先經過同儕的審查。

print [prɪnt] [v] 印刷

Please **print** 10 copies of event rundown for the meeting.
請複印十份活動流程作為會議用。

printing ['prɪntɪŋ] [n] 印刷業；印刷

The duplex **printing** function reduces paper use.
雙面列印的功能減少紙張的用量。

書籍雜誌和手冊

book [buk] [n] 書

In conclusion, it is a good **book** to read.
總之，這是一本好書。

volume ['vɑljəm] n 卷；冊；體積

This engineering textbook consists of two **volumes**.
這本工程學課本有兩冊。

magazine [ˌmægə'zin] n 雜誌

Newsweek **magazine** reported that GE will invest more money next year.
據新聞週刊報導，明年通用電氣將會提高投資額。

manual ['mænjʊəl] n 手冊

You should read the **manual** before using the refrigerator.
在使用冰箱前你應該先閱讀手冊。

傳單小冊子

leaflet ['liflɪt] n 傳單

He received a part time job of giving out **leaflets** on the street.
他得到了一份在街上發放傳單的兼職工作。(give out 分發)

pamphlet ['pæmflɪt] n 小冊子

The museum issues **pamphlets** to visitors upon admission.
在參觀者入場時，博物館會分發小冊子。

brochure [bro'ʃʊr] n 小冊子

This is a **brochure** advertising the newly built theme park.
這是一本宣傳新建好主題樂園的小冊子。

● 聯想主題／出版印刷、價格和價值

poster ['postə-] n 海報

This **poster** has the picture of the pretty actress on one side and her autograph on the reverse.
這張海報一面有美麗女演員的照片，反面還有她的簽名。(on the reverse 相反的)

bulletin ['bulətɪn] n 公告

All new announcements are posted on the **bulletin** board.
所有的新公告都會張貼在布告欄上。

價格和價值

price [praɪs] n 價格

According to the report, the **price** of steel will continue rising.
根據此報告，鋼鐵的價格還會繼續上漲。

priceless ['praɪslɪs] adj 無價的

Never risk the company's goodwill; it is **priceless**.
永遠不要拿公司的信譽冒險，因為信譽無價。

value ['vælju] n 價值

These ancient Persian carpets' **value** was beyond our imagination.
那些古波斯地毯的價值超乎我們想像。

valuable ['væljuəbl] adj 貴重的

This antique camera is now very **valuable**.
這台古董相機現在非常值錢。

出版印刷
價格和價值

080

valuables ['væljuəbḷz] n 貴重物品

Always keep all valuables at a secured place.
隨時將所有的貴重物品放置在安全的地方。

devalue [di'vælju] v 貶值

The building of nuclear power plant devalues the property nearby.
核電廠的興建讓附近的房地產貶值了。

depreciate [dɪ'priʃɪ,et] v 降低

The value of a car will depreciate over time.
車的價值會隨著時間降低。

depreciation [dɪ,priʃɪ'eʃən] n 降價

The accumulated depreciation of this building is approximately two million dollars.
這棟大樓總共跌價約兩百萬美元。

『at a ~ price』

at a low price 低價

Jack desperately needed cash, so he sold his car at a low price.
由於傑克急需現金，因此低價拋售了他的車子。

at a reasonable price 以合理的價格

Bill dedicated all his energy to the auction and finally got what he wanted at a reasonable price.
比爾把他所有精力都投在了拍賣會上，最後終於以合理的價格買到了他想要的東西。

price tag [praɪs] [tæg] 價格標籤

Jack misread the price tag and received only ten dollars for selling the sweater which was worth 100 dollars.
傑克看錯了標價，把價值一百美元的毛衣以十美元賣掉了。

price war [praɪs] [wɔr] 價格戰

We managed to beat off our opponents in the price war.
我們設法在價格戰中成功擊退競爭對手。(beat off 打敗；擊退)

lower the price 降低價格

That is to say, we have no choice but to lower the price.
也就是說，我們唯一的選擇就是降價。

half the price 半價

He was in luck to have bought the cell phone at half the price.
他很幸運的以半價買下了這部手機。(in luck 運氣好)

價格起伏

rise [raɪz] v 上升

Underestimated by people, the price of oil is now rising.
被大家低估的油價，現在開始漲了。

up [ʌp] adv 向上

In conclusion, it is clear that the price of the stock will go up.
總之，股價很明顯將會上漲。

價格和價值

價格起伏和變動

down [daʊn] adv 向下

The price of petroleum has finally gone **down**.
油價終於下降了。

drop [drɑp] v 下降；n 下降

There was a **drop** in the value of U.S. dollar.
美金價值曾一度下跌。

價格增加降低和變動

on the increase　漲；正在增加

Prices of raw materials are **on the increase**.
原物料價格正在上漲。

on the decrease　降低

A local newspaper remarked that crime is **on the decrease**.
一家地方報紙評論說犯罪案件正在減少。

fluctuate [ˈflʌktʃʊˌet] v 波動

The price of watermelons **fluctuates** seasonally.
西瓜的價格隨季節變動。

fluctuation [ˌflʌktʃʊˈeʃən] n 波動

Our quotation will be subject to market **fluctuation**.
我方的報價隨市場變動。

● 聯想主題／成本和利潤

capital ['kæpətl] n 資本；首都

The company is in need of **capital** injection.
這家公司需要注入新資本。

∨
∨

fund [fʌnd] n 資金

Chances for collecting enough **funds** for the project are low.
能夠籌到足夠資金來支持這項計畫的機率很低。

∨
∨

cost [kɔst] n 成本；v 花（錢或時間）

To maximize our profit, we have to take **cost** into account.
為了使利潤最大化，我們必須要考慮成本。(take … into account 將…列入考慮)

income ['ɪnˌkʌm] n 收入

Some people may see annual **income** as business secrets.
有些人會把年收入視為商業機密。

∨
∨

profit ['prɑfɪt] n 利潤

Tom made good use of his expertise and made **profit** on the stock market.
湯姆充分利用他的專長，在股市中賺了一筆。(make use of 利用；使用)

∨
∨

profitable ['prɑfɪtəbl̩] adj 有利的

Tom is engaged in a very **profitable** business.
湯姆正從事一項利潤豐厚的生意。(be engaged in 忙於)

∨
∨

成本和利潤

revenue [ˈrɛvəˌnju] **n** 收益

Due to sliding **revenues**, I think it is best for our CEO to resign.
鑒於我們下滑的業績，我覺得我們的總裁主動辭職會比較好。

費用和花費

charge [tʃɑrdʒ] **v** 索取；**n** 費用

Our company provides unlimited access to the Internet for a fixed monthly **charge**.
我們公司提供每月固定收費的無限量上網服務。

budget [ˈbʌdʒɪt] **n** 預算

This expensive luggage has exceeded my **budget**.
這個昂貴的行李箱已超出我的預算。

expense [ɪkˈspɛns] **n** 費用

Does the insurance cover medical **expenses** on injury caused by work?
這份保險包括工作傷害所產生的醫療費用嗎？(medical expenses 醫療費用)

全價和折扣

full price [fʊl] [praɪs] 全價

Adults have to buy **full price** tickets.
成人必須買全價票。

competitive price [kəmˈpɛtətɪv] [praɪs] 競爭價格

Many stores nowadays sell products at a **competitive price**.
時下有很多商店都以競爭價格販賣商品。

● 聯想主題／費用和折扣

discount ['dɪskaunt] n 折扣

Show me your student ID and you can have a 10% discount.
出示你的學生證就能得到九折優惠。

coupon ['kupɑn] n 減價優待券

Customers receive 5% discount when they purchase with a coupon.
當顧客持有優惠卷消費時，就享有百分之五的折扣。

【 值得相關片語句型 】

worth + 金錢

This is a really big deal; it is worth 10 million dollars.
這真的是一筆大買賣，它價值一千萬美元。

worth + 動名詞

Jim wants to do something worth doing.
吉姆想做一些值得做的事情。

worth one's while 值得的；值得某人去…

This reward was worth one's while.
這份報酬相當有價值。

be worthy of + 名詞／動名詞 值得

Are there any new movies worthy of watching?
有哪幾部新電影是值得觀看的嗎？

travel ['trævl] n 旅行

We will **travel** around the world on condition that I had enough money.
如果我有足夠的金錢，我們就去環遊世界。(on condition that 如果)

journey ['dʒɝnɪ] n 旅行

They will have a long **journey** crossing the Sahara Desert.
他們將踏上橫跨撒哈拉沙漠的漫長旅程。

trip [trɪp] n 行程

It'll be more interesting to have a friend with you on a **trip** than to travel alone.
旅遊時，有個朋友陪伴會比獨自一人更加有趣。(on a trip 在旅途中)

voyage ['vɔɪɪdʒ] n 航海

The one month **voyage** on the sea was unforgettable.
那段在海上一個月的旅程真是令人難忘。

sightseeing ['saɪt,siɪŋ] n 觀光

I like to take a **sightseeing** bus around the city.
我喜歡搭著觀光巴士遊覽城市。

tour [tur] n 旅行

The **tour** group will stop off at Shanghai for a short period of time.
旅遊團將在上海稍作停留。(stop off 稍作停留)

● 聯想主題／觀光旅行

tour guide [tur] [gaɪd] 導遊

The tour guide explained to us the history of this church.
導遊向我們解說這座教堂的歷史。

tourism ['turɪzəm] n 旅遊

Night market tourism is attractive to foreign visitors.
夜市觀光很吸引外國遊客。

旅客旅行社

visitor ['vɪzɪtɚ] n 訪問者；觀光者

You may ask for direction at the visitor center.
你可以向遊客中心詢問方向。

tourist ['turɪst] n 旅遊者

The number of tourists from Southeast Asia has increased.
從東南亞來的旅客增加了。

traveler ['trævlɚ] n 旅行者

Travelers withdrew from the trip after hearing the storm forecast.
旅客們聽到暴風雨的氣象預測後，決定退出旅行。(withdraw from 退出)

traveler agency ['trævlɚ] ['edʒənsɪ] 旅行社

I purchased the air ticket from the traveler agency.
我向旅行社購買機票。

風景景色

scenery ['sinərɪ] n 風景

Switzerland is famous for its mountain **scenery**.
瑞士的山景很有名。

scene [sin] n 場面

The rescue team arrived at the **scene** in good time.
營救小組及時趕到了案發現場。(at the scene 在現場)

sight [saɪt] n 景色

Mary fainted at the **sight** of blood.
瑪麗一見到血就暈了過去。(at the sight of 一看到…)

landscape ['lænd,skep] n 風景

The beauty of the **landscape** was truly beyond description.
景色的美實在難以言喻。(beyond description 難以言喻)

觀光旅行

tour guide

scenery
landscape

tourist

traveler

◉ 聯想主題／交通以及交通工具

traffic ['træfɪk] n 交通

I was late for an hour because of the heavy traffic.
因為交通繁忙，我遲到了一個小時。

traffic jam ['træfɪk] [dʒæm] 交通阻塞

There is a traffic jam because a car broke down and got on the way.
前方有交通堵塞，因為一輛汽車拋錨擋到了路。

traffic congestion ['træfɪk] [kən'dʒɛstʃən] 交通擁擠

Because of traffic congestion, we'll be late for the concert.
因為塞車的關係，我們會趕不上音樂會。

heavy traffic ['hɛvɪ] ['træfɪk] 繁忙的交通

From my point of view, every city can not avoid heavy traffic.
在我看來，每個城市無法避免交通堵塞的問題。

traffic rule ['træfɪk] [rul] 交通規則

Every driver must obey traffic rules.
每位駕駛人都必須遵守交通法規。

交通以及交通工具

traffic jam / traffic congestion / heavy traffic

陸地交通工具及其衍生

car [kɑr] n 汽車

There was a **car** accident on the highway.
高速公路上發生一起車禍。

limousine (limo) ['lɪmə,zin] n 豪華轎車

The manager will be fetched from the airport with a **limousine**.
會有一輛加長型禮車到機場接送經理。

truck [trʌk] n 卡車

This **truck** delivers fresh vegetables to the market every morning.
這輛卡車每天早上運送新鮮蔬菜到市場。

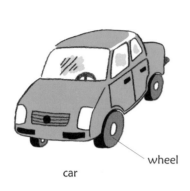

car

wheel

truck　a steering wheel

taxi ['tæksɪ] n 計程車

During rush hour, all the **taxis** are occupied.
在尖峰時段，所有的計程車都客滿了。

bus [bʌs] n 公車

The **bus** should arrive soon; it comes every 15 minutes.
公車每十五分鐘來一班，應該很快就會到了。

shuttle ['ʃʌtl] n 穿行的車輛

The hotel has a **shuttle** bus to the airport.
飯店有接駁巴士到機場。

hotel

shuttle bus

airport

subway ['sʌb,we] n 地下鐵

It is always crowded on the **subway** during rush hours.
尖峰時間，地鐵上總是很擁擠。

driver ['draɪvɚ] n 駕駛員；司機

The bus **driver** is friendly and greets every passenger.
這位友善的公車司機都會向每位乘客打招呼。

taxi

driver

TAXI

⚫ 聯想主題／交通以及交通工具

海上交通工具及其衍生

ship [ʃɪp] n 船

I will mail this package to you by **ship**.
我會以海運把包裹寄給你。

boat [bot] n 小船

We will take the **boat** to the island.
我們將搭小船到那座小島。

captain ['kæptɪn] n 船長；機長

The **captain** announced the plane will land in 10 minutes.
機長廣播宣布飛機將在十分鐘內降落。

空中交通工具及其衍生

airplane ['ɛr,plen] n 飛機

This **airplane** can accommodate 300 passengers.
這架飛機可容納三百名乘客。

plane [plen] n 飛機

Cell phones should be switched off on **plane**.
在飛機上，行動電話應關機。

pilot ['paɪlət] n（飛機）駕駛員

The **pilot** announced that the airplane was ready for take off.
機長宣布飛機已準備好起飛。

搭乘交通工具

by car 乘汽車

It is more convenient to go to work **by car**.
開車上班方便多了。

by bus 搭公共汽車

Most students go to school **by bus**.
絕大部分的學生都搭公車上學。

by boat 乘船

We will go to the island **by boat**.
我們將搭小船到那座小島。

by train 乘火車

My dream is to tour around Taiwan **by train**.
我的夢想是搭火車遊遍臺灣。

by subway 乘地鐵

You can go to many attractions **by subway**.
你可以搭地鐵到很多景點。

take a bus 坐公共汽車

How will we **take a bus** to the science center?
我們該如何搭公車到科學中心？

take a train 乘火車

You can enjoy the sea scenery when you **take a train**.
搭火車時，可以欣賞海景。

ride a bicycle 騎腳踏車

It is relaxing to **ride a bicycle** by the riverside.
在河岸邊騎腳踏車真是放鬆。

交通以及交通工具

by airplane 搭飛機

I am going to Japan **by airplane**.
我將搭飛機到日本。

by air 乘飛機

It is unwise to travel to France **by air** in such a foggy weather.
在起大霧時坐飛機去法國旅行是很不明智的。

board the airplane 登機

She was on the point of **boarding the airplane** when her mother called.
就在她登機之際，母親打了通電話過來。

go on board 上飛機；上火車

I just **went on board** when the train pulled out of the station.
我才剛剛登上火車，它便駛出了車站。

go abroad 去國外

The manager will **go abroad** for training next week.
經理下週要出國接受培訓。

動身前往

leave for 動身前往

He'll be leaving for Paris.
他即將動身前往巴黎。

be bound for 開往

The train is bound for Paris.
這輛火車將開往巴黎。

head for 出發

It is time for employees to head for home.
現在該讓員工回家了。

飛機和機場

airplane ['ɛr‚plen] n 飛機

It is sad to hear that an airplane crashed.
聽到飛機墜毀的消息真令人悲傷。

airport ['ɛr‚port] n 機場

The airport announced a delay in the next flight to San Diego due to dense fog.
機場通知，因為受濃霧影響，下一班開往聖地牙哥的飛機將延誤。

airport tax ['ɛr‚port] [tæks] 機場稅

Airport tax has been included in the air ticket.
機場稅已包含在機票裡。

⊙ 聯想主題／飛機和機場

飛機和機場

customs ['kʌstəmz] n 海關

Citizens can usually go through the **customs** faster than foreigners.
通常公民可以比外國人更快通過海關。

declare [dɪ'klɛr] v 申報；宣布

I do not have anything to **declare** at the customs.
我沒有任何需要在海關申報的東西。

declaration [ˌdɛklə'reʃən] n 申報；宣告

Foreign visitors are required to fill out the customs **declaration** form.
外國遊客需要填寫海關申報表。

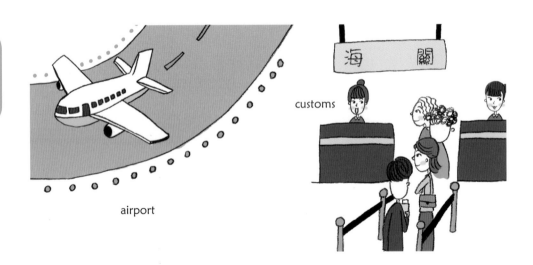

customs

airport

『 airport 』 及其衍生

airport ['ɛr,port] n 機場

I am waiting for a transfer flight at the **airport**.
我在機場等待轉機。

port [port] n 機場；航空站；港

I can see the **port** from our cruise.
我可以從油輪上看到港口。

porter ['portə-] n 搬運工

You can just give the luggage to the **porters**.
你把行李交給搬運工就行了。

 艙等

first class 頭等艙

First class passengers can board the plane first.
頭等艙的乘客可以優先登機。

business class 商務艙

I would like an upgrade from economy class to **business class**.
我想要從經濟艙升等到商務艙。

economy class 經濟艙

He has booked two **economy class** tickets.
他訂了兩張經濟艙的票。

起程和到達

depart [dɪ'pɑrt] n 啟程

No matter what time you leave, call me before your flight **departs**.
無論你什麼時候離開，請在飛機起飛前撥通電話給我。

飛機和機場

◉ 聯想主題／飛機和機場

departure [dɪ'pɑrtʃɚ] n 離開

The airplane is ready for **departure** in 5 minutes.
飛機已準備好在五分鐘內起飛。

airport ['ɛr,port] n 機場

The **airport** is closed because of a typhoon.
機場因為颱風而關閉。

arrival [ə'raɪvl] n 到達

The estimated time of **arrival** is 8:15 a.m..
預計抵達的時間是早上八點十五分。

arrive [ə'raɪv] v 到達

The experts' team will soon **arrive**.
專家團隊馬上就會到達。

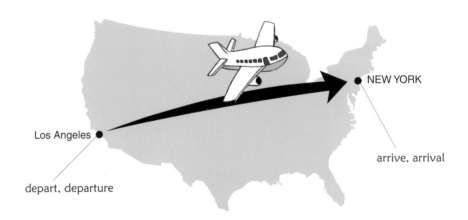

飛機和機場

送行和起飛

see off 送行

He **saw** me **off** at the airport.
他在機場幫我送行。

take off 起飛

The plane will take off soon.
飛機即將起飛。

登機和航程

check in [tʃɛk] [ɪn] 報到；辦理登機手續

We checked in at the airport an hour before the plane took off.
我們在飛機起飛前一小時於機場辦理登機手續。

check in

baggage

fly [flaɪ] v 飛行

The airplane just **flew** across an island.
飛機剛飛過一座小島。

flight [flaɪt] n 航班；航程；飛行

It is a long **flight** from Australia to Korea.
從澳洲飛到韓國是一趟漫長的航程。

flight attendant [flaɪt] [əˈtɛndənt] 空服員

Flight attendants are serving food now.
空服員正在提供餐點。

crew [kru] n 全體機員

The cabin **crew** need to ensure passengers' safety.
空服員需要確保乘客的安全。

登機和行李

flight attendant

航程可能產生的問題

turbulence ['tɝ·bjələns] n 亂流

It's common to encounter turbulence during a flight.
飛行途中遇到亂流，很常見的。

airsick ['ɛr,sɪk] adj 暈機的

I got airsick because of the turbulence.
因為亂流我暈機了。

jet lag [dʒɛt] [læg] 時差感

I had jet lag after flying from Taiwan to Italy.
從臺灣飛到義大利後我有時差。

證件機票等等

passport ['pæs,port] n 護照

My passport will expire in 6 months.
我的護照將在六個月內過期。

visa ['vizə] n 簽證

You need a passport to apply for visa.
你需要護照才能申請簽證。

ticket ['tɪkɪt] n 票

The custom officer will check your air ticket.
海關人員會檢查你的機票。

◉ 聯想主題／登機和行李

boarding pass ['bordɪŋ] [pæs] 登機證

Your seat number is printed on the boarding pass.
你的座位號碼就印在登機證上。

traveler's check 旅行支票

Bring a traveler's check is safer than bringing lots of cash.
帶旅行支票比帶大量的現金安全多了。

a one-way ticket 單程票

This is a one-way ticket to Seattle.
這是一張到西雅圖的單程票。

a round-trip ticket 往返票

I'd like to book a round-trip ticket to Macao on Eve Air.
我想訂一張夏娃航空到澳門的來回機票。

行李包裹及其衍生

luggage （英式） n 行李

There's a weight limit to check-in luggage.
托運行李有重量限制。

luggage tag 行李牌

Remember to check the luggage tag before collection.
記得拿行李前先確認行李牌。

登機和行李

carry-on luggage　隨身攜帶的行李

Only one piece of carry-on luggage is allowed on the plane.
只允許一件隨身攜帶的行李登機。

a piece of luggage　一件行李

She only brings a piece of luggage with her.
她只帶一件行李。

baggage　（美式）n 行李

You can put your baggage on the cart.
你可以把行李放在推車上。

baggage claim　行李認領

You may pick up your baggage at the baggage claim.
你可以在行李提領處取行李。

baggage allowance　行李限重

You should find out the baggage allowance with your airline.
你應該向航空公司詢問行李的限重限額。

a piece of baggage　一件行李

Although he only carries a piece of baggage, it's overweight.
雖然他只帶一件行李，但是這件行李超重了。

登機和行李

105

旅館和住處

hotel [ho'tɛl] n 旅館

All the five-star **hotels** in London have been booked on Christmas Eve.
平安夜當天，倫敦所有五星級飯店都被訂滿了。

inn [ɪn] n 客棧

We will be staying at the **inn** for a night.
我們會在小旅館待一晚。

lodging ['lɑdʒɪŋ] n 寄宿；住所

What is the **lodging** expense for this trip?
這次旅行的住宿花費是多少？

accommodation [ə,kɑmə'deʃən] n 住處；膳宿

We called to check if the hotel has enough **accommodations**.
我們打電話向飯店詢問是否有足夠的房間。

accommodate [ə'kɑmə,det] v 能容納

This room can **accommodate** up to 6 people.
這間房間可以容納六個人。

空房和預訂

available [ə'veləbl̩] adj 可用的；有空的

May I ask if there are three seats **available** for tomorrow's Broadway performance?
請問明天的百老匯演出還有三個空位嗎？

vacancy ['vekənsɪ] n 空白；空房

There is no more vacancy left at B&B (bed and breakfast).
民宿已經沒有空房間了。

reservation [,rɛzə'veʃən] n 保留；預訂

In addition to room reservation, the international hotel also offers services such as ticket booking and meal delivering.
除了提供房間預訂之外，這家國際旅舍還提供票務訂購和運送膳食等服務。

make a reservation 預訂

You can make a reservation on the hotel's website.
你可以在飯店的網頁預訂房間。

fill in the registration form 填寫登記表

Please fill in the registration form for the class.
請填寫課程的申請表格。

check in [tʃɛk] [ɪn] 報到

Let's check in and put our baggage in the room.
我們去辦理住宿登記手續然後把行李放在房間裡。

check out [tʃɛk] [aʊt] 結帳離去；辦妥手續離去

Tom was checking out when we reached the hotel.
我們到達酒店時，湯姆正在結帳準備離開。

安全密碼

valuable ['væljʊəb!] adj 有價值的

Someone broke into the house and stole everything that was **valuable**.
有人闖進房子，偷走了所有值錢的東西。(break into 闖入)

safe [sef] adj 安全的

Is it **safe** to bring all the cash with you?
你將所有的現金都帶在身上安全嗎？

lock [lɑk] n 鎖；v 鎖（門）

Did you **lock** the door when you left the room?
你離開房間的時候有鎖門嗎？

code [kod] n 代碼；密碼

You need to enter a **code** to access the room.
你需要輸入代碼才能進入房間。

旅館和旅館服務

lobby ['labɪ] n 大廳

Our group members are waiting for us at the lobby.
我們的團員在大廳等我們。

the dining room （家中的）飯廳；餐廳

You may have the cake on the dining room table.
你可以吃飯廳桌上的蛋糕。

a beauty salon 美容院

I am going to a beauty salon for nail painting.
我要到美容院做指甲彩繪。

a barber shop 理髮店

Should I get my hair cut at a barber shop?
我應該在理髮院剪頭髮嗎？

restaurant ['rɛstərənt] n 飯店；餐廳

Which restaurant would you choose to hold your birthday party?
你要選擇在哪家餐廳舉行生日派對？

steak house [stek] [haus] 牛排館

My friend had her family gathering at a steak house.
我的朋友在牛排館辦家庭聚餐。

⦿ 聯想主題／餐廳和餐飲服務

café [kə'fe] n 咖啡館

She's meeting with her career partner at the café.
她跟事業夥伴約在咖啡廳見面。

buffet ['bʌfɪt] n 自助餐

Girls are crazy about this dessert buffet.
女孩們都對這甜點自助餐瘋狂。

bar [bɑr] n 酒吧

There will be a live band performance at the bar tonight.
今晚在酒吧裡會有現場的樂團表演。

nightclub ['naɪt,klʌb] n 夜總會

She often goes to nightclub to dance.
她經常到夜總會跳舞。

餐廳服務人員

cook [kʊk] n 廚師；v 烹調

She can cook a variety of Indian food.
她會煮好幾樣印度食物。

chef [ʃɛf] n 主廚

The chef has been to Thailand to learn traditional Thai food.
主廚曾到泰國學習傳統的泰國料理。

waiter ['wetɚ] n 侍者

Waiters attend to every customer's need at the restaurant.
餐廳裡的服務生會注意每位客人的需求。

waitress ['wetrɪs] n 女服務生

The waitress just served our last dish.
服務生剛端來我們的最後一道菜。

wait [wet] v 等待

The students waited in line to see the artwork in turn.
學生們排隊輪流欣賞藝術品。(wait in line 排隊)

各國食物

Chinese food ['tʃaɪ'niz] [fud] 中國食物

Chinese food in England is surprisingly delicious.
英國的中國食物意外地美味。

Japanese food [ˌdʒæpə'niz] [fud] 日本食物

Sushi and ramen are well known Japanese food worldwide.
壽司和拉麵是在世界各地都知名的日本料理。

Korean food [ko'riən] [fud] 韓國食物

Korean food has a lot of side dishes.
韓國食物有很多小菜。

聯想主題／餐廳和餐飲服務

Thai food [taɪ] [fud] 泰國食物

Tom yum is my favorite **Thai food**.
泰式酸辣湯是我最喜歡的泰國食物。

recipe ['rɛsəpɪ] n 食譜

Where can I find **recipes** for Mediterranean cuisine?
我到哪裡可以找到地中海餐的食譜？

各種不同的食物

steak [stek] n 牛排

I prefer medium-well to well-done **steak**.
我喜歡七分熟多過於全熟的牛排。

pizza ['pitsə] n 批薩

What would you like to put on your **pizza**?
你想在你的批薩上加什麼料呢？

noodle ['nudḷ] n 麵條

Beef **noodles** are one of my favorites.
牛肉麵是我的最愛之一。

spaghetti [spə'gɛtɪ] n 義大利麵條

Ashley had eaten three dishes, one plate of **spaghetti** and the two plates filled with sandwiches.
艾希莉已經吃了三盤東西，一盤義大利麵，和兩盤堆得滿滿的三明治。

sushi ['suʃɪ] n 壽司

It is easy to make a **sushi** roll.
做壽司卷是很簡單的。

sandwich ['sændwɪtʃ] n 三明治

This tuna **sandwich** is bought from a convenient store.
這個鮪魚三明治是從便利商店買的。

hot pot [hɑt] [pɑt] 火鍋

I love eating **hot pot** in winter.
我喜歡在冬天吃火鍋。

cook

steak

pizza

食物味道

sour ['saʊr] adj 酸的；n 酸味

This **sour** dipping sauce is for the meat.
這個酸的沾醬是沾肉用的。

◉ 聯想主題／餐廳和餐飲服務

sweet [swit] adj 甜的

This donut is too **sweet** for me.
這個甜甜圈對我來說太甜了。

bitter ['bɪtɚ] adj 苦的

Most people don't like the **bitter** taste of herbs.
大多數人不喜歡草藥的苦味。

spicy ['spaɪsɪ] adj 辣的

Most Thai cuisines are sour and **spicy**.
大部分的泰國料理都又酸又辣。

salty ['sɔltɪ] adj 鹹的

Eating too much **salty** food is not good for health.
吃太多鹹的食物對健康沒有好處。

delicious [dɪ'lɪʃəs] adj 美味的

These chocolates are really **delicious**; no wonder so many people like them.
這些巧克力真的很好吃，難怪那麼多人喜歡。

tasty ['testɪ] adj 可口的

The environment of this restaurant is not good enough, but the desserts here are **tasty**.
這個飯店的環境不夠好，但甜點很可口。

公共空間

public place ['pʌblɪk] [ples] 公共場所

Smoking in **public places** amounts to ruining other people's health.
在公共場所吸煙等於危害他人健康。

public space ['pʌblɪk] [spes] 公共空間

Parks and libraries are considered **public space**.
公園和圖書館都算是公共空間。

town square [taʊn] [skwɛr] 城市廣場

There's an event going on at the **town square**.
廣場上正在舉辦活動。

forum ['forəm] n 討論會

Anyone can voice his opinions at this **forum**.
任何人都可以在這個討論區發表意見。

park [pɑrk] n 公園

This national **park** is famous for its waterfall.
這個國家公園以其瀑布著名。

parking lot ['pɑrkɪŋ] [lɑt] 停車場

There's no more space left at the **parking lot**.
停車場裡沒有位子了。

parking lot

公共建築物

museum [mjuˈzɪəm] n 博物館

We visited the **museum** as well as the library in the city.
我們參觀了城市裡的圖書館和博物館。

library [ˈlaɪˌbrɛrɪ] n 圖書館

I am going to the **library** to return books.
我正要去圖書館還書。

theater [ˈθɪətɚ] n 劇場

The **theater** is always crowded with people during weekends.
劇院在週末總是擠滿了人。

court [kort] n 法庭

He's attending the **court** as a witness.
他以證人的身份出席法庭。

公共空間和公共建築物

hospital ['hɑspɪtl] n 醫院

Our daughter coughed heavily this morning; perhaps we should take her to the **hospital**.
我們的女兒這個早上咳得很嚴重，或許我們應該帶她去醫院。

『public』的衍生

public interest ['pʌblɪk] ['ɪntərɪst] 公共利益

Government policies should conform to the **public interests**.
政府政策應該符合公眾利益。

public telephone ['pʌblɪk] ['tɛlə,fon] 公共電話

Cellular phones enable communication when **public telephones** are not available.
沒公共電話時，手機讓人們得以通訊。

public library ['pʌblɪk] ['laɪ,brɛrɪ] 公共圖書館

She donated books to the **public library**.
她捐書給公立圖書館。

public affair ['pʌblɪk] [ə'fɛra] 公共事務

He's a **public affair** specialist working for the government.
他是為政府工作的公眾事務專家。

public relations ['pʌblɪk] [rɪ'leʃənz] 公共關係

Public relations professionals help corporations create good public images.
公共關係的專家會幫助企業創造良好的公共形象。

◎ 聯想主題／公共空間和公共建築物、銀行

public health ['pʌblɪk] [hɛlθ] 公共衛生

Immunization is an important **public health** measure.
預防接種是一項重要的公共衛生措施。

『public』的反義『private』的衍生

private school ['praɪvɪt] [skul] 私立學校

The **private school** promised to answer for its teaching methods.
這家私立學校承諾為其教學方式負責任。

private club ['praɪvɪt] [klʌb] 私人俱樂部

There are many **private clubs** who limit their membership to important business people.
有很多私人俱樂部只接受重要商業人物作為會員。

in private [ɪn] ['praɪvɪt] 私下；祕密的

The board of directors decided to sell the firm **in private**.
董事會決定私下賣掉公司。

in public [ɪn] ['pʌblɪk] 公開；在公共場所

The political scandal is now out **in public**.
這個政治醜聞現在被公開了。

銀行及其相關

bank [bæŋk] n 銀行

You can apply for credit card at the **bank**.
你可以在銀行申請信用卡。

bank account [bæŋk] [ə'kaunt] 銀行帳戶

Peter found a large amount of money in his **bank account**, but he doesn't know how it came about.
彼得發現銀行帳戶裡有很大一筆錢，但是他不知道那是從哪裡來的。

bank manager [bæŋk] ['mænɪdʒɚ] 銀行經理

Tom said that being a **bank manager** is the best job on earth.
湯姆說當銀行經理是世界上最好的工作。

transfer [træns'fɝ] Ⓥ **轉帳**

Only if you **transfer** the money to our account will we send you the commodities.
你先把錢匯到我們的帳戶上，我們才會把商品寄給你。

存款和貸款

saving ['sevɪŋ] Ⓝ **積蓄**

I can't afford the vacation because it would eat up my **savings**.
我付不起這筆旅遊費用，這將會耗盡我的積蓄。(eat up 耗盡)

deposit [dɪ'pɑzɪt] Ⓥ **存款**

The salary will be **deposited** into your bank account.
薪水將會存進你的銀行帳戶。

debtor ['dɛtɚ] Ⓝ **債務人**

The **debtor** owed him more than 5,000 dollars.
債務人欠他超過五千美元。

銀行

◎ 聯想主題／銀行

loan [lon] v 借出；n 貸款

She has to apply for a student **loan** from the bank.
她必須要向銀行申請學生貸款。

in debt [ɪn] [dɛt] 欠債

Many people are **in debt** at a young age.
很多人在年輕時就負債了。

in heavy debt [ɪn] ['hɛvɪ] [dɛt] 負債累累

Having lost a great deal of money in gambling, Tom was **in heavy debt**.
由於賭博損失了一大筆錢，湯姆負債累累。

overdue ['ovɚ'dju] adj 未兌的；過期的

Our records show that some of your debts are still **overdue**.
我們的紀錄顯示你有一些債務還沒有償清。

in heavy debt

銀行

貸款和破產

loan [lon] n 借款；v 借出

Although he was very poor, we did not consent to his request for **loans**.
雖然他很窮，我們依然沒有同意他申請貸款的請求。

on credit [ɑn] ['krɛdɪt] 賒帳

Tony always buys things **on credit**.
托尼買東西時總是賒帳。

bankruptcy ['bæŋkrəptsɪ] n 破產

The cause of our company's **bankruptcy** is still under investigation.
我們公司破產的原因還在調查中。

bankrupt ['bæŋkrʌpt] adj 破產的

There is no point in keeping a fancy car when everyone knows we are nearly **bankrupt**.
大家都知道我們瀕臨破產，何必還要留住那部昂貴的汽車。

go bankrupt [go] ['bæŋkrʌpt] 破產

He's heavily in debt and might **go bankrupt**.
他負債累累而且有可能會破產。

跟錢有關的常見用法

pocket money 零用錢

I spent all my **pocket money** on CD and candy.
我把所有的零用錢全花在買唱片和糖果上了。

121

◉ 聯想主題／銀行

save money 省錢

Mary had to cut back on expenditures to save money for a new laptop.
為了購買新的筆記型電腦，瑪麗只好省錢減少開銷。

borrow money 借錢

John had to borrow money from his friends to get through the toughest time of the year.
約翰不得不向朋友借錢以度過一年之中最艱難的時候。

make money 賺錢

In order to make more money, he worked overtime.
他為了賺更多的錢而超時工作。

earn a lot of money 大賺一筆

We will earn a lot of money if we can finish the project within two weeks.
如果我們能在兩個星期內完成這個計畫，就能大賺一筆了。

worth the money 值回票價

Buyers will be satisfied if they think their purchase is worth the money.
如果買家認為他們購買的東西物有所值，他們就會感到滿意。

a waste of time and money 既浪費金錢又浪費時間

Mr. Wang thinks that the investment on the project is a waste of time and money.
王先生認為對那個項目的投資既浪費金錢又浪費時間。

post office [post] ['ɔfɪs] **郵局**

By the way, do you have any idea where the **post office** is?
順便問一下，您知道郵局在哪裡嗎？

mail [mel] n **郵件**；v **郵寄**

I just received a **mail** from my friend.
我剛收到一封朋友寄來的郵件。

mailbox ['mel,bɑks] n **郵箱**

There's a letter from the bank in my **mailbox**.
郵箱裡有一封銀行寄來的信。

mailman ['mel,mæn] n **郵差**

The **mailman** usually delivers mails to us in the morning.
郵差通常在早上把郵件送給我們。

airmail ['ɛr,mel] n **航空郵件**

Items will be mailed to overseas buyers with **airmail**.
物品將會以航空郵件寄給海外的買家。

post office

mailman

mailbox

信件和郵票

letter ['lɛtɚ] n 信件；字母

She had written many **letters** before she realized that she didn't have enough envelopes.
在她發現信封不夠前，她已經寫完很多封信了。

envelope ['ɛnvə,lop] n 信封

Delivery failed because the address on the **envelope** was wrong.
遞送失敗是因為信封上的地址錯誤。

stamp [stæmp] n 郵票

Peter, my colleague, enjoys collecting foreign **stamps**.
我的同事彼德喜歡收集外國郵票。

postage ['postɪdʒ] n 郵費

What's the **postage** for a registered mail?
掛號郵件的郵資是多少？

郵局

cancel ['kænsl] v 蓋銷（郵票）；撤銷

These stamps were all **cancelled**.
這些郵票都蓋銷了。

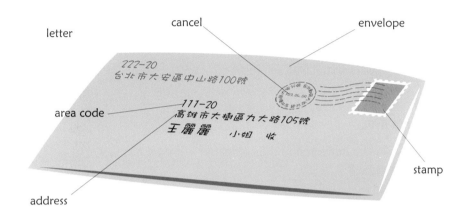

運送傳送

deliver [dɪ'lɪvɚ] v 投遞；寄送

I will check the records again to assure commodities had been **delivered**.
我會再次確認紀錄，確保商品已送出。

delivery [dɪ'lɪvərɪ] n 投遞；交貨

Jack, the owner of the logistics company, assured us that he would make special arrangements for our **delivery**.
物流公司的老闆傑克保證會為我們的貨運做特殊安排。

carrier ['kærɪɚ] n 運送人

The seller has sent the goods to the **carrier**.
賣家已經把貨品交給送貨員。

carry ['kærɪ] v 運；拿

Would you **carry** the books here for me?
能幫我把書搬來這裡嗎？

package ['pækɪdʒ] n 包裹

John was certain that he had mailed the important **package** two weeks ago.
約翰確信他兩個星期前有寄出那個重要的包裹。

parcel ['pɑrsl] n 小包

When will the **parcel** be delivered to the company?
包裹什麼時候會寄到公司？

醫院診所

hospital ['hɑspɪtl] n 醫院

Linda's friend came to the **hospital** to ask after her.
琳達的朋友來到醫院探望她。

clinic ['klɪnɪk] n 診所

Ha has been to the **clinic** for a checkup.
他到過診所做檢查。

醫生和治療相關單字

doctor ['dɑktɚ] n 醫生

At one time, Lucy hoped to become a **doctor**.
露西曾經希望成為一名醫生。

nurse [nɝs] **n** 護士

Young **nurses** have to take night shifts.
年輕護士要上晚班。

patient ['peʃənt] **n** 病人

The doctor can't help making the **patient** feel better.
醫生無法讓病人舒服一點。

cure [kjur] **v** 治療

It is difficult to **cure** Lily's father of smoking, for the habit was formed too many years ago.
要讓莉莉的爸爸改掉吸煙的毛病是有困難的，因為這個惡習太多年以前就已經養成了。
(cure…of 治癒)

heal [hɛl] **v** 治癒

We hope his wound will **heal** up soon, so he can get back to work.
我們希望他的傷口儘快痊癒，那樣他就可以回去工作了。(heal up 痊癒)

treatment ['tritmənt] **n** 治療；對待

Thanks to your **treatment**, the senior citizen did not die from heart attack.
多虧您的治療，那位老年人才沒有死於心臟病。

relief [rɪ'lif] **n** 緩和；減輕

It's such a **relief** to know she passed the exam.
知道她考試合格真讓人寬心。

◆ 聯想主題／醫院和疾病

health [hɛlθ] **n** 健康

Drinking is bad for one's **health**.
喝酒有害人體健康。

healthy ['hɛlθɪ] **adj** 健康的

As far as sports are concerned, playing football is a good way to keep one **healthy**.
就體育而言，踢足球是保持健康的好方法。

醫院和疾病

illness ['ɪlnɪs] **n** 疾病

It is the doctor's duty to cure patients of **illnesses**.
為病人治病是醫生的職責。

ill [ɪl] **adj** 生病的

He worked too much and fell **ill**.
他因為工作過量而生病了。

sickness ['sɪknɪs] n 疾病

After surgery, John's **sickness** is now in control.
手術後，約翰的病情得到了控制。

sick [sɪk] adj 噁心的；生病的

John is too **sick** to attend the meeting.
約翰病得很重，不能參加會議。

sick leave [sɪk] [liv] 病假

Employees take more **sick leaves** in autumn than at any other time.
與其他季節相比，員工更容易在秋季請病假。

購物及購物場所

shopping ['ʃɑpɪŋ] n 購物

I always do grocery **shopping** at this store.
我都在這家店購買食品雜貨。

go shopping [go] ['ʃɑpɪŋ] 去購物

Let's **go shopping** during the great sale.
我們在特賣會的時候一起去購物吧。

go window shopping [go] ['wɪndo] ['ʃɑpɪŋ] 逛商店

Would you like to **go window shopping** with me?
你想要和我一起去逛街嗎？

department store [dɪˈpɑrtmənt] [stor] 百貨公司

The **department store** is full of people since the sales promotion is on the run.
百貨公司內因為正在進行促銷活動而擠滿了人。(on the run 活動；正在)

⇩
⇩

mall [mɔl] n 購物中心

You can go to the **mall** on foot; it's only a three-minute walk from here.
你可以走路去那個商場；那邊離這裡只有三分鐘路程。(on foot步行)

> 各種不同的市場

market [ˈmɑrkɪt] n 市場；需求

John is good at opening the foreign **market**.
約翰擅長於開發國外市場。

⇩
⇩

supermarket [ˈsupɚˌmɑrkɪt] n 超級市場

To buy some drinks, he went to the **supermarket**.
他為了買些飲料，去了超級市場。

⇩
⇩

flea market [fli] [ˈmɑrkɪt] 跳蚤市場

You can buy things at a good bargain at **flea markets**.
你可以在跳蚤市場買到便宜的東西。

> 貨幣形式和付款方式

逛街購物

money [ˈmʌnɪ] n 錢

Do you have enough **money** to pay for the rent?
你有足夠的錢付房租嗎？

⇩

cash [kæʃ] n 現金；v 把…兌現

She always tries to **cash** in by selling second hand clothes online.
她總是依靠在網路上販賣二手衣物來賺錢。

coin [kɔɪn] n 硬幣

This vending machine only accepts **coins**.
這個販賣機只收硬幣。

bill [bɪl] n 帳單

You can pay utility **bills** at convenient stores.
你可以在便利商店繳水電帳單。

check [tʃɛk] n 支票

I'd like to find a bank to cash a **check**.
我想找一家銀行來兌現這張支票。(cash a check支票兌現)

credit card ['krɛdɪt] [kɑrd] 信用卡

I am sorry that the **credit card** is overdue.
很抱歉，您的信用卡已過期。

coin

credit card

money

◎ 聯想主題／時間和行程

時間

time [taɪm] n 時間；時光

What is the current **time** in London?
倫敦目前的時間是幾時？

on time 準時

In order to get there **on time** tomorrow morning, we'd better get up earlier.
為了明天早上能準時到達，我們最好早點起床。

overtime ['ovɚ͵taɪm] n 加班；超時；adv 超過地

As the manager of the shopping center, George always works **overtime**.
作為購物中心的經理，喬治經常加班。

timely ['taɪmlɪ] adj 及時的；adv 及時地

Please submit your report in a **timely** manner.
請在時間內提交你的報告。

in time 及時

You arrive just **in time** for the discussion session.
你剛好趕上討論會。

in good time 及時地

She arrived at the concert **in good time**.
她及時到達演奏會。

時間和行程

132

行程和日曆

timetable ['taɪm,tebl̩] n （火車等的）時刻表

When will the bus arrive according to the **timetable**?
根據時刻表，公車什麼時候會到？

schedule ['skɛdʒul] n （火車等的）時刻表；日程安排表

The bus arrived in New York ahead of **schedule**.
巴士提前到達了紐約。(ahead of schedule 提前)

itinerary [aɪ'tɪnə,rɛrɪ] n 旅程

Do you have any suggestion about the **itinerary**?
你對這個旅遊計畫有任何建議嗎？

agenda [ə'dʒɛndə] n 日程

This is the **agenda** for our meeting today.
這是今天會議的議程。

calendar ['kæləndɚ] n 日曆

Today is the 15th on the lunar **calendar**.
今天是農曆十五號。

delay [dɪ'le] v 耽擱；使延期

The baseball game would be **delayed** until the storm passed over.
棒球比賽將被延遲至暴風雨過後。(pass over 越過)

時間和行程

◎ 聯想主題／和時間有關的片語

deadline ['dɛd,laɪn] **n** 截止期限；（報紙）截稿時間

Tomorrow is the **deadline**. I have to burn the midnight oil to finish the work.
明天就是截止日了，我得挑燈夜戰來完成任務。(burn the midnight oil 開夜車)

跟『now』有關的片語

right now 馬上；現在

Lily is not available **right now**, so you can cross her name off the list.
莉莉現在沒有空，所以你可以把她的名字從名單上刪除。

up to now 直到現在

Up to now, Mick hasn't explained to me why the business failed.
直到現在，米克還沒有向我解釋生意失敗的原因。

from now on 從現在開始

From now on, we will be colleagues, as well as friends.
從現在起，我們既是同事也是朋友。

every now and then 時常；有時

He always did well in school in spite of having part time jobs **every now and then**.
儘管他不時有一些兼差工作，但他在學校裡的表現總是很好。

now or never 僅有的機會

Perhaps we should give it a shot, it's **now or never**.
或許我們應該嘗試看看，勿失良機。

now that 既然

Now that he is here, we might as well give him a chance.
既然他已經來了，我們不如給他一次機會。

ever since 自從

Ever since becoming the director, he became another man.
自從升為主管後，他就變了一個人。

跟『day』有關的片語

day by day 一天天地；每天

Day by day, Bob does the same boring job.
每天鮑伯都做著同樣的無聊工作。

day in and day out 日以繼夜；每天

Jeff operates the machine day in and day out.
傑夫日以繼夜的操作著那部機器。

day and night 日以繼夜；不停地

The scientists worked on the experiments day and night.
那些科學家日以繼夜的做實驗。

in the day 在白天（= in the daytime）

Cats sleep in the day and go out at night.
貓白天睡覺，夜晚活動。

◉ 聯想主題／和時間有關的片語、建築物

＊ 跟『date』有關的片語

to date　迄今為止

To date, the basketball team has not lost a single game.
迄今為止，這支籃球隊還沒輸過任何一場比賽。

fix a date for　為（某事）安排日期

Mary and Jane fixed a date for the next movie.
瑪麗和珍約好了下次一起看電影的時間。

out of date　過時的（＝old-fashioned）

My membership at this club is out of date.
我在這家俱樂部的會員資格已過期。

up to date　現代化的；最新的；合乎潮流的（＝updated）

I keep myself up to date by listening to news on the radio.
我透過收聽廣播電台播放的新聞來確保自己能夠收到最新的消息。

＊ 建築和建築師

build [bɪld] ⓥ 建築

This museum was built in honor of the great artist.
這座美術館是為了紀念那名偉大的藝術家而建立的。(in honor of 為了紀念)

building ['bɪldɪŋ] ⓝ 建築物

The round building ahead of us is the school's cafeteria.
前方的圓形建築是學校的食堂。

architect [ˈɑrkəˌtɛkt] **n** 建築師

Gaudi was a famous **architect**.
高地是一位很有名的建築師。

architecture [ˈɑrkəˌtɛktʃɚ] **n** 建築學；建築（風格）

She loves taking pictures of Gothic **architecture**.
她熱愛拍攝歌德式建築的照片。

construct [kənˈstrʌkt] **v** 建造

This church is **constructed** by a famous architect.
這間教堂是一位有名的建築師建造的。

constructor [kənˈstrʌktɚ] **n** 建設者；施工者

The **constructor** requested to extend the deadline.
營造商要求延後最後期限。

construction [kənˈstrʌkʃən] **n** 建設

You must wear a helmet at the **construction** site.
在建築工地你必須戴安全帽。

各種不同的建築物

house [haʊs] **n** 房子

You will find a beautiful garden behind the **house**.
你會在房子後面發現一座漂亮的花園。

● 聯想主題／建築物

apartment [ə'partmənt] n 公寓

When I grow up, I plan to rent an **apartment** and live by myself.
等我長大，我打算租一間公寓，自己生活。

flat [flæt] n 住宅

She rented a **flat** beside the train station.
她在車站旁租了一間公寓。

dormitory ['dɔrmə,torɪ] n 學生宿舍

He lives with her wife at the staff **dormitory**.
他和太太住在員工宿舍。

mansion ['mænʃən] n 大廈

I was amazed to see this gorgeous **mansion**.
看到這棟華麗的大廈真令我驚豔。

villa ['vɪlə] n 別墅

The **villa** by the beach is owned by a businessman.
海邊的那棟別墅是一位商人所擁有的。

real estate ['riəl] [ɪs'tet] 房地產

You can find **real estate** for sale online.
你可以在網路上找到出售中的房地產。

possession [pə'zɛʃən] n 財產；所有物

She claimed that this house is her **possession**.
她聲稱這間房子是她的所有物。

property ['prɑpɚtɪ] n 所有物

This land is the only property given by his father.
這塊地是他父親給他的唯一資產。

apartment   villa   dormitory

建
築
物

建築材料及其衍生

board [bord] n 木板

I'll use the board to make a table for you.
我會用這片木板做一張桌子給你。

timber ['tɪmbɚ] n 木材

This coffee table is made of timber.
這張咖啡桌是木頭做的。

lumber ['lʌmbɚ] n 木材

This stack of lumber is freshly cut.
這堆木材是剛被砍下的。

wood [wud] n 木頭

All the furniture in this room is made by **wood**.
這個房間裡所有的家具都是木製的。

wooden ['wudn] adj 木的

Sofas are more comfortable than **wooden** chairs.
沙發比木製椅子坐起來舒服。

cement [sɪ'mɛnt] n 水泥

This building is made purely of **cement**.
這棟建築物是純水泥建造。

concrete ['kɑnkrit] adj 具體的；n 混凝土

Concrete is made from cement mixed with sand and water.
混凝土是用水泥混合著沙和水做成的。

solidify [sə'lɪdə,faɪ] v 使堅固

The pudding will **solidify** in the fridge.
布丁會在冰箱裡凝固。

adhesive [əd'hisɪv] adj 有黏性的

This band-aid is not **adhesive** to my skin.
這塊OK繃無法黏著在我的皮膚上。

詞類變化篇

第 2 篇

accept
[ək'sɛpt]
v 接受

★ Whether you like it or not, you have to **accept** the demotion.
不管你是否喜歡，你都得接受這次降職。

acceptable
[ək'sɛptəbl̩]
adj 可以接受的

★ What he said was **acceptable**.
他所說的話是可以接受的。

accident
['æksədənt]
n 意外事件；事故

★ Who is to blame for the traffic **accident**?
誰該負責這起交通事故？

accidentally
[ˌæksə'dɛntl̩ɪ]
adv 偶然地；
意外地

★ I read that report **accidentally**.
我偶然讀到那篇報導。

accommodate
[ə'kamə͵det]
v 提供膳宿；
提供方便

★ This theater can **accommodate** a thousand people at most.
這個劇場最多能容納一千人。（at most 最多）

accommodation
[ə͵kamə'defən]
n 調和；膳宿；
方便設施

★ They made the **accommodations** for the new clients.
他們安排新客戶的住宿事宜。

advance
[əd'væns]
v 推進；促進；
n 前進

★ He knew in **advance** that he was going to be fired.
他早就知道自己要被解雇了。

advanced
[əd'vænst]
adj 年邁的；超
前的；高級的

★ This mini disc player is the most **advanced** device on the market.
這台迷你光碟播放機是市面上最先進的設備。

affect
[ə'fɛkt]
v 影響

★ Some services were omitted, but it doesn't seem to have **affected** the sale.
一些服務內容被省略了，但是那似乎並不影響銷售情況。

affection
[ə'fɛkʃən]
n 影響；傾向；
愛情

★ Neither the poor quality nor the high price can change her **affection** for this adorable mobile phone.
不佳的品質和過高的訂價都影響不了她對這部可愛手機的喜愛程度。

afford
[ə'ford]
v 給予；擔負
得起

★ We can't **afford** to take a trip to Europe this year, maybe next year.
今年我們付不起去歐洲旅遊，也許明年去吧。

affordable
[ə'fordəbl]
adj 負擔得起的

★ One on one English lessons are not really **affordable** for me right now.
我現在不太能夠負擔一對一的英語課。

agent
['edʒənt]
n 代理商；密探

★ The **agent** secretly investigated the bribery.
這位探員暗中調查賄賂案件。

agency
['edʒənsɪ]
n 專業行政部
門；代理行

★ Our travel **agency** provides a package tour to the Philippines.
我們的旅行社提供菲律賓套裝旅遊。

amazing
[ə'mezɪŋ]
adj 令人驚異的

★ He said he could finish the project in merely one day, which was **amazing**.
他說他能在僅僅一天之內完成這項工程，這很讓人吃驚。

amazed
[ə'mezd]
adj 驚奇的；
吃驚的

★ Alice was **amazed** that her father counted her out of their travel plans.
愛麗絲很震驚她的爸爸把她排除在旅行計畫之外。

◗ 詞類變化

amuse
[ə'mjuz]
v 提供娛樂；
逗樂

★ Tom makes up stories to **amuse** his little brother.
湯姆編故事逗他的小弟弟。

amusement
[ə'mjuzmənt]
n 娛樂；消遣

★ Many Taiwanese people like to go to karaokes or shop for **amusement**.
很多臺灣人以去唱歌或購物作為娛樂。

announce
[ə'nauns]
v 預告；宣布；
聲稱

★ An important decision will be **announced** after the meeting.
會議結束後，一個重大的決定將被宣布。

announcement
[ə'naunsmənt]
n 一項公告；
宣告；發表

★ President Lincoln made his famous Emancipation Proclamation **announcement**.
林肯總統發表著名的解放奴隸宣言。

appear
[ə'pɪr]
v 出現

★ When Andy Lau **appeared** on the stage, the audience cheered with one voice.
當劉德華登上舞台時，所有觀眾一致歡呼。

appearance
[ə'pɪrəns]
n 外貌

★ The twin sisters are so alike in **appearance**.
這對雙胞胎姊妹外貌好像。

appreciate
[ə'priʃɪ,et]
v 欣賞

★ Your dedication to work will be highly **appreciated** by the boss.
你對工作的投入將受老闆很大的讚賞。

appreciation
[ə,priʃɪ'eʃən]
n 欣賞；感謝

★ His boss gave him a BMW as a token of **appreciation** to his contributions.
他的老闆送他一輛BMW作為感謝他的貢獻的象徵。

applicant
['æpləkənt]
n 申請人

★ The company asked all the **applicants** to send a CV before the dead line.
公司要求每位申請者在最後期限之前遞上簡歷。

application
[ˌæplə'keʃən]
n 應用

★ The period from a new concept to a new **application** is short nowadays.
這些年來，從新概念的提出到實現的週期縮短了。

approve
[ə'pruv]
v 贊許；認可

★ Her parents don't **approve** of her spending so much time with her new boyfriend.
她的父母親不贊成她花那麼多時間陪她的新男朋友。

approval
[ə'pruvl̩]
n 贊成；認可

★ It seems improper to cut out the third paragraph without writer's **approval**.
不經作者同意就刪掉第三段好像不合適吧。

★ The group ended up with an excellent report which won a lot of **approval**.
這個小組最後做出一份精彩的報告，贏得一片肯定。

arrive
[ə'raɪv]
v 到達；到來

★ When our new director **arrived**, he received a warm welcome.
當我們的新總裁到來時，他受到熱烈的歡迎。

arrival
[ə'raɪvl̩]
n 到達物；到達；到達者

★ We'll forward our goods on the **arrival** of your check.
收到你們的支票後，我們就會出貨。

assign
[ə'saɪn]
v 指派；分配

★ After John was promoted, he was **assigned** to be in charge of the entire department.
約翰獲得升職以後，被指定負責整個部門。

assignment
[ə'saɪnmənt]
n 工作；功課；任務

★ The director found it difficult to find someone equal to the **assignment**.
主管發現要找一名能夠勝任這份工作的人很困難。

145

詞類變化

assist
[ə'sɪst]
ⓥ 協助；說明

⭐ Since you can't finish the work alone, I'll arrange for another clerk to **assist** you.
既然你無法獨立完成工作，我另會安排一名員工來協助你。

assistant
[ə'sɪstənt]
ⓝ 助理；助手

⭐ Molly has been working in this company as a manager's **assistant** for two years, and she is now considering changing her job.
茉莉在這家公司當經理助理已經兩年了，她正在考慮換個工作。

associate
[ə'soʃɪ,et]
ⓥ 使聯合；結交；ⓝ 同事；夥伴；合夥人

⭐ Success is usually **associated** with hard work.
成功往往與勤奮相聯。

⭐ Most of my **associates** play online games to kill time.
我大多數的同事都玩網路遊戲來打發時間。

association
[ə,sosɪ'eʃən]
ⓝ 聯合；交往；社團

⭐ It is very easy to take part in our **association**.
參加我們協會很簡單。

assure
[ə'ʃur]
ⓥ 確保；使放心

⭐ Before you wash your clothes, **assure** your pockets are empty.
在你洗衣服之前，確保你的口袋是空的。

assurance
[ə'ʃurəns]
ⓝ 保證；確信；擔保；斷言

⭐ Quality **assurance** should always be our golden rule.
品質的確保是我們不變的指導原則。

attract
[ə'trækt]
ⓥ 吸引

⭐ Many restaurants have their house special in order to **attract** more customers.
許多飯店為了吸引更多的顧客都有自己的招牌菜。

attractive
[ə'træktɪv]
ⓐⓓⓙ 有吸引力的；引起注意的；吸引的

⭐ The digital camera show is excellent and **attractive**.
這個數位相機秀很精彩，很吸引人。

author
['ɔθɚ]
n 作者;著作家

★ The **author** used three exclamation marks at the end of the last sentence to wake up the readers.
作者在最後一句用了三個驚嘆號,以引起讀者的注意。

---

authority
[ə'θɔrɪtɪ]
n 權威;權力

★ The boss was on vacation, and Mary had the **authority** to solve the issue.
老闆在渡假,瑪麗擁有處理事務的權力。

詞類變化

automobile
['ɔtəmə,bɪl]
= auto n 汽車

★ All the **automobile** manufacturers are up against the fierce competition.
所有汽車生產商都面臨激烈競爭。

---

automatic
[,ɔtə'mætɪk]
adj 自動手槍;
自動的

★ My **automatic** coffee maker begins to brew coffee at six o'clock sharp every morning.
我的自動咖啡機每天早上六點整準時開始泡咖啡。

---

bare
[bɛr]
adj 赤裸的;
光禿的

★ While we were in India, we saw a man walking on hot coals with his **bare** feet.
我們在印度的時候,看到一個人赤腳走在熱炭上。

---

barely
['bɛrlɪ]
adv 幾乎不;
只不過;僅僅

★ He can **barely** read.
他幾乎不會讀書。

---

beg
[bɛg]
v 乞討;懇求

★ She fell on her knees to **beg** the king for forgiveness.
她跪下,懇求國王寬恕她。

---

beggar
['bɛgɚ]
n 乞丐

★ The little girl counted out a dollar in change and gave it to the **beggar**.
小女孩數了一美元的零錢給乞丐。

詞類變化

◐ 詞類變化

believe
[bɪ'liv]
v 相信

★ But that I saw it, I wouldn't have believed it.
要不是我親眼目睹，簡直不敢相信。

believable
[bɪ'livəbl̩]
adj 可信的

★ The conclusion, based on enough evidences, is believable.
基於足夠證據所做出的結論是值得相信的。

bleeding
['blidɪŋ]
n 流血

★ You have to apply pressure on the cut in order to stop the bleeding.
你必須用力壓在傷口上以止血。

blood
[blʌdɪ]
n 血

★ Written with fake blood, the note looks terrifying.
用假血寫的紙條看起來很恐怖。

breath
[brɛθ]
n 微風；氣息；呼吸

★ The children ran around the playground until they were out of breath.
孩子們不斷圍繞著遊樂場奔跑，直到他們上氣不接下氣。

breathe
[brið]
v (低聲地) 說出；呼吸；喘氣

★ People with asthma have difficulty breathing at times.
哮喘病患有時候會呼吸困難。

calculation
[ˌkælkjə'leʃən]
n 計算

★ Prior to the invention of computers, people had to spend much time doing math calculations.
在電腦發明之前，人們不得不花大量時間做數學計算。

calculator
['kælkjə,letɚ]
n 計算機

★ A calculator is very useful when you do business.
做生意的時候，計算機很有用。

capital
['kæpətl]
n 資本；首都；
adj 可處死刑
的；大寫的

★ Troops put down a rising in the capital.
部隊平息了發生在首都的叛亂。

capitalization
[,kæpətlə'zeʃən]
n 資本；資本額

★ The market capitalization of Koogle is huge, and who can believe the promoters are two young boys?
Koogle的市值巨大，誰又能相信它的創始人居然是兩個小伙子呢？

cash
[kæʃ]
n 現金；v 把…
兌現

★ Some oil companies attempted to cash in on energy crisis.
某些石油公司企圖從能源危機中撈到好處。

cashier
[kæ'ʃɪr]
n 出納

★ Lucy is a cashier.
露西是個收銀員。

champion
['tʃæmpɪən]
n 冠軍者；
優勝者

★ He became the new champion of this season.
他成為本季新冠軍。

championship
['tʃæmpɪən,ʃɪp]
n 冠軍；優勝；
擁護

★ To date, it is the only football team that keeps 5 successive championships.
到現在為止，那是唯一一支保持五連冠的足球隊。

charm
[tʃɑrm]
n 魅力；符咒；
v 吸引；迷住

★ Cary was a handsome young man whose charm overwhelmed all the ladies present the other night.
凱瑞是位英俊的年輕人，那天晚上他的魅力傾倒了在場所有女士。

◎ 詞類變化

charming
['tʃɑrmɪŋ]
adj 嬌媚的；迷人的

★ Actually, the design of the computer is **charming** to young people, but the price is too high.
實際上，這部電腦的設計很吸引年輕人，但是價格過高。

chemist
['kɛmɪst]
n 藥劑師；化學家；藥商

★ Jason is a **chemist**.
傑森是化學家。

chemistry
['kɛmɪstrɪ]
n 化學

★ Her accomplishments in the fields of **chemistry** and physics won her three prizes.
她在化學和物理領域的成就讓她得獎三次。

clothes
[kloz]
n 衣服

★ A laundry is a store where **clothes** are washed and ironed.
洗衣店是洗熨衣服的地方。

clothing
['kloðɪŋ]
n (衣著) 服裝

★ Janet left for New York, one of the most fashionable cities in the world, to begin her career as a **clothing** designer.
珍妮去了紐約，這個世界上最時尚的城市之一，開始了她服飾設計師的職業生涯。

combine
[kəm'baɪn]
v 聯合；結合；化合

★ Diligence, **combined** with intelligence, will lead to success.
勤奮再加上才智能夠帶來成功。

combination
[ˌkɑmbə'neʃən]
n 結合；聯盟

★ Could you give out the latest news about the **combination** of the two unions?
你能給我關於這兩個聯盟合併的最新消息嗎？

comfort
['kʌmfɚt]
n 安慰；v 安慰

★ Government officials shall **comfort** the grieving parents.
政府官員應該慰問這些傷心的父母親。

comfortable
['kʌmfə·təbl]
adj 舒適的

★ The survey shows that people are not very **comfortable** with what the government did.
調查顯示，人們對政府的所作所為不太滿意。

command
[kə'mænd]
n 命令；掌握
v 命令；指揮

★ After years of work, you will have a good **command** of the skills.
經過多年的工作後，你會很好地掌握這些技能。

★ Jeff is now directly under the **command** of the boss.
傑夫現在在老闆的直接指揮下。

commander
[kə'mændə·]
n 司令官；指揮官

★ When the army got lost, the **commander** decided to go just the other way around.
當軍隊迷路時，指揮官決定由反方向繞過去。

commerce
['kɑmɜ·s]
n 貿易；商業

★ To survive the **commerce** competition, you need a smart mind.
為了在商業競爭中生存下來，你必須擁有聰明的頭腦。

commercial
[kə'mɜ·ʃəl]
adj 商業的；
n 商業廣告

★ A good **commercial** can attract many people's attention.
好的商業廣告可以吸引很多人的注意。

communicate
[kə'mjunə,ket]
v 傳達；連接；
傳染；交流

★ Now we **communicate** with our customers through emails.
現在我們用電子郵件和客戶溝通。

communication
[kə,mjunə'keʃən]
n 通信工具；
交流；通訊

★ Our life has improved a lot since modern **communication** methods are widely used.
自從現代通訊技術普及以來，我們的生活有了很大進步。

competition
[,kɑmpə'tɪʃən]
n 比賽

★ They concentrate on the track and field **competition** again.
他們又全神貫注地觀看田徑比賽了。

詞類變化

competitive
[kəm'pɛtətɪv]
adj 好競爭的；
競爭的

★ Universities can help students become qualified and **competitive**.
大學可以幫助學生成長得更合格、更有競爭力。

compose
[kəm'poz]
v 創作；組成；
使平靜

★ This book is **composed** of six main parts.
這本書包含六大部分。

composition
[,kampə'zɪʃən]
n 作品；創作；
組成；結構

★ Apart from some spelling mistakes, your **composition** is well written.
除了幾處拼寫錯誤，你的作文寫的很好。

conclude
[kən'klud]
v 結束；推斷出

★ Mark talked so nervously that we **concluded** he wasn't telling the truth at all.
馬克說話時如此緊張，以至於我們認為他根本沒有說實話。

conclusion
[kən'kluʒən]
n 結尾；締結；
結論

★ In **conclusion**, fiscal policy is different from monetary policy.
最後，可以總結出財政政策和貨幣政策是不同的。

concern
[kən'sɝn]
v 關於；關心；
n 關心

★ As far as I'm **concerned**, this is a pretty nice working place.
就我所關心的方面來說，這是一個不錯的工作場所。

concerning
[kən'sɝnɪŋ]
prep. 關於

★ Please inform me of your new plan **concerning** that project.
請告訴我你關於那個專案的新計畫。

conduct
[kən'dʌkt]
v 表現；n 舉止

★ Her heroic **conduct** of fighting against the bad man was counted to her credit.
她和壞人戰鬥的英雄行為受到讚揚。

conductor
[kən'dʌktɚ]
n 指揮者

★ The **conductor** lifted his baton.
指揮舉起了他的指揮棒。

confuse
[kən'fjuz]
v 搞亂；使糊塗

★ New and surprising things are always happening to excite people or to **confuse** them.
總是發生各種新鮮驚人的事物，使得人們要麼為之興奮，要麼為之困惑。

confusion
[kən'fjuʒən]
n 混淆；困惑；混亂

★ The little park was an oasis of calm amid the noise and **confusion** of the urban jungle.
這個小公園是嘈雜混亂城市叢林中的一塊安靜綠洲。

congratulate
[kən'grætʃə,let]
v 道喜；祝賀

★ You should **congratulate** her for having done such a good job.
她工作做得這麼出色，你應該祝賀她。

congratulation
[kən,grætʃə'leʃən]
n 祝賀

★ On hearing that John started a new business, Mary gave her **congratulations** to him.
聽到約翰開始了新的生意，瑪麗向他表示祝賀。

considerate
[kən'sɪdərɪt]
adj 體諒的；體貼的

★ Is it very **considerate** of him to remember my birthday every year?
他每年都記得我生日，是不是很體貼？

consideration
[kənsɪdə'reʃən]
n 關心；考慮

★ We should take into **consideration** his difficulties and forgive him.
我們應該考慮到他的難處，並且原諒他。

consist
[kən'sɪst]
v 在於；組成；存在於

★ The new machine **consists** of three parts.
新機器由三個部分組成。

詞類變化

consistent [kən'sɪstənt] adj 一致的;符合的;堅持的	★ Tina deserved to be promoted because of her **consistent** good work. 因為她一貫優異的工作表現,蒂娜應該得到晉升。
construction [kən'strʌkʃən] n 建造物;建造;結構	★ The cost for the school's **construction** amounted to two million dollars. 建造那所學校的費用共計兩百萬美元。
construct [kən'strʌkt] v 對…進行構思;建造	★ The workers have been **constructing** a library. 工人們一直在建造圖書館。
contribute [kən'trɪbjut] v 投稿;捐獻	★ All members should **contribute** to the Fund. 所有會員都應向基金會捐款。
contribution [,kantrə'bjuʃən] n 捐款;貢獻	★ Nash made a great **contribution** to the game theory. 納許對博弈論貢獻卓著。
cooperate [ko'apə,ret] v 配合;合作;協作	★ Mary and Jane have decided to put aside their misunderstandings and **cooperate** from now on. 瑪麗和珍決定由現在起拋開誤解,互相合作。
cooperation [ko,apə'reʃən] n 合作	★ In order to improve the **cooperation** between us, we need to have a long talk. 為了增進彼此間的合作,我們需要長談。
create [krɪ'et] v 創造	★ The Constitution of the U.S. **created** a government of balanced power. 美國的憲法使政府的權力分開平衡。

creative
[krɪ'etɪv]
adj 有創造力的；
創造性的

★ He is **creative** enough to come up with all different ideas.
他有足夠的想像力，能想出各種不同的主意來。

creature
['kritʃɚ]
n 創造物；生物

★ Human being is the only **creature** that cares for their parents.
人類是唯一會關心父母的生物。

critic
['krɪtɪk]
n 評論家；
批評家

★ **Critics** have deemed Britney Spears the next Madonna.
評論家們認為小甜甜布蘭妮是下一個瑪丹娜。

critical
['krɪtɪkl]
adj 批評的；
決定性的

★ Economists of main stream are **critical** to the reforms of that enterprise.
主流經濟學家對這個企業的系列改革提出批評。

criticize
['krɪtɪ,saɪz]
v 評價；批判

★ He has been **criticized** by the director many times.
他已經被導演批評很多次了。

criticism
['krɪtə,sɪzəm]
n 評論（文章）；指責

★ Tom went ahead with his work regardless of others' **criticism**.
湯姆不顧別人的批評，繼續做他的工作。

dancing
['dænsɪŋ]
n 舞蹈

★ Mary's **dancing** skills wasted away due to lack of practice.
由於缺少練習，瑪麗的舞蹈技能退步了。

dancer
['dænsɚ]
n 舞蹈家；舞女

★ He is not more a **dancer** than a singer.
與其說他是個舞蹈家倒不如說他是個歌手。

詞類變化

definite
['dɛfənɪt]
adj 一定的;
明確的

★ The report is so vague that we can't get any **definite** information from it.
這報告主題太模糊了,我們無法從中得到任何確切的資訊。

definitely
['dɛfənɪtlɪ]
adv 明確地

★ You will **definitely** fail the final exam if you don't start reviewing the lessons.
如果你還不開始複習,期末考試一定會不及格。

definition
[,dɛfə'nɪʃən]
n 清晰;定義

★ We need to clear up some **definitions** before we make the final decision.
在做最終決定之前,我們必須弄清一些定義。

deliver
[dɪ'lɪvɚ]
v 傳送;投遞

★ The goods you ordered will be **delivered** within three days.
您訂的商品會在三日內送達。

delivery
[dɪ'lɪvərɪ]
n 投遞

★ Mary decided to overlook the delay of the **delivery**.
瑪麗決定不追究送貨遲延的事。

dependable
[dɪ'pɛndəbl̩]
adj 可靠的;
可信任的

★ We can assure you that the quality of the computer is **dependable**.
這台電腦的品質我們可以保證。

dependent
[dɪ'pɛndənt]
adj 依賴的;
依靠的

★ Children are always **dependent** on their parents.
孩子們總是依賴他們的父母。

desperate
['dɛspərɪt]
adj 極嚮往的;
不顧一切的;絕
望的

★ She felt **desperate** and sad.
她感到又絕望又難過。

desperately
['dɛspərɪtlɪ]
adv 絕望地；
拚命地

★ The company is **desperately** in quest of a big deal.
這家公司正在急切地找尋一項大型交易。

determine
[dɪ,tɜ-mə'neʃən]
v 決定

★ Nancy was **determined** to become a consultant after her graduation.
南茜決定畢業後去當諮詢員。

determination
[dɪ,tɜ-mə'neʃən]
n 確定；決心

★ Due to the lack of **determination**, we may lose the competition.
由於缺乏果斷，我們可能會輸掉比賽。

develop
[dɪ'vɛləp]
v 使成長

★ The **developed** countries should take steps to cope with the environmental problems.
發達國家應採取措施以解決環境汙染問題。

development
[dɪ'vɛləpmənt]
n 發展；生長

★ Collecting information from the market is very useful for company's **development**.
從市場上收集資訊對於公司的發展很有幫助。

devote
[dɪ'vot]
v 將…奉獻給

★ In spite of all the effort he **devoted** to the book, it failed in coming out.
儘管他全心全意寫書，但還是沒能出版。

devotion
[dɪ'voʃən]
n 投入；熱愛

★ Learning English well calls for great patience and **devotion**.
學好英語需要極大的耐心和投入。

discuss
[dɪ'skʌs]
v 討論

★ The project is still being **discussed**.
這個項目現在還在討論中。

discussion
[dɪ'skʌʃən]
n 討論

★ They had a heated **discussion** on whether to cancel the plan or not.
他們為是否取消該計畫進行激烈的討論。

詞類變化

dramatic
[drə'mætɪk]
adj 戲劇性的；
引人注目的

★ A **dramatic** rescue at sea took place yesterday.
昨天上演了激動人心的海上救援。

dramatically
[drə'mætɪklɪ]
adv 戲劇性地

★ The rate of car accidents increased **dramatically**.
汽車事故率大大地升高。

ease
[iz]
v 減輕；緩和；
n 悠閒；容易；
adj 簡單的

★ Since Mary came to help me, my job became much **easier**.
自從瑪麗來幫忙之後，我的工作就簡單多了。

easily
['izɪlɪ]
adv 無疑地；肯
定地；容易地

★ My trip down the Amazon River has **easily** been the greatest
adventure of my life.
我沿著亞馬遜河下行的旅行顯然是我這輩子最大的冒險。

economy
[ɪ'kanəmɪ]
n 充分利用；經
濟（制度）；節
約

★ John commented that the report on **economy** was too
optimistic.
約翰對於那份經濟報告的評價是它過於樂觀。

economic
[,ikə'namɪk]
adj 經濟學的；
經濟上的；經濟
的

★ Everyone is expecting to usher in the **economic** boom.
大家都期待迎接經濟增長的到來。

edition
[ɪ'dɪʃən]
n 版本

★ The press is bringing out a new **edition** of dictionary.
這家出版社正出版新編辭典。

editorial
[ˌɛdə'tɔrɪəl]
adj 社論的；
n 社論

☆ Peter loved reading the editorial section of the newspaper.
彼得喜歡看報紙的社論版。

education
[ˌɛdʒʊ'keʃən]
n 教育

☆ The current education system is not welcome.
現行的教育制度並不受歡迎。

educational
[ˌɛdʒʊ'keʃənl]
adj 教育的

☆ Her educational background is quite good.
她的教育背景相當好。

employee
[ˌɛmplɔɪ'i]
n 雇員；雇工

☆ Steve is one of the most promising employees in our office.
史蒂夫是我們辦公室最有前途的員工之一。

employer
[ɪm'plɔɪɚ]
n 雇主；雇傭者

☆ The employer should be sincere and smart.
雇主應該又真誠又聰明。

entertain
[ˌɛntɚ'ten]
v 招待；使快樂

☆ Comedies entertain the public, including the elderly and the young.
喜劇娛樂了大眾，無論老少。

entertainment
[ˌɛntɚ'tenmənt]
n 招待；娛樂

☆ To businessmen, holding parties is more than entertainment.
對於商人，舉行派對不只是娛樂而已。

enthusiastic
[ɪn,θjuzɪ'æstɪk]
adj 熱情的；
熱心的

☆ Mary was very enthusiastic about her new position.
瑪麗對她的新職位很期待。

enthusiasm
[ɪn'θjuzɪˌæzəm]
n 熱心；熱情

☆ It calls for patience, wisdom and enthusiasm to be a good teacher.
當個好教師，需要的是耐心，智慧和熱情。

● 詞類變化

詞類變化

environmental
[ɪn͵vaɪrən'mɛntl̩]
adj 環境的；
周圍的

★ The **environmental** condition calls for people's attention.
環境狀況需要人們的關注。

environmentally
[ɛn͵vaɪrən'mɛntlɪ]
adv 有關環境方面

★ This machine runs on renewable energy and is pollution free. In a word, it is **environmentally** friendly.
這部機器使用可再生能源且不會製造汙染，簡而言之，它是環保產品。

exact
[ɪg'zækt]
adj 精確的；
確切的

★ Does your secetary know the **exact** time of the meeting?
你的祕書知道會議的確切時間嗎？

exactly
[ɪg'zæktlɪ]
adv 嚴密地；
正確地

★ Zoe knows **exactly** which actions need to be taken to deal with during the slowing down economy.
佐伊清楚地知道在經濟增長緩慢的情況下該採取什麼措施。

examine
[ɪg'zæmɪn]
v 檢查

★ The doctors have been **examining** the patient.
醫生們一直檢查該病人。

examination
[ɪg͵zæmə'neʃən]
n 檢查；考試

★ I know Jim failed in the **examination**, but after all, he has tried best.
我知道吉姆考試沒及格，但是畢竟他還是盡力了。

excite
[ɪk'saɪt]
v 刺激；使激動

★ Did you tell our boss some good news? She is **excited** now.
你告訴老闆什麼好消息了嗎？她現在很興奮。

excitement
[ɪk'saɪtmənt]
n 令人興奮的事；
刺激；興奮

★ Peter was trembling with **excitement** when he received the award.
彼得拿到獎項時興奮地發抖。

explode
[ɪk'splod]
v 使爆炸；
爆發；激增

★ All of a sudden, the car **exploded** on the highway.
突然之間，車子就在高速公路上爆炸了。

explosion
[ɪk'sploʒən]
n 激增；爆發

★ It came out that the **explosion** was caused by a cigarette.
真相大白了，這次爆炸是由一根香煙引起的。

extend
[ɪk'stɛnd]
v （範圍）
達到；提供

★ If you want to stay here longer, you have to have your visa **extended**.
如果你想在這停留長一點時間的話，你必須延長你的簽證。

extent
[ɪk'stɛnt]
n 寬度；程度

★ When the volcano erupts, the **extent** to which our homes will be destroyed is immeasurable.
火山爆發時，我們家園被毀壞的程度是不可估量的。

faith
[feθ]
n 信仰；信任；
信心

★ Whatever may happen, we shall continue to strive and never lose **faith**.
無論發生什麼，我們都應該繼續努力奮鬥而決不失去信念。

faithful
['feθfəl]
adj 如實的；盡
職的；忠誠的

★ Jim was not **faithful**.
吉姆不忠誠。

fluent
['fluənt]
adj 流暢的；
流利的

★ Being able to speak **fluent** English, Jack was sent on a business trip to the USA.
因為英語流利，傑克被派遣到美國出差。

fluently
[fl'uəntlɪ]
adv 流利地；
流暢地

★ Nowadays many companies need employees who can speak English **fluently**.
如今許多公司都需要英語流利的員工。

詞類變化

fortune
['fɔrtʃən]
n 運氣；財產

★ Experience means **fortune** for every businessman.
對於商人來說經驗就是財富。

---

fortunately
['fɔrtʃənɪtlɪ]
adv 幸虧；
幸運地

★ **Fortunately**, I got into my dream company in the end.
幸運的是，我最終進入我夢想的公司。

---

forbid
[fɚ'bɪd]
v 禁止；不許

★ The government imposed a new law to **forbid** rally.
政府透過新法律禁止大型集會。

---

forbidden
[fɚ'bɪdn]
adj 不允許的

★ Smoking is **forbidden** here. Please put your cigarette out.
這裡禁止吸煙，請將您的煙熄滅。

---

found
[faund]
v 創辦；創立；
創建

★ Lisa **founded** this popular cosmetic shop two years ago.
莉莎在兩年前創立了這家受歡迎的化妝品店。

---

founder
['faundɚ]
n 奠基人；鑄
工；創始人；
翻沙工

★ Louis Vuitton was named in honor of his **founder**.
路易威登是為了紀念創始人而以其名字命名的。

---

gamble
['gæmbl]
v 孤注一擲；賭
博；投機；n 冒
險；賭博

★ Some people do not **gamble** for money, but for the excitement.
有些人賭博不是為了贏錢，而是為了刺激。

---

gambling
['gæmblɪŋ]
n 賭博

★ John likes **gambling**, but his bad hand caused him to lose a lot of money.
約翰喜歡賭博，但因為手氣不好輸掉了很多錢。

general
['dʒɛnərəl]
adj 普遍的；普通的

★ The receptionist is responsible for answering **general** questions.
服務台負責回答一般問題。

generally
['dʒɛnərəlɪ]
adv 通常；一般地

★ **Generally** speaking, it's not uncommon to get nervous before you make a speech.
總的來說，在演講前緊張是最普通不過的事了。

graduate
['grædʒu,et]
n 畢業生；
v （使）畢業

★ We **graduated** from our middle school two years ago to the day.
我們從中學畢業剛好兩年。

graduation
[,grædʒu'eʃən]
n 畢業典禮；畢業

★ Getting a job with a salary of 3000 dollars right after **graduation** is impossible.
一畢業就找到個月薪三千美元的工作是不可能的。

high
[haɪ]
adj 高的；高級的

★ Most buyers are adolescents who are still in **high** school.
大多數的購買者都是還在就讀高中的青少年。

highly
['haɪlɪ]
adv 非常贊許地；高度地；非常

★ Success can be **highly** related to one's strong point.
成功與個人優勢有很大關聯。

imagine
[ɪ'mædʒɪn]
v 想像

★ Can you **imagine** that one day we will have our own house with a large garden?
你能想像我們有天將擁有一棟附有大花園的房子嗎？

imagination
[ɪ,mædʒə'neʃən]
n 想像；想像力；空想

★ Writing such a story requires a stretch of the **imagination**.
要寫出這樣的故事得發揮想像力。

● 詞類變化

immediate
[ɪ'midɪɪt]
adj 立即的；
直接的

★ Facing the accident, Jane was calm enough to take **immediate** actions.
面對意外，珍冷靜地及時採取行動。

immediately
[ɪ'midɪɪtlɪ]
adv 直接地；
立即

★ If he comes to the office, tell him to come to my office **immediately**.
如果他進辦公室的話，請他立刻到我的辦公室來。

impression
[ɪm'prɛʃən]
n 印記；印象；
感覺

★ What she has done later corresponded with our initial **impression** of her.
她後來所做的事情與我們對她的第一印象是相符的。

impressive
[ɪm'prɛsɪv]
adj 給人印象深刻的

★ Tom's achievement in our company is **impressive**.
湯姆在公司所取得的成績令人敬佩。

increase
[ɪn'kris]
n 增加；v 增加

★ The company's sales have been **increasing** these years.
公司的銷售額幾年來一直在增加。

increasingly
[ɪn'krisɪŋli]
adv 越來越多地；日益

★ Judy began to grow **increasingly** agitated as she waited for her name to be announced.
在等著被叫到她名字的時候，茱蒂開始越來越激動。

inform
[ɪn'fɔrm]
v 通知；報告

★ The manager was **informed** of an unexpected visit by some VIPs.
經理被告知有幾位貴賓將突然來訪。

information
[ˌɪnfɚ'meʃən]
n 消息；報導；資訊

★ Mike was asked to fill out personal **information** when he applied for a credit card.
邁克申請信用卡的時候被要求填寫個人資訊。

instructive
[ɪn'strʌktɪv]
adj 有益的；
教育性的

☆ Participating in some volunteering work is **instructive**.
參加志工活動是有建設性的。

instructor
[ɪn'strʌktɚ]
n 講師；教師

☆ Neither of the students has turned in his term papers to the **instructor** yet.
還沒有學生把學期論文交給老師。

invest
[ɪn'vɛst]
v 投資；投入

☆ If you want to be a rich man, observe and **invest** wisely.
如果你想成為一個富翁的話，那就聰明地觀察和投資吧。

investment
[ɪn'vɛstmənt]
n 投入

☆ Helen came up with a new problem about the risk of the **investment** plan.
海倫提出關於這項投資案風險的新問題。

late
[let]
adj 晚的；慢的

☆ In future, anyone that comes **late** will be fired.
今後，任何遲到的人都會被開除。

lately
['letlɪ]
adv 不久前；
最近

☆ Why is she skipping so much class **lately**?
她最近為什麼曠了這麼多堂課？

library
['laɪˌbrɛrɪ]
n 圖書館

☆ Using the Internet, students can check out book records of the university **library**.
透過網路，學生可以查詢大學圖書館的藏書紀錄。

librarian
[laɪ'brɛrɪən]
n 圖書館館長；
圖書館員

☆ **Librarians** can help students find books in a very short time.
圖書管理員能在很短的時間內幫學生找到書。

loyal
['lɔɪəl]
adj 忠誠的

☆ Japanese people believe that employees should be **loyal** to their companies.
日本人認為員工應該對公司忠心。

● 詞類變化

詞類變化

loyalty
['lɔɪəltɪ]
n 忠誠

★ Above all, one must bear **loyalty** to one's family.
做人最重要的是對家庭忠誠。

luck
[lʌk]
n 好運；吉祥物；僥倖

★ Bob said he got the position due to good **luck**.
鮑伯說他得到這個職位只是因為運氣好。

luckily
['lʌkɪlɪ]
adv 幸運地

★ **Luckily**, I passed the exam.
幸運的是，我通過了測驗。

manage
['mænɪdʒ]
v 設法做到；經營

★ No one knows how he **managed** to get away from the prison.
沒人知道他是怎樣逃離監獄的。

management
['mænɪdʒmənt]
n 經營

★ The company has been in the red these years due to poor **management**.
由於管理不善，這家公司的財政赤字已經持續了幾年。

mean
[min]
adj 平均的；
v 意謂

★ When he said the plan needed further improvement, he **meant** he was not satisfied with your work.
當他說這個計畫還要進一步改進時，他的意思是他對你的工作不太滿意。

meaningful
['minɪŋfəl]
adj 意味深長的

★ The boss is going to have a **meaningful** talk with the customers.
老闆將和顧客進行一次深層的談話。

natural
['nætʃərəl]
adj 自然的；
天然的

★ It is **natural** for a fashion designer to be fashionable.
時裝設計師追求時髦是很自然的。

166

naturally
['nætʃərəlɪ]
adv 自然地；
天生地

★ He has skipped most of the classes this semester. **Naturally**, he won't pass the exams.
他這學期翹掉了大多數的課，因此他理所當然不會通過考試。

neighbor
['nebɚ]
n 鄰居

★ She has always been more efficient than her **neighbors**.
她總是比她的鄰居更有效率。

neighborhood
['nebɚ‚hʊd]
n 鄰近地區

★ The inhabitants of the **neighborhood** now share a common idea called water preserving.
附近的居民現在都有一個叫做護水的共同念頭。

normal
['nɔrml]
adj 標準的；
正常的

★ My score did not come up to a **normal** level.
我的成績沒有達到標準水平。

normally
['nɔrmlɪ]
adv 按慣例；
正常地

★ Health teachers **normally** discourage students from eating without first washing their hands.
衛生老師通常不讓學生們吃東西前不洗手。

obvious
['ɑbvɪəs]
adj 平淡無奇
的；明顯的

★ Even without investigation, it is **obvious** what actually brought on the riot.
不用調查，引發騷亂的原因也是顯而易見的。

obviously
['ɑbvɪəslɪ]
adv 顯然地

★ **Obviously** the plan will bring us great benefits in a short time.
這個計畫顯然可以讓我們在短期內大賺一筆。

oppose
[ə'poz]
v 反對；反抗

★ Mary **opposed** to the plan.
瑪麗反對這項計畫。

詞類變化

opposite
['ɑpəzɪt]
adj 相對的；
n 對立面；
adv 在對面

★ Teenagers often feel shy when talking to the **opposite** sex.
青少年在和異性談話的時候常常會感到害羞。

patient
['peʃənt]
adj 有耐心的；
n 病人

★ Bell attended to all the **patients** by herself; this cost her a lot of time.
貝爾親自照料所有病人，這花費了她大量的時間。

patiently
['peʃəntlɪ]
adv 耐心地

★ The waiter stood next to the table **patiently**, waiting to take their lunch orders.
服務員耐心的站在桌子旁，等著幫他們點午餐。

perfect
['pɝfɪkt]
adj 完美的；
理想的

★ A museum is the **perfect** place to take your child to during the summer vacation.
博物館是暑假帶領孩子參觀的好去處。

perfectly
['pɝfɪktlɪ]
adv 完美地

★ You will get promoted on the condition that you solve these problems **perfectly**.
若你能圓滿解決這些問題，你將獲得晉升。

perfection
[pɚ'fɛkʃən]
n 完善（的人）

★ His character ensured the **perfection** of each and every report he ever made.
他的個性確保了他所完成的每一份報告都完美無缺。

perform
[pɚ'fɔrm]
v 表演；履行；
行動

★ In the course of the game, John **performed** very well.
比賽過程中，約翰表現得非常好。

performance
[pɚ'fɔrməns]
n 實行；性能；
表演

★ The pub has a **performance** every other day: Monday, Wednesday and Friday.
酒吧每隔一天就有演出，即週一、週三、週五有。

persistence
[pə'sɪstəns]
n 堅持

★ **Persistence** may lead to progress, achievements and successes.
堅持不懈能夠帶來進步、成就和成功。

---

persistent
[pə'sɪstənt]
adj 持續的；持久的

★ The **persistent** practice of English everyday has made him a fluent English speaker.
每天堅持練習英語的習慣使他能說一口流利的英語。

---

possess
[pə'zɛs]
v 擁有

★ In comparison to her sister, Grace has more talent in music, but **possesses** less scientific knowledge.
相較於她的妹妹，葛雷絲更有音樂天賦，但比較缺乏科學知識。

---

possession
[pə'zɛʃən]
n 財產；擁有

★ Tom is in **possession** of this company.
湯姆擁有這間公司

---

possible
['pasəbl]
adj 可能的

★ Could you reply to the clients' letter as soon as **possible**?
你可以儘快答覆客戶的信嗎？

---

possibility
[,pasə'bɪlətɪ]
n 可能發生的事；可能性

★ By working hard, you will have a higher **possibility** of receiving a raise.
你努力工作，加薪的機會便會增加。

---

prepare
[prɪ'pɛr]
v 準備

★ A contract in black and white must be **prepared** before our cooperation.
在我們合作之前必須先準備書面合同。

---

preparation
[,prɛpə'reʃən]
n 預習；預備

★ It is always important to make good **preparations**.
做好準備工作很重要。

詞類變化

詞類變化

produce
[prə'djus]
v 製造;生產

★ Mini disc players **produce** better sound quality than regular CD players.
迷你唱片隨身聽比一般CD隨身聽的音質更好。

producer
[prə'djusɚ]
n 製作人;
生產者

★ Mr. Smith is a movie **producer**.
史密斯先生是一位電影製作人。

profit
['prɑfɪt]
n 利潤;v 獲
益;有益於

★ Our products sold well but the **profit** was little.
我們的產品賣得很好但是利潤卻不多。

profitable
['prɑfɪtəbl]
adj 有益的;
盈利的

★ The point is how **profitable** the product will be after its release.
問題在於這商品投放市場後能帶來多大的利潤。

prosper
['prɑspɚ]
v（使）繁榮

★ Sometimes I thought that it was God that **prospered** my business.
我有時認為一定有神保佑我的事業繁榮發展。

prosperity
[prɑs'pɛrətɪ]
n 成功;繁榮

★ History witnessed the **prosperity** of the ship-making industry.
歷史見證了造船業的繁榮。

qualify
['kwɑlə,faɪ]
v 取得資格

★ On what condition will I be **qualified** for this team?
我需要通過哪些條件才能加入這支球隊?

★ After passing the difficult exam and getting a license, you are a **qualified** accountant.
通過困難的考試又取得了執照,你已經是位合格的會計師了。

qualification
[,kwɑləfə'keʃən]
n 資格;歸屬;
品質

★ Some companies raised their recruitment standards to ensure the **qualification** of their employees.
一些公司都提高了雇傭標準來確保雇員的品質。

refer
[rɪˈfɝ]
v 涉及；參考

★ Mary is often **referred** to as a cat.
瑪麗常被比喻成一隻小貓。

---

reference
[ˈrɛfərəns]
n 參照；證明

★ Please check up these **references** before you hand in the report.
在提交報告之前請核對一下參考資料。

---

relation
[rɪˈleʃən]
n 關係；敘述

★ This organization is in **relation** to the United Nations.
這個組織和聯合國有關聯。

---

relate
[rɪˈlet]
v 有關；敘述

★ After the success of the movie, many **related** products followed up.
電影成功後，許多相關產品行動也跟進了。

---

research
[rɪˈsɝtʃ]
n 調查；**v** 調查

★ They collaborated with each other to do **research** about the project.
他們互相合作研究此專案。

---

researcher
[riˈsɝtʃɚ]
n 調查者；研究員

★ Today, **researchers** affirm that cloning is possible but yet illegal.
如今，研究者確信無性繁殖有可能，但不合法。

---

satisfy
[ˈsætɪsˌfaɪ]
v 滿足

★ Do we have enough food to **satisfy** our hungry guests?
我們有足夠的食物來滿足我們饑腸轆轆的客人嗎？

---

unsatisfactory
[ˌʌnsætɪsˈfæktərɪ]
adj 令人不滿的

★ Your proposal has been turned down because of **unsatisfactory** aspects.
由於未盡人意的方面，你的提議被拒絕了。

---

scare
[skɛr]
v 驚嚇；**n** 驚恐

★ The cat **scared** the mouse off.
那隻貓把老鼠嚇跑了。

詞類變化

scary
['skɛrɪ]
adj 膽小的;
引起驚慌的

★ Jill, I want to hear a **scary** story.
吉爾,我想聽恐怖的故事。

secure
[sɪ'kjur]
v 保衛; adj 安全的

★ The building is so **secure** that even employees must have their identities verified.
這棟樓很安全,連員工也要被驗證身份。

security
[sɪ'kjurətɪ]
n 安全;證券

★ Not until the age of forty did John show his talent in **security** investment.
直到四十歲,約翰才顯示了他在證券投資上的才華。

settle
['sɛtl]
v 定居;解決;結帳

★ Bill and Tom asked the manager to **settle** the argument once for all.
比爾和湯姆要求經理為他們徹底解決爭論。

settlement
['sɛtl̩mənt]
n 殖民(地);解決;安頓

★ She accepted the **settlement** of five million dollars.
她接受了五百萬美元的賠償金。

starve
[starv]
v 挨餓;饑餓

★ A lot of people **starve**.
很多人挨餓。

starvation
[star'veʃən]
n 饑餓

★ There should be freedom from hunger and **starvation**.
應該不再有饑餓災荒了。

state
[stet]
v 聲明;陳述

★ It has been **stated** that anyone violating these rules will be punished.
已經規定違犯這些規則者都要受到懲罰。

statement
['stetmənt]
n 聲明;報告單

★ We're to submit the accounting **statement** on time.
我們準時提交財務報表。

support
[sə'port]
v 支持；支撐

★ Tom **supports** the company's new policy with his heart and soul.
湯姆全力支持公司新政策。

supportive
[sə'portɪv]
adj 支援的

★ All the way, Mary had been **supportive** on John's studies.
瑪麗一直都非常支持約翰的研究工作。

technological
[tɛknə'ladʒɪkl]
adj 技術的

★ **Technological** development didn't make it easier to deal with the social problems.
科技進步並沒有使社會問題更加容易解決。

technology
[tɛk'nalədʒɪ]
n 技術；術語

★ New **technology** is always out of date before the old people can be familiar with it.
新技術總是在老人們能夠熟練掌握之前就過時了。

teen
[tin]
n 青少年；
adj 十幾歲的

★ The economic development of the country is in its **teens**.
這個國家的經濟發展還在起步階段。

teenage
['tin,edʒ]
adj 十幾歲的

★ Most **teenage** girls wish they could be slim and beautiful super models.
大多數十幾歲的女孩希望自己能成為既苗條又漂亮的超級模特兒。

tense
[tɛns]
adj 引起緊張
的；n 時態

★ It's unreal to cool the **tense** situation down just by offering mediation.
僅僅依靠提供斡旋就想使緊張的局勢得以緩和，這是不現實的。

tension
['tɛnʃən]
n 繃緊；緊張狀況

★ Because of all the **tension**, the couple decided to move out of the apartment.
由於緊張，這對夫婦決定搬離這個公寓。

threat [θrɛt] n 威脅；構成威脅的人	★ What you're saying amounts to a **threat** and I will never acknowledge it. 你所說的等於是威脅，我永遠不會聽的。
threaten ['θrɛtn] v 威脅；預示	★ The kid stopped crying when his father **threatened** to throw him out of the window. 當他父親威脅說要把他從窗戶扔出去時，這個小孩不哭了。
true [tru] adj 真實的；忠誠的	★ Is it **true** that the neighbors have been talking about Joseph lately? 最近鄰居們真的都在談論約瑟夫嗎？
truth [truθ] n 事實；真相；真理	★ In **truth**, 2009 wasn't the best year for General Motors. 事實上，2009年對於通用汽車而言並不是最好的一年。
unable [ʌn'ebl] adj 不能的；不能勝任的	★ He is **unable** to escape from this prison. 他不可能從這個監獄逃出去。
able ['ebl] adj 能；有能力的；能幹的	★ When I was at your age, I was **able** to dress up all by myself. 我在你這個年紀的時候，我都能自己穿衣服了。
ability [ə'bɪlətɪ] n 能力；才幹	★ His brilliant management **ability** began to come out in this crisis. 在這次危機中他傑出的管理能力開始顯現出來。
capable ['kepəbl] adj 有技能的；有能力的	★ All of them are **capable** of operating the machine. 他們都能操作此機器。

union
['junjən]
n 結合；聯盟

★ In order to prevent strikes, government officials negotiated with labor **unions**.
為了提防罷工，政府官員和勞工聯盟談判。

unite
[ju'naɪt]
v 聯合；統一

★ America began with thirteen **united** colonies.
美國最初只是十三個聯合的殖民地。

various
['vɛrɪəs]
adj 各種各樣的；不同的

★ **Various** barricades blocked off the main streets of the city.
各種路障封鎖住了城市裡的主要道路。

variety
[və'raɪətɪ]
n 多樣化；種類

★ Students arrive at school late for a **variety** of reasons.
學生有一堆上學遲到的理由。

work
[wɝk]
v 工作

★ She has been **working** for 15 years.
她已經工作十五年了。

★ Oversea **working** experience helped him to find a well-paid job in China.
海外工作的經驗讓他在中國找到了一份待遇優厚的工作。

workshop
['wɝk,ʃɑp]
n 小工廠；作坊

★ Everyone in the **workshop** works carefully.
工作坊裡的每個人小心謹慎地工作。

worthy
['wɝðɪ]
adj 值得的；有價值的

★ The car is **worthy** of buying for its good quality.
這部汽車值得買，它的品質很好。

★ Is there any movie that is **worthy** of watching?
有沒有什麼值得一看的電影？

worthless
['wɝθlɪs]
adj 無價值的；無用的

★ Tom looked pale when he discovered the vase he bought was **worthless**.
當湯姆知道他買的花瓶一文不值時臉色變得蒼白。

worthwhile
['wɝθ'hwaɪl]
adj 有真實價值
的;值得做的

★ I am going to do my utmost and to most of all make my efforts **worthwhile**.
我會全力以赴,要使我的努力有所值。

同義反義篇

第 3 篇

● 同義反義

abandon [ə'bændən] Ⅴ 放棄	★ Because of the failure in this examination, Peter **abandoned** himself to despair. 由於考試失利,彼得心灰意冷。
quit [kwɪt] Ⅴ 停止;離開	★ Let's **quit** talking and pretend to do our assignments. 別說話了,裝作做作業吧。
acquire [ə'kwaɪr] Ⅴ 獲得;學到	★ People **acquire** the smoking habit out of curiosity. 人們因為好奇養成抽煙習慣。
obtain [əb'ten] Ⅴ 得到	★ I am going to try my best and to most of all **obtain** their approval. 我會全力以赴,力求爭得他們的同意。
agree [ə'gri] Ⅴ 同意	★ I don't think Jack will **agree** to attend that party. 我覺得傑克不會同意參加那場宴會。 ★ By signing your name here, it means that you **agree** to the terms of this agreement. 在這裡簽名之後,就表示你同意這份合同內的條款。
disagree [ˌdɪsə'gri] Ⅴ 不適宜; 不一致	★ As a matter of fact, all the parents **disagree** with the new regulation. 事實上,所有家長都反對新條例。
allow [ə'lau] Ⅴ 允許	★ You were not **allowed** to attend this conference. 你不允許進入會議。
permit [pə'mɪt] ⓝ 許可證;執 照;Ⅴ 許可	★ I will travel a lot if my wallet **permits**. 如果我的荷包允許,我會多去旅行。

同義反義

break
[brek]
v 打破；折斷

★ They were obviously preparing to **break** off the negotiation.
很明顯，他們準備終止談判。

crack
[kræk]
n 裂縫；v 劈啪
地響

★ Many prisoners **cracked** up after jailing for 15 years.
經過十五年的囚禁，許多囚犯都崩潰了。

chance
[tʃæns]
n 機會；v 偶然
遇到

★ Everyone has to be confronted with many challenges and **chances** in his life.
每個人在一生當中都必須面對許多挑戰和機遇。

opportunity
[ˌɑpɚˈtjunətɪ]
n 機會；時機

★ Treasure the **opportunity** this time.
好好珍惜這次的機會。

arrange
[əˈrendʒ]
v 整理；安排

★ Tom's friend **arranged** a blind date for him.
湯姆的朋友替他安排了一場相親。

disarrange
[ˌdɪsəˈrendʒ]
v 弄亂；擾亂

★ Bad weather **disarranged** all the plans.
壞天氣擾亂了所有的計畫。

cautious
[ˈkɔʃəs]
adj 謹慎的；
小心的

★ Scientists who are **cautious** have more chances to acquire accurate results from their experiments.
小心謹慎的科學家更有機會從實驗中獲取精確結果。

careful
[ˈkɛrfəl]
adj 小心的；
仔細的

★ Everyone is **careful** and cautious when working in the factory.
每個人在工廠工作要小心謹慎。

● 同義反義

certain
['sɝ·tən]
adj 確信的；
可靠的

★ I am very **certain** of what I saw with my own eyes.
我對於親眼所見之事十分確定。

uncertain
[ʌn'sɝ·tn]
adj 不明確的；
不確定的

★ The boss is **uncertain** of the result for the production.
老闆不知道生產的結果如何。

check
[tʃɛk]
v 檢查；n 檢查；支票

★ His daughter was wide-awake every time Marcus went to **check** on her.
每次馬克司查看他的女兒，她都完全清醒著。

inspect
[ɪn'spɛkt]
v 檢查

★ Buses are thoroughly **inspected** before a long drive.
在長途行駛前，公共汽車被徹底地檢查過了。

cigar
[sɪ'gɑr]
n 雪茄煙

★ Always buying luxury **cigars**, John often couldn't make ends meet.
約翰總是買昂貴的雪茄，常常入不敷出。

cigarette
[,sɪgə'rɛt]
n 捲煙；香煙

★ If you keep on smoking 5 **cigarettes** a day, you will end up in lung cancer.
如果你再繼續每天吸五支煙，你會死於肺癌的。

clarify
['klærə,faɪ]
v 闡明；澄清

★ She was about to **clarify** her proposals, which she presented to her customers.
她打算把介紹給客戶的建議說清楚。

interpret
[ɪn'tɝ·prɪt]
v 解釋

★ The sentence admits of being **interpreted** in many ways.
這個句子可以從許多方面加以解釋。

client
['klaɪənt]
n 客戶；當事人

★ Communication with **clients** is very important for those who work as salesmen.
對於銷售員來說，與客戶的交流是非常重要的。

customer
['kʌstəmə]
n 顧客

★ The **customer** booked for us the most comfortable hotel in the city.
客戶為我們訂了該市最舒適的酒店。

complicated
['kɑmplə,ketɪd]
adj 難懂的；
複雜的

★ It was a very **complicated** task.
這項任務很複雜。

complex
['kɑmplɛks]
adj 複雜的；複合的；n 情結；綜合體

★ What does the more and more **complex** Crop Circles stand for?
越來越複雜的麥田怪圈代表著什麼？

confess
[kən'fɛs]
v 承認；坦白

★ She **confessed** to having hit him with a book.
她承認用書打過他。

admit
[əd'mɪt]
v 容許；承認

★ She finally **admitted** her mistake.
她終於承認錯誤。

conference
['kɑnfərəns]
n 討論；會議

★ The **conference** went on from 9 a.m. to 6 p.m..
會議從早上九點開到晚上六點。

meeting
['mitɪŋ]
n 會議

★ The **meeting** was postponed because of heavy traffic.
會議因交通擁擠而延遲。

corporation
[,kɔrpə'reʃən]
n 公司

★ The famous multinational **corporation** has come down in the world.
這家著名的跨國公司已經敗落破產。

enterprise
['ɛntə,praɪz]
n 企業

★ Innovation and teamwork are the **enterprise** cultures of our company.
創新和團結是我們公司的企業文化。

● 同義反義

decrease
[dɪ'kris]
v 降低；n 降低

☆ Since John is not suitable for the job, why don't you **decrease** his salary?
既然約翰不稱職，你為何不將他減薪呢？

increase
[ɪn'kris]
v 增大；n 增加

☆ The boss promised me a wage **increase**.
老闆答應加我薪水。

defense
[dɪ'fɛns]
n 防禦工事；保護

☆ Women today have learned to arise in **defense** of their legal rights.
現今婦女學會起來保護她們的合法權利。

protection
[prə'tɛkʃən]
n 保護

☆ Four main points will be discussed, one of which is about environmental **protection**.
有四個主要問題要討論，其中之一是關於環境保護的。

disease
[dɪ'ziz]
n 不健全；疾病；弊端

☆ Many people don't like smoking because it not only causes **disease**, but also dirties the air.
很多人都不喜歡抽菸，因為抽菸不僅會致病，還會汙染空氣。

illness
['ɪlnɪs]
n 疾病；病

☆ The medicine is not appropriate to your **illness**.
這些藥並不適合你的病情。

discipline
['dɪsəplɪn]
n 訓練；紀律；v 處罰；訓導

☆ Self-**discipline** means one holds a tight control of his or her behavior.
自律就意味著嚴格支配個人行為。

train
[tren]
v 訓練

☆ After **training**, Andy is now capable of finishing 3000 meters running.
經過訓練，安迪現在可以完成三千公尺的長跑了。

engage
[ɪn'gedʒ]
v 保證；雇

☆ Who can **engage** your company and pay the money back on time?
誰能保證你們公司能夠按時付錢？

promise
['prɑmɪs]
v 保證；允諾；承諾；n 保證

★ I can't **promise** you anything.
我不能向你承諾什麼。

eventually
[ɪ'vɛntʃʊəlɪ]
adv 最後；終於

★ **Eventually**, Tom compromised under the great pressure of the government.
最終，湯姆在政府的強大壓力下讓步了。

finally
['faɪn̩lɪ]
adv 最後

★ Though doing their best, the basketball team **finally** missed the championship.
儘管盡了全力，這支籃球隊最終沒能獲得冠軍。

evidence
['ɛvədəns]
n 證據；根據

★ Even though no **evidence** can prove the existence of God, Christians still believe in Him.
即使沒有證據能夠證明上帝的存在，基督徒仍然信仰上帝。

proof
[pruf]
n 檢驗證據；證明

★ I will not comment on the company without any **proof** or evidence.
我不會在沒有任何證據的情況下評論這家公司的。

faithful
['feθfəl]
adj 忠實的

★ Lucy was dismissed by her boss because she was not **faithful**.
露西被老闆解雇了，因為她不忠誠。

reliable
[rɪ'laɪəbl̩]
adj 可靠的；可信賴的

★ The information put down by pens is more **reliable** than that by memory.
用筆記下來的資訊要比用腦袋記下來的可靠的多。

famous
['feməs]
adj 出名的；著名的

★ Jack was **famous** for his outstanding achievements to the company.
傑克因為他對公司的傑出貢獻而聞名。

distinguished
[dɪ'stɪŋgwɪʃt]
adj 著名的;高貴的;卓著的

★ Peter is a **distinguished** economist.
彼得是位出色的經濟學家。

---

well-known
['wɛl'non]
adj 出名的;著名的

★ Phoop is a **well-known** electronic factory, especially in the LCD area.
飛歐浦是有名的電子公司,特別在液晶螢幕領域。

fortunately
['fɔrtʃənɪtlɪ]
adv 幸虧;幸運地

★ **Fortunately**, the fire didn't cause much damage to the factory.
幸運地,大火沒有對工廠造成很大的損壞。

---

unfortunately
[ʌn'fɔrtʃənɪtlɪ]
adv 不幸地

★ **Unfortunately**, opportunities are very slim now. Can you find another solution?
不幸的是,目前機會非常渺茫。你還有其他的解決辦法嗎?

gain
[gen]
v 獲得

★ In business, nothing ventured, nothing **gained**.
在商場上,沒有冒險就沒有收益。

---

lose
[luz]
v 丟失;遺失

★ The factory is closing up, so the workers also **lose** their jobs.
工廠要關門了,所以工人們也就失業了。

guarantee
[,gærən'ti]
v 保證

★ I cannot **guarantee** anything.
我不能保證什麼。

---

assure
[ə'ʃʊr]
v 確保;使放心

★ We **assure** that the television you ordered will be delivered immediately.
我們保證即刻寄出您訂的電視。

guilty
['gɪltɪ]
adj 有罪的；
內疚的

★ Andy felt **guilty** for confusing the orders.
安迪因為弄混訂單而愧疚。

innocent
['ɪnəsn̩t]
adj 無罪的

★ Andy was **innocent**.
安迪是無辜的。

include
[ɪn'klud]
v 包含

★ The people who knew about the secret **included** Jane, Judy and Anna.
知道這個祕密的人包括珍、茱蒂和安娜。

involve
[ɪn'vɑlv]
v 牽涉；使捲入

★ Your pet dog was **involved** in a car accident so it's dead.
你的寵物狗死了，它被車撞了。

injury
['ɪndʒərɪ]
n 傷害；損害

★ His **injury** has gone from bad to worse.
他的傷勢越來越惡化。

harm
[hɑrm]
n 傷害；v 損害

★ For its own sake, a company is willing to **harm** the customers.
一家公司可以做傷害消費者的事來維護自己的利益。

inferior
[ɪn'fɪrɪɚ]
adj 下級的；劣等的；n 下屬；下級

★ Temporary workers were considered **inferior** to regular employees.
臨時工被認為次於正式員工。

superior
[sə'pɪrɪɚ]
adj 上級的；較優的

★ Mary is not popular because she considers herself **superior** to others.
瑪麗不受歡迎，因為她覺得自己優於其他人。

● 同義反義

jam
[dʒæm]
v 塞緊；堵塞；
n 擁擠

★ Being caught in a traffic **jam** on my way to work, I'm late again.
在去工作的路上塞車了，我又遲到了。
（traffic block = traffic jam 交通阻塞）

block
[blɑk]
v 阻塞；阻止；
n 阻塞

★ We will **block** up this entranceway.
我們將封鎖此入口。

lack
[læk]
n 缺乏；v 缺乏

★ Despite his **lack** of enthusiasm, Jack still answered the teacher's questions.
雖然缺乏熱情，傑克還是回答老師的問題。

shortage
['ʃɔrtɪdʒ]
n 匱乏；不足

★ Due to a **shortage** in supplies, the price of raw material rose 3 times.
由於供應緊縮，原材料的價格上漲了三倍。

lecturer
['lɛktʃərɚ]
n 講師；講演者

★ Professor Yang, a famous **lecturer**, is fond of collecting baseball cards.
楊教授是個著名的演說家，他喜歡收集棒球卡片。

professor
[prə'fɛsɚ]
n 教授

★ **Professors** find it hard to prevent students from doing research by Internet.
教授們發現很難防止學生們用網際網路做研究。

meeting
['mitɪŋ]
n 會議

★ The committee **meeting** is held on Monday morning as usual.
委員會會議像往常一樣在週一早上召開。

appointment
[ə'pɔɪntmənt]
n 約會；職位

★ Let's make an **appointment** with Mr. Lee.
我們和李先生預約一下吧。

modern
['mɑdɚn]
adj 近代的；
現代的

★ The computer is a **modern** invention.
電腦是現代的發明。

ancient
['enʃənt]
adj 古代的

★ Plato is one of the most distinguished philosophers in **ancient** Greek.
柏拉圖是古希臘傑出的哲學家之一。

participate
[parˈtɪsəˌpet]
v 參與；參加

★ The semester grade is based on how you **participate** in class.
學期成績取決於你參與上課的程度。

attend
[əˈtɛnd]
v 出席；參加

★ He is supposed to be **attending** a meeting now.
他現在應該是在參加會議。

attendance
[əˈtɛndəns]
n 出席

★ Robert was the first one to call and inform me of his **attendance**.
羅伯特是第一個打電話告訴我他會出席的人。

pay
[pe]
n 薪水；v 付

★ How will you **pay** for the digital camera, by cash or by credit card?
您要透過什麼方式買下這台數位相機？付現金還是用信用卡？

salary
[ˈsælərɪ]
n 薪水

★ My boss's attitude about my **salary** was ambiguous.
老闆對我的薪水的態度模糊。

project
[prəˈdʒɛkt]
n 計畫；專案

★ He finished his **project** on time.
他準時完成了他的計畫。

plan
[plæn]
n 計畫；v 計畫

★ As soon as I arrived, we began discussing our **plan**.
我一到，我們就開始討論計畫了。

professional
[prəˈfɛʃənl]
adj 職業的；職業上的

★ He's a **professional** tennis player.
他是個職業網球選手。

◎ 同義反義

amateur
['æmə,tʃur]
adj 業餘愛好的；n 外行

★ She is an **amateur** pianist.
她是個業餘鋼琴師。

promote
[prə'mot]
v 促進；晉升

★ Determination to be **promoted** made Angela energetic.
晉升的決心使安琪拉精力充沛。

encourage
[ɪn'kɝɪdʒ]
v 促進；助長

★ His optimism **encouraged** the whole group.
他的樂觀鼓舞整個團體。

provide
[prə'vaɪd]
v 提供；撫養；預防

★ Salesmen like to have dealings with customers who can **provide** business opportunities.
銷售員喜歡和能夠帶來生意的客戶打交道。

offer
['ɔfɚ]
v 提供；提議；n 提供；提議；出價

★ The young man looked happy after being told that he got the **offer** from the company.
得知自己被那家公司錄用了，年輕人看起來很高興。

quarrel
['kwɔrəl]
n 爭論；v 爭論

★ By courtesy of the mothers-in-law, the couple stopped **quarreling**.
由於岳母和婆婆出面，夫妻倆才停止爭吵。

argue
['ɑrgju]
v 爭論

★ Many people **argue** that he is wrong.
很多人爭論他錯了。

reasonable
['riznəbl]
adj 合理的；有理性的

★ By comparison, it is a more **reasonable** and systematic method.
相較之下，這個方法更合理，更有系統。

logical
['lɑdʒɪkl]
adj 合理的；
合邏輯的

★ His reaction is **logical**.
他的反應合乎邏輯。

refrigerator
[rɪ'frɪdʒə,retə-]
n 冰箱

★ Milk goes bad easily without putting in **refrigerator**.
牛奶不放在冰箱裡，很容易變質。

container
[kən'tenə-]
n 集裝箱；容器

★ The cup, a convenient **container**, can help you drink water without wetting yourself.
杯子是個很方便的容器，能用來喝水而不會弄溼你。

refuse
[rɪ'fjuz]
v 拒絕

★ I **refused** to speak with John because he lied to me.
我拒絕和約翰說話，因為他騙我了。

accept
[ək'sɛpt]
v 接受

★ The investment plan was **accepted** by the board of directors.
董事會批准這項投資案了。

salary
['sælərɪ]
n 薪水

★ The **salary** is paid in cash at the end of every month.
公司每個月月底以現金方式發放薪水。

wages
['wedʒɪs]
n 工資

★ Unlike the inheritors, we earn **wages** in return for our labor.
不像那些財產繼承人，我們靠勞力換取工資。

suitcase
['sut,kes]
n 旅行用手提箱

★ The airline lost our **suitcase**.
航空公司弄丟了我們的旅行用手提箱。

baggage
['bægɪdʒ]
n 行李

★ Tom gave Mary a hand when she was lifting her **baggage**.
瑪麗提行李的時候，湯姆幫了她一把。

同義反義

同義反義

同義反義

surprise [sə'praɪz] v 驚訝；n 驚訝	☆ Tom got here in a flash and we were all **surprised**. 湯姆瞬間就到這了，我們都感到驚訝極了。
astonish [ə'stɑnɪʃ] v 使吃驚； 使驚訝	☆ We were all **astonished** that the boss went to work by bike. 老闆騎腳踏車來上班讓我們十分吃驚。
task [tæsk] n 工作；作業	☆ For all the effort they put in, they still can not finish the **tasks** in advance. 儘管很努力了，他們仍然不能提前完成任務。
job [dʒɑb] n 工作	☆ What you learn from your first **job** is important. 從第一份工作中你能學到什麼很重要。
unite [ju'naɪt] v 統一；使團結	☆ Marriage **unites** lovers who commit themselves to love each other forever. 結婚將兩個願意永遠彼此相愛的戀人結合起來。
combine [kəm'baɪn] v 聯合；結合	☆ He **combines** passion and patience in his dealings with customers. 他在對待客戶時既熱情又有耐心。

形似篇

第 4 篇

○ 形似

accompany [ə'kʌmpənɪ] Ⅴ 陪伴；伴奏	★ The dog **accompanied** the blind man all the way home. 那隻狗陪著盲人一路到家。
accomplish [ə'kamplɪʃ] Ⅴ 實現；完成；達到	★ The construction of the bridge will have been **accomplished** by the time we come here next month. 我們下個月來這裡的時候，這座大橋就會建造完畢了。
accuse [ə'kjuz] Ⅴ 指控；指責	★ Lily **accused** him of stealing her car. 莉莉控告他偷她的車。
accuracy ['ækjərəsɪ] ⁿ 準確性；正確性	★ His **accuracy** with Chinese to English translations won him the position at the firm. 他精確的中譯英能力，為他贏得了公司的職位。
administration [əd,mɪnə'streʃən] ⁿ 經營；管理部門；實施	★ It's said that our **administration** manager has decided to resign, is that true? 據說我們的行政經理決定辭職了，這是真的嗎？
collaboration [kə,læbə'reʃən] ⁿ 合作	★ The two groups worked in **collaboration** to build the house. 兩群人齊心協力地蓋房子。
adapt [ə'dæpt] Ⅴ 使適應	★ I have not **adapted** to the new condition. 我不適應這個新的環境。
adopt [ə'dɑpt] Ⅴ 收養；採用；接受	★ The boy was **adopted** by old George. 男孩被老喬治收養了。

advanced
[əd'vænst]
adj 高級的；
超前的

★ The company offered several **advanced** courses for the new employees.
公司對新的雇員提供了多門高級課程。

---

advertisement
[,ædvɚ'taɪzmənt]
n 廣告

★ Mary was reading the recruitment **advertisement** carefully.
瑪麗仔細的看招聘廣告。

---

approach
[ə'protʃ]
n 方法；接近；
v 接近；即將到
達

★ The Browns dare not **approach** the forest in fear of being harmed by wild animals.
因為害怕被野生動物傷害，布朗一家不敢接近森林。

---

approximately
[ə'praksəmɪtlɪ]
adv 大概

★ The population of the United States is **approximately** 280 million.
美國大約有兩億八千萬人口。

---

aspect
['æspɛkt]
n 方向；方面

★ There are some **aspects** of the class I find interesting.
我發現這課有些方面挺有趣的。

---

aspirin
['æspərɪn]
n 阿斯匹林

★ I need to keep some **aspirin** in my bag.
我需要在包包裡放些阿斯匹靈。

---

assassinate
[ə'sæsɪn,et]
v 行刺；暗殺

★ A total of four presidents were **assassinated** while holding office.
總共有四位總統在執政期間被暗殺。

★ President Lincoln, one of America's greatest presidents, was **assassinated**.
林肯，美國最偉大的總統之一，是被暗殺的。

形似

assistant
[ə'sɪstənt]
n 助理；助手

★ Do you know how many people will attend the forum? I think you'd better ask the **assistant**. She is the one who sent the invitations.
你知不知道有多少人會來參加討論會？我覺得你最好問問助理，邀請函是她發的。

---

assignment
[ə'saɪnmənt]
n 任務；功課

★ To be frank, I have some difficulties with the **assignment**.
坦白說，這項任務對我來說有些困難。

---

assure
[ə'ʃur]
v 確保；使放心

★ Our teacher has **assured** that the next test will be easier.
我們老師保證下次考試會簡單些。

---

associate
[ə'soʃɪ,et]
v 使聯合；
n 合夥人

★ We usually **associate** poverty with misery.
一說到貧窮，人們往往聯想到悲慘的境遇。

---

astonish
[ə'stɑnɪʃ]
v 驚訝

★ It **astonished** us that Frank made such a blunder.
我們很驚訝法蘭克會犯這樣的大錯。

---

astronaut
['æstrə,nɔt]
n 太空人；
宇航員

★ American **astronauts** were the first men to walk on the moon.
美國太空人是第一批在月球上行走的人。

---

attach
[ə'tætʃ]
v 配屬；貼上

★ The little chicks became **attached** to Mary after she fed them some rice.
當瑪麗用一些米飯餵過小雞以後，牠們就跟著她了。

---

attempt
[ə'tɛmpt]
n 企圖；嘗試；
v 企圖；嘗試

★ They had made many **attempts** to persuade him to give up smoking.
他們多次嘗試勸他戒煙。

attend
[ə'tɛnd]
Ⅴ 出席；參加

★ I think you should spare some time to attend his wedding ceremony.
我想你應該抽點時間去參加他的結婚典禮。

---

attention
[ə'tɛnʃən]
ⓝ 照料；注意；注意力

★ Tony did not pay attention to the teacher in the class.
湯尼在課堂上沒有認真聽老師上課。

---

await
[ə'wet]
Ⅴ 將降臨到…身上；等候

★ Jane passed her internship interview and she awaits the next stage.
珍通過了實習工作的面試，並等待著下個階段來臨。

---

award
[ə'wɔrd]
ⓝ 獎品；獎金；
Ⅴ 授予

★ On the contrary, we should award the staff who spoke up.
相反的，我們應該獎勵那位勇於發言的員工。

形
似

---

backpack
['bæk,pæk]
ⓝ 登山用的背包

★ Due to a robbery, everyone's backpack was checked on his or her way out.
由於搶劫案，出去時每個人的背包都要接受檢查。

---

background
['bæk,graund]
ⓝ 背景；出身背景

★ Universities gathers students with different social statuses and family backgrounds.
大學聚集了具有不同社會地位和家庭背景的學生。

---

balance
['bæləns]
ⓝ 天平；結存；平衡

★ Bray is very good at keeping balance, so it took him a very short period of time to learn to ride a bike.
布雷平衡感很好，因此花費很少時間就學會了騎腳踏車。

---

ballet
['bæle]
ⓝ 芭蕾舞劇；芭蕾舞樂曲；芭蕾舞

★ Mr. and Mrs. Eric spent a great deal of money pushing their kid to learn ballet.
艾瑞克夫婦花費了大量金錢逼迫他們的小孩學習芭蕾舞。

ban
[bæn]
v 禁止;取締;
n 禁令;禁止

★ It's a good policy to **ban** smoking in the conference room.
會議室內不得吸煙是條很好的規定。

---

bankrupt
['bæŋkrʌpt]
adj 破產的; v
使破產; n 破產
者

★ Consumers have been on the decline these months, which caused the **bankrupt** of the supermarket.
幾個月來顧客量的減少使超市倒閉了。

---

barrier
['bærɪr]
n 障礙;屏障

★ Peter's selfishness is the biggest **barrier** for him to get promoted.
彼得的自私是他晉升的最大阻礙。

---

bargain
['bɑrgɪn]
n 交易; v 討價
還價;預料

★ I didn't **bargain** Mary coming so soon.
我沒想到瑪麗來的這麼快。

---

battery
['bætərɪ]
n 一系列;電池
(組);排炮

★ My cell phone has lost power; I need to recharge the **battery**.
我的手機沒電了,電池需要再充電。

---

battle
['bætl]
n 決鬥;戰鬥;
v 作戰;鬥爭

★ The patient is still in **battle** against virus in his body.
病人仍在和他體內的病毒抗爭。

---

bloom
[blum]
n 青春煥發(時
期);花;開花
(期); v 開花

★ The IT industry is in **bloom**.
IT產業正處於朝氣蓬勃之時。

bond
[bɑnd]
n 公債；聯結；債券；合同；v 結合

★ Many people shy away from purchasing **bonds**.
許多人害怕購買債券。

brake
[brek]
n 煞車；v 煞車；煞住（車）

★ The **brakes** on my scooter aren't working so well, so don't ride too fast.
我摩托車上的煞車不太靈敏，所以你不要騎太快。

brand
[brænd]
n 牌子；商標

★ IBM and HP are the top two notebook **brands** in the market.
國際商務機器公司和惠普是筆記型電腦市場上頂尖的兩個牌子。

bracelet
['breslɪt]
n 手鐲

★ While walking along the beach, Mike found a diamond and a gold **bracelet** in the sand.
沿著沙灘走，邁克在沙子裡發現了一顆鑽石和一個金手鐲。

bravery
['brevərɪ]
n 剛毅；勇敢

★ The captain was recommended by the general to receive a medal for his **bravery**.
上尉因為表現英勇，得到將軍推薦獲得一枚勳章。

campaign
[kæm'pen]
n 戰役；運動；v 參加競選

★ John will initiate a **campaign** against the discrimination toward females.
約翰將發起一場反對歧視女性的運動。

camping
['kæmpɪŋ]
n 露營；野營

★ The school arranged a **camping** trip on Saturday for the graduates.
學校在週六為畢業生安排了露營活動。

career
[kə'rɪr]
n 職業

★ Lucy told me not to risk my **career** by offending my boss.
露西叫我不要冒犯老闆，因為那會危及我的事業。

形似

carriage
['kærɪdʒ]
n 馬車；（火車）客車廂

★ The train is longer than the airplane because it has more **carriages**.
火車比飛機長，因為火車的車廂較多。

cart
[kɑrt]
n 手推車；小車

★ What you did was putting the **cart** before the horse. Do you understand what you should do first?
你做事本末倒置了，你知道什麼事情應該先處理嗎？

ceremony
['sɛrə,monɪ]
n 禮節；典禮

★ As the sports meeting came to a close, the president gave the closing **ceremony** speech.
運動會快要結束了，主席致閉幕詞。

certificate
[sə'tɪfəkɪt]
n 執照

★ The **certificate** should be sent soon.
這張證書應該趕快寄出去。

client
['klaɪənt]
n 客戶；委託人；當事人

★ Nick has a way of persuading his **clients** to buy products.
尼克在把產品推銷給顧客方面很有一套。

cliff
[klɪf]
n 峭壁；懸崖

★ Standing on the brink of the **cliff**, we can feel the howling gale.
站在懸崖邊緣，我們能夠感受到強風呼嘯而過。

collapse
[kə'læps]
v 崩潰；n 倒塌；突然失敗

★ Due to heavy smoking, his body began to **collapse**.
由於他大量吸煙，他的身體狀況開始崩潰了。

collar
['kɑlə]
n 頸圈；衣領

★ It's important to take some physical exercise regularly, particularly for those white-**collar** workers.
有規律地運動很重要，對白領階級而言尤為如此。

commit
[kə'mɪt]
v 使承擔義務；犯（罪）

★ He **committed** a crime.
他犯罪了。

commission
[kəˈmɪʃən]
n 佣金；授權

★ It's said Tom sold ten cars in a day. He earned a lot of **commission**.
據說湯姆一天之內賣掉了十輛車。他賺了很多佣金。

condition
[kənˈdɪʃən]
n 環境；狀況

★ You will be given a bonus on the **condition** that you can sell 10 cars.
如果你能賣出十輛汽車的話，你將獲得獎勵。

connection
[kəˈnɛkʃən]
n 關係

★ Mary went to see the doctor in **connection** with her serious cough.
咳嗽的厲害，瑪麗去看了醫生。

confess
[kənˈfɛs]
v 承認；坦白

★ John **confessed** to having broken the glass.
約翰承認是他打破了玻璃。

★ The little boy **confessed** to breaking the vase, so his mother punished him by asking him to clean the kitchen.
小男孩坦承打破花瓶的事，因此母親懲罰他清洗廚房。

confidence
[ˈkɑnfədəns]
n 信心；信任

★ Cathy gave a speech; she was full of **confidence**.
凱西充滿自信的發表了演講。

content
[kənˈtɛnt]
adj 滿意的；v 使滿足；n 目錄；滿足；內容

★ They will not be **content** with the victory they already got.
他們不會滿足已取得的勝利。

★ We had to read the book part by part in order to fully understand the **content**.
我們必須逐步閱讀這本書，才能完全理解其中的內容。

contest
[ˈkɑntɛst]
n 比賽

★ Simon won the first prize in the English **contest** yesterday.
西蒙在昨天的英語比賽中獲得第一名。

context
[ˈkɑntɛkst]
n 上下文；背景

★ The word can be understood even without **context**.
即使沒有上下文也能理解這個單字的意思。

形
似

contract ['kɑntrækt] n 契約	★ We were asked to put down the **contract** in black and white. 我們被要求把合同以書面形式記下來。
contact ['kɑntækt] n 聯絡;接觸; v 聯絡	★ She has been unavailable for a month and we could hardly **contact** her. 她已經一個月都沒有空了,而且我們幾乎聯絡不到她。
contrast ['kɑn,træst] n 對比;v 形成 對比;對照	★ The brightness of his work was in **contrast** to his own sad nature. 他明亮的作品與本身哀傷的個性形成對比。
costume ['kɑstjum] n 服裝;裝束	★ Reputable **costume** designers shape today's fashion trends. 著名時裝設計師塑造了現今的時裝潮流。
counter ['kaʊntɚ] n 櫃檯;櫃檯式 長桌;v 反抗	★ The ATM is out of service, and I have to go to the **counter**. 自動櫃員機壞了,我不得不去櫃檯。
courtesy ['kɜ·təsɪ] n 禮貌;謙恭; 贊助	★ All fresh water comes by **courtesy** of the store nearby school. 所有的純淨水由學校旁邊的商店贊助。
count [kaʊnt] v 計算;數	★ The opening ceremony is being **counted** down from ten seconds. 開幕式已經進入十秒鐘倒數計時。
counter ['kaʊntɚ] n 籌碼;櫃檯; v 反抗	★ Displayed on the top of the **counter** are the new products. 櫃上展示的是新產品。

crack
[kræk]
n 破裂聲；裂縫；v 打；（使）破裂

★ The government decided to **crack** down drug trafficking.
政府決定嚴厲取締毒品販賣。

crash
[kræʃ]
n 碰撞；破裂聲；墜毀；v 撞擊；（電腦）當機

★ This computer had **crashed** four times since we bought it last week.
自從上個星期我們買下這部電腦，它已經當機四次了。

deceive
[dɪ'siv]
v 蒙蔽；欺騙

★ The salesman **deceived** us into buying the Life Accident Insurance.
銷售人員欺騙我們購買人身意外傷害險。

decline
[dɪ'klaɪn]
v 衰退；下降；謝絕；n 下降

★ Wheat production is on the **decline**.
小麥正減產。

decade
['dɛked]
n 十年

★ For the past few **decades**, football has become increasingly popular.
過去幾十年裡，橄欖球變得更加流行了。

declare
[dɪ'klɛr]
v 斷言；聲明；申報；表態

★ Since the two companies could not resolve the problem peacefully, they decided to **declare** war upon each other.
既然兩家公司無法和平解決問題，雙方決定互相宣戰。

delight
[dɪ'laɪt]
n 快樂；v 感到高興；使欣喜

★ The teacher takes **delight** in criticizing his students.
這個老師以責備他的學生為樂。

○ 形似

elect
[ɪˈlɛkt]
v 選擇;決定;選舉;adj 選定的

★ Being **elected** to the board of directors delighted Johnson.
強森很高興被選為董事會成員。

despite
[dɪˈspaɪt]
prep 儘管;不管

★ **Despite** my hunger, I continued to work without rest.
儘管我很餓,我還是繼續工作,沒有休息。

destroy
[dɪˈstrɔɪ]
v 消滅;破壞

★ Francesca cunningly **destroyed** all the evidence this morning.
今天早上,法蘭西卡狡猾地銷毀了所有的證據。

destination
[ˌdɛstəˈneʃən]
n 目的地

★ Jim finally arrived at the **destination** on time.
吉姆最終還是準時到達了目的地。

deficient
[dɪˈfɪʃənt]
adj 不足的;缺乏的

★ The flood is caused by the city's **deficient** drainage system.
水災是由於該市不完善的排水系統造成。

due
[dju]
adj 到期的;欠款的

★ She finished her paper before its **due** date that afternoon.
在到期前的那個下午,她完成論文了。

duration
[djuˈreʃən]
n 持續期間;持續

★ The doctor advised his patient to rest for the **duration** of the week.
醫生建議病人休息一個星期。

encouragement
[ɪnˈkɝɪdʒmənt]
n 鼓勵

★ What John needs is not criticism but **encouragement**.
約翰需要的不是批評而是鼓勵。

形似

202

development
[dɪ'vɛləpmənt]
n 發展；生長

★ Females play a more and more important role in our country's **development**.
女性在我國發展的過程中扮演著越來越重要的角色。

establish
[ə'stæblɪʃ]
v 確定；建立

★ Refusing to work as an employee, John decided to **establish** his own company.
約翰不想只做一名員工，他要開自己的公司。

estate
[ɪs'tet]
n 莊園；地產

★ Almost 1/5 of the real **estate** market in London is occupied by this company.
倫敦大約五分之一的房地產市場被這家公司占有了。

exchange
[ɪks'tʃendʒ]
n 匯兌；交換；
v 交流

★ It is not worth it to sacrifice your health in **exchange** of excitement.
為刺激而犧牲你的健康是不值得的。

change
[tʃendʒ]
n 改變；v 改變

★ I do hope that your mood will **change** for the better.
我真的希望你的心情變得更好。

expand
[ɪk'spænd]
v 膨脹；擴大

★ Seeing our products are in great demand, we need to **expand** our production.
有鑒於我們的產品需求量極大，我們需要擴大生產。

experiment
[ɪk'spɛrəmənt]
n 試驗；實驗

★ Our **experiment** fell flat owing to the small mistake.
由於這個細小的錯誤，整個實驗徹底失敗。

expectation
[,ɛkspɛk'teʃən]
n 預期；期待

★ Does the result answer to your **expectation**?
結果符合你們的期望嗎？

expense
[ɪk'spɛns]
n 開支；價錢

★ We must cut back on **expenses** so as to tap the new market.
我們必須縮減開支以開拓新市場。

exhaust
[ɪgˈzɔst]
v 使精疲力盡；
n 廢氣

★ People nowadays can not help breathing in car **exhaust**.
如今人們不得不吸入汽車廢氣。

---

exhibition
[ˌɛksəˈbɪʃən]
n 展覽（會）

★ The most expensive picture in this **exhibition** is this abstract painting.
展覽中最貴的作品是這幅抽象畫。

---

flame
[flem]
n 火舌；火焰

★ The huge fire left the building in **flames**.
這場大火讓大樓在烈焰中燃燒。

---

flash
[flæʃ]
n 閃光燈；閃爍；
v 飛馳；閃光；
閃現

★ In a **flash**, he realized that the boss wasn't satisfied with his answer.
他立刻意識到老闆對他的回答並不滿意。

---

flavor
[ˈflevɚ]
n 特色；味；v 加味於；調味

★ The new **flavor** for coke is in great demand.
新口味可樂的需求量很大。

---

flesh
[flɛʃ]
n 肉體；果肉；肉

★ Humans cannot live forever, for we are only **flesh** and blood.
人類不過是血肉之軀，不可能永遠地存活下去。

---

float
[flot]
v （使）漂流；飄動；n 浮動

★ Can you imagine the day when buildings will **float** in the sky?
你能想像大樓在天空中飄的日子嗎？

---

flock
[flɑk]
n 一群；v 聚集；成群

★ Thousands of Americans **flocked** west in search of gold.
成千上萬的美國人湧入西部淘金。

形
似

grab
[græb]
v 抓住（機會）；
n 奪；抓

★ I will **grab** some water for you while you are here buying the tickets.
我去拿些水，你在這裡買票。

---

grammar
['græmɚ]
n 文法

★ The class was pretty easy, but the **grammar** is quite difficult.
課程非常簡單，但是文法相當的難。

---

grant
[grænt]
v 同意；授予；
准予；n 授予物

★ Please **grant** me more time, I will give you my new design next week.
請再給我一點時間，我下星期會把新的設計方案交給你。

---

grasp
[græsp]
v 抓住；n 理
解；抓緊

★ We should **grasp** that opportunity because it's now or never.
這是僅有的機會，我們應該緊握住它。

---

gratitude
['grætə,tjud]
n 感謝

★ Jim would like to extend his **gratitude** on behalf of his parents.
吉姆想要代表他的父母表示感謝。

---

attitude
['ætətjud]
n 看法；態度

★ Whether I go or I stay depends on the **attitude** of my boss.
我走人或者留下完全取決於我老闆的態度。

---

harm
[harm]
n 危害；傷害；
v 危害；傷害

★ As we all know, rising dollars will do **harm** to the economy of America.
眾所周知，美元上揚會對美國經濟造成傷害。

---

harmony
['harmənɪ]
n 融洽；和諧

★ Human being should develop the society in **harmony** with nature.
人類應該在與自然和諧相處的前提下推進社會的發展。

形
似

hesitation [,hɛzə'teʃən] n 躊躇；猶豫	★ The appearance of the hat caught my eye, so I bought it without **hesitation**. 帽子的外形吸引了我，所以我毫不猶豫的買下了。
determination [dɪ,tɝmə'neʃən] n 堅定；決心	★ A boss should have the **determination** to overcome all the difficulties. 老闆應該有決心克服所有困難。
inflation [ɪn'fleʃən] n 膨脹；通貨膨脹	★ The **inflation** was kept in check. 通貨膨脹得到控制。
influential [,ɪnflu'ɛnʃəl] adj 有權勢的；有影響力的	★ The cram school is **influential** because many people take courses there. 補習班很有影響力，因為很多人都去那上課。
lawn [lɔn] n 草坪；草地	★ There are two tall buildings and a small **lawn** in between. 那邊有兩棟高樓，大樓中間有一小塊草地。
launch [lɔntʃ] v 發射；使開始從事；n 發行；（新產品）投產	★ New models for mobile phones are **launched** every month. 新款手機每個月都被推出。
lively ['laɪvlɪ] adj 愉快的；栩栩如生的	★ Dining-room is **lively** and concise. 餐廳明快簡潔。
alive [ə'laɪv] adj 活著的；存在的	★ Had she seen the doctor earlier, Mary would still be **alive**. 要是瑪麗早一點去看醫生，瑪麗還會活著。

mankind
[mæn'kaɪnd]
n 人類

★ Some questions can't be answered by **mankind**.
有些問題人類沒法回答。

---

mansion
['mænʃən]
n 官邸；大廈

★ It would be fantastic to live in a three-story **mansion** on the mountains.
住在山上的三層大樓裡真奇妙。

---

manual
['mænjuəl]
n 鍵盤；手冊；
adj 體力的

★ We have sent him user **manual** in reply to his inquiry.
回應他的詢問，我們已經寄用戶手冊給他了。

---

mental
['mɛntl]
adj 精神的；內心的；智力的

★ Playing online games is bad for one's physical and **mental** health.
玩網路遊戲對身心健康有害。

---

mention
['mɛnʃən]
v 提名表揚；提到；n 傳令嘉獎；提及

★ Thank you for writing, but the lighting system's problem you have **mentioned** still needs to be examined.
感謝您的來函，但是您所提及的關於照明系統的問題還有待檢查。

---

meter
['mitɚ]
n 公尺

★ There is about 25 **meters** of space between the tall buildings.
高樓之間約有二十五公尺的空間。

---

metro
['mɛtro]
n 地下鐵道；捷運

★ The **metro** station was crowded with students and adults on their way home.
捷運站擠滿了要回家的學生和成人。

---

method
['mɛθəd]
n 方法

★ **Methods** of cooking have barely changed in the last ten years.
烹飪方法在過去十年幾乎沒有改變。

measure
['mɛʒɚ]
n 方法；v 測量

★ These **measures** can lessen the present tension.
這些措施可以緩和現在的緊張局勢。

motivate
['motə,vet]
v 刺激；激發

★ Nothing could **motivate** Jason in that company, so he chose to leave.
那個公司已經沒有什麼可以激發傑森了，所以他選擇離開。

activation
[,æktə'veʃən]
n 啟動

★ The **activation** fee for your account is $10.
你戶頭的啟動費用是十美元。

native
['netɪv]
adj 天生的；n 土著；本地人

★ Kelly speaks Chinese so fluently because she is a **native** speaker.
凱莉說中國話很流利，因為中國話是她的母語。

national
['næʃənl]
adj 國家的

★ The quality is in accord with the **national** standards.
品質符合國家標準。

negotiation
[nɪ,goʃɪ'eʃən]
n 談判

★ This **negotiation** will contribute to the further cooperation between the two companies.
這次談判將有助於兩家公司之間的進一步合作。

suggestion
[sə'dʒɛstʃən]
n 建議

★ I hope your **suggestion** will contribute to solving the problem.
我希望你的建議有助於解決這個問題。

outline
['aut,laɪn]
v 概述；n 概要

★ If you agree to the terms **outlined** in the contract, please sign your name.
如果你同意契約裡的條款，請你簽字。

outstanding
['aut'stændɪŋ]
adj 未解決的；傑出的

★ You deserve the promotion because you are the most **outstanding** in our company.
這次晉升是你應得的，因為你是公司中最出類拔萃的。

形
似

overlook
[ˌovɚˈluk]
v 忽略；俯瞰

★ Your first delay of settling the account is usually **overlooked** by the bank.
銀行常常不追究你第一次拖延結清帳款。

overnight
[ˈovɚˈnaɪt]
adv 通宵；adj 一整夜的

★ The wealth is not built **overnight**. It is accumulated day by day.
財富不是一夜之間獲得，必須一天天的積累。

owe
[o]
v 欠債

★ I must finish the work in time because I **owe** it to Tom.
我得對湯姆負責任，因此我必須及時完成工作。

own
[on]
v 有；adj 自己的

★ The great American dream is for each family to own their **own** land.
實現偉大的美國夢，是讓每個家庭都能擁有自己的一塊土地。

pace
[pes]
n 速度；一步；v 踱步

★ The mayor **paced** around the stage.
市長在台上走來走去。

Pacific
[pəˈsɪfɪk]
n 太平洋；adj 太平洋的

★ In the South **Pacific** Ocean lie many small islands.
在南太平洋座落著很多小島。

parade
[pəˈred]
n 閱兵典禮；遊行

★ Thousands of people gathered on the city's sidewalks to watch the **parade**.
成千上萬的人集合在城裡的人行道上觀看遊行。

paradise
[ˈpærəˌdaɪs]
n 天堂

★ The voyagers set out in the early morning in search of a hidden **paradise**.
為找尋失落的天堂，航海者們大清早就出發了。

◎ 形似

形

似

passage
['pæsɪdʒ]
n 通路；通行；
航行；文章

★ Read this **passage** and pick up mistakes from it right now.
馬上讀讀這篇文章，然後找出錯誤。

---

passport
['pæs,port]
n 通行證；護照

★ Make sure your **passport** isn't out of date; we will go to Europe this week.
要確保你的護照沒有過期，我們這星期要去歐洲。

---

post
[post]
n 郵件；郵箱；
職位

★ Only applicants with a PHD will be considered for the new **post**.
這個新職位只考慮有博士學位的申請者。

---

postpone
[post'pon]
v 延遲

★ The press conference must be **postponed**, for the general manager has not arrived yet.
由於總經理尚未到場，記者會必須延遲舉行。

---

pound
[paund]
v 猛擊；n 磅

★ Carla became the angel of beauty after she lost twenty **pounds**.
卡拉減了二十磅體重後成了美女天使。

---

pour
[por]
v 傾瀉；倒

★ For Jack who failed the exam twice in a row and then broke his legs, it never rains but it **pours**.
傑克兩次考試都不及格，又摔斷了腿，真是禍不單行。

---

presence
['prɛzns]
n 出席；面前

★ Jack had to behave himself in the **presence** of Mary.
傑克在瑪麗面前必須表現得體。

---

presentation
[,prizɛn'teʃən]
n 報告；提供；
介紹

★ The manager told Mary to get the **presentation** started as soon as possible.
經理告訴瑪麗儘快開始報告。

preview
['pri,vju]
n 預習；v 預習；試映

★ The teacher's suggestions is to **preview** the lesson before class.
老師的建議是課前預習。

previous
['priviəs]
adj 先前的

★ Just different in appearance, the new cell phone's function is all the same as the **previous** model.
除了外觀不同，新型手機的功能居然與老型號完全相同。

progress
['prɑgrɛs]
n 前進；v 前進

★ The company's technical innovation is in **progress**.
公司正在進行技術創新。

promptly
[prɑmptlɪ]
adv 敏捷地；立即地

★ In response to the crisis, the government had failed to act **promptly**.
政府未能及時應對危機。

prohibit
[prə'hɪbɪt]
v 妨礙；禁止

★ Slavery was legal in America until it was lawfully **prohibited**.
直到法律禁止奴隸制，它在美國是合法的。

pronunciation
[prə,nʌnsɪ'eʃən]
n 發音

★ To read English aloud every day will help perfect your **pronunciation**.
每天大聲朗讀英語有助於完善你的發音。

refugee
[,rɛfju'dʒi]
n 難民

★ Though they have escaped from the dangerous area, the **refugees'** fates are still questionable.
雖然逃出了危險的區域，那些難民的命運仍然處於不確定狀態。

regardless
[rɪ'gɑrdlɪs]
adv 無論如何

★ **Regardless** of the safety, he ran into the fire to save the little girl.
他不顧自身安全，衝入火海中救了那個小女孩。

regulation
[,rɛgjə'leʃən]
n 條例；規章；管理

★ The new **regulation** brought great losses on the export.
新規定帶來了巨大的出口損失。

形
似

⭕ 形似

relatively ['rɛlətɪvlɪ] **adv** 相對地	★ Teachers should pay more attention to students with **relatively** poor academic performance. 老師應該多多關注在校表現相對較差的學生。
relax [rɪ'læks] **v** 鬆弛；緩和	★ **Relax**, or you will get mad under such pressure. 放鬆一下，不然在這種壓力下你會瘋掉。
release [rɪ'lis] **v** 釋放；**n** 發行；通訊稿	★ After the analysis was **released**, the truth finally dawned on everyone. 當分析公布後，真相終於大白了。
rescue ['rɛskju] **n** 援救；**v** 營救	★ Linda fell into the river. Right on cue, a passerby **rescued** her. 琳達掉到河裡，一位路人正好經過，救了她。
resemble [rɪ'zɛmbl̩] **v** 類似	★ She **resembles** her sister in appearance. 她和她姊姊外貌相似。
rise [raɪz] **n** 上升；**v** 上升；增加	★ Steel is going up in price; therefore, the price of construction is **rising**. 鋼鐵價格上揚導致建築的成本增加。
arise [ə'raɪz] **v** 升起；出現	★ No problems **arise**. 沒有問題發生。
series ['siriz] **n** 連續；系列	★ A **series** of accidents made the company be on the verge of bankruptcy. 一連串的意外使得公司處於破產的邊緣。
serious ['sɪrɪəs] **adj** 嚴重的；嚴肅的	★ He was very **serious**. 他很嚴肅。

形似

shortage
['ʃɔrtɪdʒ]
n 匱乏；不足

★ Due to shortage in supplies, the price of gold tends upward.
因為供不應求，金價上漲。

---

shortcut
['ʃɔrt,kʌt]
n 快捷方式

★ Jim always took the shortcut through the forests.
吉姆總是抄近路穿過森林。

---

situation
[,sɪtʃu'eʃən]
n 形勢；職位

★ We are not sure whether the situation is under control.
我們不確定情況是否受到控制。

---

site
[saɪt]
n 地點；場所

★ The emergency crew arrived at the accident site to help the survivors.
急救人員趕到事故現場去幫助倖存者。

---

stadium
['stedɪəm]
n 運動場

★ A new stadium has been built in preparation for the Olympic Games.
一個新的體育館已經建成，為奧運會做準備。

---

staff
[stæf]
n （全體）工作人員

★ Our staff is comprised of people from different countries.
我們的職員是由不同國家的人組成的。

---

stare
[stɛr]
v 凝視；n 瞪眼

★ The dog stared at me while I was having my meal.
我吃飯的時候，這隻狗盯著我看。

---

start
[stɑrt]
n 開始；開端；
v 開始

★ Bob started to run his own business after graduation.
畢業後鮑伯開始經營自己的生意。

---

statue
['stætʃu]
n 塑像；雕像

★ The statue was built in 2000 to commemorate his great accomplishments.
這座雕像建於西元兩千年，用來紀念他偉大的成就。

◯ 形似

status
['stetəs]
n 地位；狀況

★ Most white-collar workers are not satisfied with their **status** quo.
大部分的白領工作者對現狀不滿意。

stretch
[strɛtʃ]
v 伸出；拉緊；
n 伸展

★ The majestic Rocky Mountains **stretches** across many parts of the United States.
雄偉的落磯山脈穿過美國許多州。

strategy
['strætədʒɪ]
n 戰略；策略

★ The general manager is considering a new **strategy** that would eliminate unnecessary paperwork in the office.
總經理正在考慮一項可能減少辦公室裡不必要的文書工作的新策略。

strict
[strɪkt]
adj 嚴厲的；
嚴謹的

★ Boys and girls, you must be **strict** with yourselves.
男孩子們，女孩子們，你們必須嚴格要求自己。

strip
[strɪp]
n 帶；v 剝；
拆卸

★ The American flag has thirteen white **stripes** and fifty white stars.
美國國旗有十三條白色條紋和五十顆白色星星。

suicide
['suə,saɪd]
n 自殺

★ If we give our competitors a hand, it would be like commiting chronic **suicide**.
如果我們援助我們的競爭對手，就相當於在慢性自殺。

suitable
['sutəbl]
adj 合適的

★ Perhaps he is not **suitable** for the position.
或許他並不合適擔任此職位。

surfing
['sɝfɪŋ]
n 衝浪遊戲

★ He was exhausted after hours of wind **surfing**.
數小時的風中衝浪後，他累壞了。

survey
[sə've]
n 調查；v 調查；測量

★ We designed a survey to find whether this product was popular or not.
我們做調查，看看這種產品是否受歡迎。

★ Many people got upset when the result of the survey was released.
調查結果一公布，很多人都感到不安。

---

surely
['ʃurlɪ]
adv 確實；當然；一定

★ He will surely be hungry for more success.
他一定非常渴望獲得更多的成功。

★ Eight grams of sugar is surely enough for this recipe.
八公克的糖對於這份食譜來說一定足夠。

---

suspect
[sə'spɛkt]
v 懷疑；猜想；n 嫌疑犯

★ Never had she suspected that her best friend would betray her.
她從沒有懷疑過最好的朋友會出賣她。

---

respect
[rɪ'spɛkt]
v 尊重；n 尊敬

★ People from all walks of life must be equally respected.
從事各個行業的人都應該被同樣尊重。

★ Employees should have respect for their leaders.
雇員應該尊重領導者。

---

suspense
[sə'spɛns]
n 掛慮；懸疑

★ The big earthquake kept the nation in suspense.
大地震讓全國人民處於緊張狀態。

---

swear
[swɛr]
v 發誓；詛咒

★ When witnesses testifies in court, they are always asked to swear by the Bible.
目擊者出庭作證時，都必須以聖經發誓。

---

sweat
[swɛt]
n 汗；不安；v 出汗

★ Clothes will adhere to the skin if you sweat too much.
如果你流太多汗，衣服就會黏在皮膚上。(adhere to 黏附；堅持)

◯ 形似

towards [tə'wɔrdz] prep 向；朝；關於	★ The ants slowly crawled **towards** their new home two feet away. 螞蟻們慢慢朝向兩英尺外的新家爬過去。
afterwards ['æftəwədz] adv 以後；之後；後來	★ Tom was severely injured in a car accident and died shortly **afterwards**. 湯姆在車禍中傷的很重，不久以後就死了。
tale [tel] n 傳說；總數	★ In the **tale**, once you take a look at Medusa, you will end up in her gaze. 傳說，你看一眼美杜沙，就會在她的注視下死於非命。
talented ['tæləntɪd] adj 有才幹的	★ Tom is **talented**. I think he may become the next Jim Carey. 湯姆很聰明。我想他可能成為下一個Jim Carey。
tremble ['trɛmbl] v 發抖；擔憂；搖晃；n 震動；發抖	★ Tom **trembled** severely in the face of the tiger. 湯姆在老虎面前顫抖的很厲害。
tremendous [trɪ'mɛndəs] adj 巨大的；極好的	★ **Tremendous** changes have taken place in the world during these years. 這些年來世界發生了翻天覆地的變化。
vase [ves] n 花瓶	★ You ought to have been more careful when you were dealing with that **vase**. 你在處理那只花瓶時本該更小心些的。
vast [væst] adj 廣闊的；大量的	★ The salvage team recovered a beautiful and **vast** underwater treasure from the shipwreck. 打撈隊從海難中找回了美麗且巨大的水下財寶。

形
似

worry
['wɝɪ]
v 使擔心

★ Jim's mother was so **worried** because of his not being home.
吉姆沒回家，因此他的媽媽非常擔心。

- -

worse
[wɝs]
adj 更壞的；
adv 更糟

★ They lost their way, and what made matters **worse** was that it began to rain.
他們迷路了，更糟糕的是開始下雨了。

片語篇

第 5 篇

⊙ 片語／中文詞義接近

最 常考有關『因為；由於』片語整理

💬 **due to** 由於；歸因於

The football game was put off to Wednesday **due to** bad weather.
由於天氣不好，橄欖球比賽被延期至週三舉行。

💡 **because of** 因為；由於

Because of SARS, everyone must have his or her temperature taken before entering a building.
由於 SARS 的緣故，大家在進入建築物前都必須測量體溫。

💬 **thanks to** 多虧了；由於；幸虧

Thanks to my boss. I got a raise.
謝謝老闆，我加薪了。

最 常考有關『大量；很多』片語整理

💡 **plenty of** 大量的；充裕的

They had **plenty of** spare time to do things they want.
他們有大量的空閒時間可以做自己想做的事情。

💡 **a lot of** 很多；許多；大量的

She has made **a lot of** mistakes, but she still won't admit to them.
她犯下很多錯誤，但是她不願意承認。

Buying daily supplies in bulk can save **a lot of** money.
大量購買日用品可以省下不少錢。

💬 **lots of** 許多；大量的

Tom spends **lots of** time in the lab doing experiments every day.
湯姆每天花大量時間在實驗室裡做實驗。

💡 **a great deal** 非常；大量

Since I have started working, I have changed **a great deal**.
自工作以來，我改變了很多。

🌸 **a great deal of** 大量；很多；大量的

Jim spent a great deal of time playing computer games.
吉姆花大量的時間玩電腦遊戲。

🌸 **a large amount of** 大量的

To conceive a new plan, we need a large amount of data.
我們需要大量數據來孕育一個新方案。

🌸 **a great number of** 大量的

John has a great number of English idioms at his command.
約翰掌握了大量的英語成語。

最 常考有關『負責；對…負責』片語整理

🌸 **answer for** 對…負有責任；保證

Adults should answer for their own behaviors.
成年人應該對自己的行為負責。

🌸 **be responsible for** 對…負責

Responsible for the project, Alice negotiated with government on behalf of her team.
作為工程的負責人，愛麗絲代表她的團隊和政府談判。

🌸 **in charge of** 負責

John is now in charge of the working unit.
約翰現在負責這個工作組。

🌸 （補充）**take charge of** 掌管；接管

No one wants to take charge of the food company after it went bankrupt.
食品公司破產後，沒人想要接管它。

片語／中文詞義接近

according to 根據；按照

According to the report, London has a large market for dehumidifiers.
根據這篇報告，倫敦的除溼機市場非常地大。

base on 以⋯為根據；基礎

You may only make conclusions based on facts, not your imagination.
你只能通過事實而非想像力來得出結論。

in accordance with 根據；與⋯一致

The manager ordered everyone to work in accordance with the company's rules and regulations.
經理命令大家按照公司規章制度來執行工作。

for all I know 根據我所知

For all I know, Mary is a very nice person.
據我所知，瑪麗人很好。

judge... by... 根據⋯做出判斷

You cannot judge a person by his appearance. Many liars look honest.
你不能單憑外表判斷一個人，很多騙子看起來很誠實。

to all appearances 就外表看來；根據觀察推斷

To all appearances, the red car is the most expensive one.
從外表來判斷，紅色的車是最貴的。

最 常考有關『導致；引起』片語整理

result in 導致；結果是

Peter tried every means to save the company but the attempts resulted in vain.
彼得竭盡全力要挽救公司，但是努力最終還是失敗了。

中文詞義接近

bring about 導致；引起；實現；造成

What brought about the accident is still under investigation.
引起事故的原因仍在調查中。

bring on 使發生；引起；使前進

Our contentions did bring on some gossips.
我們之間爭論的確造成了一些八卦。

最 常考有關『比較；對比』片語整理

compare... with... 與…相比

He cannot compare his writing with that of Shakespear's.
他無法將自己的作品與莎士比亞的著作相比。

in contrast with 與…相比；與…形成對比

In contrast with the weakening of the US dollar, RMB remained strong.
和美元的疲軟情況相比，人民幣依然保持強勁。

in contrast to 與…相反的；與…形成對照

In contrast to their bankruptcy, our company flourished.
與他們公司破產相反，我們公司蒸蒸日上。

最 常考有關『成功；失敗』片語整理

succeed in + 名詞／動名詞 （在…方面）成功

He will never succeed in his career because he doesn't push himself hard enough.
他的事業永遠不會成功，因為他不夠努力。

great success （某事）很成功

Manager Lin's visit was a great success; he got four new clients during this visit.
林經理的拜訪很成功，他在此期間得到了四位新客戶。

fail to 未能；失敗

Jack failed to figure out the total amount spent on this investment.
傑克計算不出這次投資所花費的總金額。

● 片語／中文詞義接近

常考有關『合作』片語整理

💡 collaborate with　與…合作；通敵

The company **collaborated with** IBM.
這家公司與IBM合作。

💡 cooperation partner　合作夥伴

AKUS is our long standing **cooperation partner**.
AKUS是我們的長期合作夥伴。

💡 improve the cooperation　提升合作關係

More communication is needed to **improve the cooperation** between us.
我們需要更加頻繁的溝通，以提升我們之間的合作關係。

最 常考有關『習慣』片語整理

💡 used to　（過去的）習慣…

When I was a child, I **used to** climb trees with my friends.
當我還是個小孩的時候，我常和朋友們一起去爬樹。

💡 be used to +　動名詞／名詞　（現在的）習慣…

In universities, many students **are** not **used to** getting up early in the morning.
在大學裡，很多學生都不習慣早起。

💡 get used to +　動名詞／名詞　習慣…

Tony is **getting used to** the new computer program.
湯尼開始習慣新的電腦程式了。

最 常考有關『樂意；榮幸』片語整理

💡 be happy to　樂意；高興做

If you have any questions about the PDA, I'd **be happy to** answer them for you.
如果您對於這部掌上型電腦有任何疑問，我將樂意為您提供解答。

💬 **be pleased to** 高興；樂意

Linda **was pleased to** hear that she would soon be promoted.
琳達聽到她馬上要晉升的消息十分高興。

💬 **be willing to** 願意；樂意

We **are willing to** be investigated at any time and any place.
我們願意在任何時間地點接受調查。

💬 **have the honor** 有幸；榮幸

May I **have the honor** of inviting you to the party?
我能有這個榮幸邀請你參加宴會嗎？

最 常考有關『需要；缺乏』片語整理

💬 **be in need of** 需要；缺乏

The country **is in need of** international help after the earthquake.
地震過後，這個國家需要國際援助。

💬 **be short of** 缺少；短缺；不夠；未達到

The factory has just opened and **is short of** workers.
工廠剛開幕，目前缺乏工人。

💬 **lack of** 缺乏

This factory's production has been cut down due to **lack of** raw material.
由於缺乏原料，工廠削減了生產量。

最 常考有關『控制』片語整理

💬 **under control** 處於控制之下

Something must be done to get the pollution **under control**.
必須採取行動，將汙染控制住。

💬 **in control of** 掌控著；控制著

When the teacher was ill, the class monitor was **in control of** the class.
老師生病的時候，由班長負責管理班級。

● 片語／中文詞義接近

最 常考有關『突然…』片語整理

all of a sudden　突然；突然間

All of a sudden, it started raining cats and dogs.
天空突然下起了傾盆大雨。

burst in on　突然出現

It was rude of him to burst in on our conversation.
他突然打斷了我們的談話，真是沒有禮貌。

burst into tears　突然哭起來

I was surprised when Jack suddenly burst into tears.
看到傑克突然大哭起來，我嚇了一跳。

burst out　突然…起來；叫嚷

After the volcano erupted, the entire city burst out in flames.
火山爆發後，大火突然延燒整個城市。

最 常考有關『時間』片語整理

sooner or later　遲早

If you always hand in your assignments late, you will be flunked sooner or later.
如果你每次都晚交作業，你遲早會被當掉。

a waste of time　浪費時間

To water the garden when it is raining is such a waste of time.
在下雨天替花澆水真是浪費時間。

for a while　暫時；一段時間

Linda has worked for 24 hours without rest; let her sleep for a while.
琳達已經連續工作二十四小時了，讓她睡一會兒吧。

quite a while　相當一陣子

The beef stew has been simmering on the stove for quite a while now.
燉牛肉已經在爐子上燉了一段時間了。

中文詞義接近

during one's leisure time　在閒暇時間

Jogging is a perfect activity to carry out during one's leisure time.
慢跑是一項極適合在閒暇時間進行的活動。

how much time　多少時間

How much time will it take to type this letter? About thirty minutes, I guess.
「打這封信需要花多少時間？」「我猜大概要三十分鐘。」

a period of time　時段；一段時間

Helen is excellent at her work, because she solved many problems in a short period of time.
海倫工作很出色，因為她在短時間內解決了很多問題。

in a short time　很快地；不久

How did Lucy finish so much work in such a short time?
露西如何在這麼短的時間內完成那麼多的工作？

in time　及時

She was too tired to get up in time and missed her flight.
她太累了，無法按時起床，因此沒趕上飛機。

on time　準時

As long as you can finish your work on time, I don't care how you do it.
只要你能準時完成工作，用什麼方法我都不在乎。

最 常考有關『意見；想法』片語整理

in my opinion　我認為

"In my opinion," Jason says, "everyone needs to work harder."
傑森說：「我認為，每個人都要更努力工作。」

have not the least idea　一點都不知道；沒有任何頭緒

I had not the least idea that he's in charge.
我完全不知道原來他就是負責人。

中文詞義接近

最 常考有關『總之；總結』片語整理

in a word 總之；簡而言之

In a word, 2012 was a year of failure to our company.
簡而言之，2012年對我們公司來說是失敗的一年。

in brief 簡言之

In brief, you have to obey the company's regulation.
簡言之，你們必須遵守公司的規定。

in conclusion 最後；總之

In conclusion, she wished her comrades a successful career.
最後，她預祝同事們事業順利。

最 常考有關『人和人體器官』片語整理

face to face 面對面

He argued face to face with his boss.
他和老闆面對面的爭吵。

strain one's eyes 用眼過度；眼睛疲勞

Studying without resting can easily strain one's eyes.
長時間讀書不休息容易造成眼睛疲勞。

foot the bill 付帳

Our boss said he would foot the bill for dinner.
老闆說晚餐由他買單。

have a severe toothache 牙疼的很厲害

I am having a severe toothache. I need to make an appointment with the dentist.
我的牙齒非常痛，我得和牙醫師做預約。

slip of tongue 說錯話

John told the secret by a slip of tongue.
約翰一不小心說出了祕密。

最 常考有關『健康狀況』片語整理

🌿 have a cold 感冒；著涼

Although he **had a cold**, Mark still came to work.
儘管感冒了，馬克仍然堅持上班。

🌿 catch a cold 感冒

I **caught a cold** and decided to see a doctor.
我感冒了，決定去看醫生。

🌿 hard of hearing 重聽的；耳聾的

It's hard to talk to Jenny because she is **hard of hearing**.
和珍妮說話很難，因為她有聽力障礙。

最 常考有關『動物』片語整理

🌿 dog's life 困苦的生活

In the old days, many families lived a **dog's life**.
過去，許多家庭都過著牛馬不如的生活。

🌿 birds of a feather 物以類聚；同類

Burglars and thieves are all **birds of a feather**.
盜賊和小偷都是一丘之貉。

🌿 rain cats and dogs 傾盆大雨

It was **raining cats and dogs** when I got off work.
我下班的時候下起了傾盆大雨。

最 常考有關『a ~ of』片語整理

🌿 a bottle of 一瓶

I saw Tom sitting on the roof, with **a bottle of** juice in hand.
我看見湯姆坐在屋頂上，手裡拿著一瓶果汁。

中文詞義接近

精準必考

◐ 片語／精準必考

🔅 a couple of 一對；一雙；兩三（個）

I have watched that movie a couple of times before, but I decided to watch it again.
那部電影我已經看了很多遍，但是我決定再看一遍。

🔅 a list of 清單

Mr. Lin showed us a list of the targets for next year.
林先生向我們展示了寫著明年目標的清單。

🔅 a pair of 一雙；一對

Mary needs a pair of sunglasses to protect her eyes.
瑪麗需要一副太陽眼鏡來保護眼睛。

🔅 a series of 系列；一連串

The firm has experienced a series of changes recently.
這個公司最近經歷了一連串變動。

🔅 a waste of 浪費

Sleeping until noon is such a waste of time.
睡到中午可真是浪費時間。

🔅 a piece of 一片；一張

Could you pass me a piece of toast?
可以遞給我一片吐司嗎？

🔅 a piece of news 一則消息

A piece of bad news suddenly reached Bob's ears while he was working.
鮑伯正在工作時，突然得知一個壞消息。

🔅 a glass of milk 一杯牛奶

Lily swallowed a glass of milk and dashed off to school.
莉莉灌下一杯牛奶，匆忙趕往學校去了。

精準必考

230

最 常考有關『a matter ~ of』片語整理

a matter of fact 事實

This is not a lie; it's **a matter of fact**.
這並非謊言，而是事實。

a matter of time 時間上的問題

It's only **a matter of time** before the company goes bankrupt.
這家公司的破產只是時間上的問題。

最 常考有關『~ about』片語整理

care about 關心

For the present, the shortsighted boss **cares** only **about** the profit.
目前這名目光淺短的老闆只關心他的利益。

complain about 抱怨；訴苦；申訴

Tom **complained about** the damp weather.
湯姆抱怨潮溼的天氣。

She never ceased to **complain about** prices.
她從不停止對物價的抱怨。

see about 檢查；處理

The police came to the scene to **see about** the accident.
警察來到現場處理這場意外。

think about 思考；考慮；想

Are you still **thinking about** telling the child the truth?
你還在考慮告訴孩子真相嗎？

whisper about 竊竊私語

The employees **whispered about** the company's financial crisis.
員工們對公司的經濟危機竊竊私語著。

● 片語／精準必考

worry about 擔心；焦慮

You needn't worry about our manager's safety.
你沒必要擔心我們經理的安全。

be mad about 對…生氣；為…瘋狂

The director is mad about the slow progress.
主管對緩慢的進展感到十分生氣。

know a thing or two about 略知一二；有初步瞭解

Although I am not working on the project, I know a thing or two about it.
雖然我沒參與這個項目，但我對它略知一二。

somewhere about 在附近

The children are playing somewhere about the park.
孩子們在公園附近玩耍。

最 常考有關『account』片語整理

on no account 決不；不論何種情況都不

On no account should a student break school regulations.
學生在任何情況下都不應該違反校規。

on account of 因…的緣故；因為；由於

The manager resigned on account of the company's bad performance.
經理由於公司業績不佳而辭職。

take ... into account 將…列入考慮；考慮

It's necessary to take all factors into account before making decisions.
做決定之前，有必要考慮所有的因素。

最 常考有關『age』片語整理

full age 成年

Dick had his full age son inherit the company.
迪克讓他成年的兒子繼承了公司。

under age 未成年

Alcohol cannot be sold to anyone under age.
酒不能被販售給未成年人。

at the age of 在…歲的時候

Tom lost his job at the age of 45.
湯姆四十五歲的時候丟了工作。

最 常考有關『ahead』片語整理

ahead of 勝過；在之前

The athlete running ahead of Peter is John.
跑在彼得前面的運動員是約翰。

ahead of schedule 提前

The work was finished ahead of schedule.
工作提前完成。

get ahead of 領先；超前

John always tries to get ahead of others at everything.
約翰總是試圖在各方面都領先他人。

最 常考有關『apart』片語整理

apart from 除…之外；除…之外 (還有)

Apart from a little money, Lily got nothing at all.
除了一點點錢以外，莉莉什麼都沒有得到。

come apart　破碎；崩潰

The phone **came apart** the first time I used it.
這部電話在我第一次使用時就解體了。

pull apart　撕開

Our company was **pulled apart** when many employees chose to leave.
在很多員工選擇離去之時，公司就已經四分五裂了。

tell ... apart　區分

It's hard to **tell** twins **apart** because they look the same.
因為長得很相似，所以雙胞胎總是很難區分。

最 常考有關『around』片語整理

around the clock　日以繼夜；晝夜不停地

You know, the job requires you to work **around the clock**.
你知道嗎，這份工作需要你日以繼夜地做事。

come around　甦醒；復原

Tom **came around** this morning after being carefully taken cared of.
受到細心照料後，湯姆今早甦醒了。

sail around　航行圍繞

As the boat **sailed around** the small island, people waved to the crew from the coast.
船隻圍繞小島行駛時，人們在岸邊向船員們揮手示意。

around the corner　即將來臨；在拐角處

At first sight of her, he felt love **around the corner**.
第一眼看到她，他便覺得愛情即將來臨。

精準必考

最 常考有關『ask』片語整理

ask the way 問路

If you get lost in the mountain, there might be no one for you to **ask the way**.
如果你在山裡迷路，你可能會找不到人問路。

ask for 要求；請求；尋找

Mike **asked for** an window seat to get some sleep.
邁克要了一個靠窗的座位以便睡覺。

ask after 探問；問候；問好

Don't forget to **ask after** your mother for me when you go back home.
你回家的時候，別忘了替我問候你的母親。

最 常考有關『at』片語整理

at best 充其量；至多

I can only eat two hamburgers in one meal **at best**.
我一餐最多吃兩個漢堡。

at breakfast 早餐時

Mary likes drinking a cup of coffee **at breakfast**.
瑪麗喜歡在早餐的時候喝一杯咖啡。

at first 最初

At first, Phoebe considered him a playboy, but later found out that he was actually a great person.
最初，菲比覺得他是個花花公子，但後來發現他其實是個很棒的人。

at intervals 隔一段時間

Nokia launches its new models **at intervals**.
諾基亞每隔一段時間就會推出新機型。

at last 最後；終於

Our attempts on improving our products failed **at last**.
我們為改進產品所做的努力最後以失敗告終。

at length 終於；終究

Although the prospect was dim, we made it **at length**.
儘管前景黯淡，我們最終還是成功了。

at leisure 悠閒；悠哉

After a whole day of work, the director decided to watch TV **at leisure**.
經過一天的工作，經理決定悠哉的看電視。

at most 最多

Jim goes to the gym three times a week **at most**.
吉姆每個星期最多去健身房三次。

at night 在夜裡；在晚上

The workers refused to work **at night**.
工人們拒絕在晚上工作。

at random 隨意；隨便

I chose the ice cream flavors **at random**.
我隨機挑選了冰淇淋的口味。

at all costs 不計代價

We will win the bid **at all costs**.
我們要不計代價贏取投標。

at the very beginning 在一開始；最初

Jack fell behind **at the very beginning**, but later caught up.
傑克一開始落後，但後來就趕上了。

at a loss 迷失；困惑

I was **at a loss** when my boss asked me about the task.
當我的老闆詢問我工作情況時，我不知道該說什麼才好。

最 常考有關『at the ～』片語整理

❀ at the bottom 在底端

It was said that the treasure was buried **at the bottom** of the lake.
傳說湖底埋藏著一筆財寶。

❀ (cf) bottom dollars 最後的賭注

Jack put his **bottom dollars** on the victory of the Lakers.
傑克把最後的賭注都押在了湖人隊的勝利上。

❀ at the moment 此時；現在；此刻

Don't touch the plate **at the moment**; it's hot.
現在還不要去碰那個盤子，它很燙。

❀ (cf) at this time 此時此刻

How can we help the new colleague **at this time**?
我們此時此刻能夠如何幫助新同事呢?

❀ (cf) at other times 平時；在其他時候

Sometimes he acts like a spoiled brat; **at other times** he's an angel.
有時候他表現得像個被寵壞的小孩，但有時候他又像個天使。

最 常考有關『at this ～』片語整理

❀ at this rate 照這個情況

At this rate, we will not finish this task before Friday.
照這個情況，我們不可能在週五前完成任務。

❀ at this speed 照這個速度

I dare say you will never finish the work **at this speed**.
我敢說，按照這個速度，你永遠也無法完成工作。

❀ at this time 此時此刻

The boss will be arriving home **at this time** tomorrow.
老闆將在明天的這個時候到達家裡。

精準必考

● 片語／精準必考

最 常考有關『at ~ of』片語整理

🗨 at the cost of 以…為代價

Paul married with Joan **at the cost of** losing his job.
保羅以失去工作為代價,與瓊安結了婚。

🗨 at the end of 結束時;在盡頭

All the clerks were given an extra bonus **at the end of** the year.
年終時每位職員都得到了一筆額外的獎金。

Betty is usually very busy **at the end of** the month; never bother her during that time.
貝蒂在月底總是十分繁忙,永遠不要選在那個時候打擾她。

🗨 at the heels of 緊跟;跟隨

John is always **at the heels of** his director.
約翰總是緊跟在主管後面。

🗨 at the mercy of 受支配

My grades are completely **at the mercy of** the teacher.
我的成績完全掌控在老師手中。

🗨 at the peak of 在高峰期

After continuous success, Mr. William was **at the peak of** his career.
在取得連續的成功之後,威廉先生迎來了事業的高峰。

🗨 at the point of 到…的地步

At the side of the river, the enemies realized that they had arrived **at the point of** no return.
當敵人抵達河邊時,他們發現自己已經無路可退了。

🗨 at the sight of 一看到…

At the sight of the director, Jeff immediately pretended to be working.
傑夫一見到主管便馬上假裝工作。

精準必考

238

🌸 **at the beginning of** 在開始

At the beginning of each class, the teacher counts the students.
每節課開始前，老師都會先點人數。

🈵 常考有關『～ away』片語整理

🌸 **die away** 逐漸消逝

The noise of the motorbike died away.
摩托車發出的噪音逐漸消逝了。

🌸 **go away** 走開；離開

Please go away and leave me alone.
請你走開，讓我一個人靜一靜。

🌸 **idle away** 浪費時間；虛度光陰

If you idle away time in college, don't blame anyone if you can't get a good job.
如果你在大學期間虛度光陰，就不要把找不到工作的責任推卸給他人。

🌸 **pass away** 過去；去世

Weekends pass away very fast.
週末過得很快。

🌸 **run away** 跑開

You had better run away right now.
你最好現在就立刻跑開。

🌸 **wear away** 消磨；消耗

Constant dropping will wear away a stone.
滴水能夠穿石。

● 片語／精準必考

最 常考有關『～away with』片語整理

💡 **do away with** 消滅；清除；取消；破除

The new manager is trying to do away with unreasonable rules.
新任經理正試圖廢除不合理的制度。

💡 **walk away with** 偷竊；帶走

The loose lock of the shop made it easy for thieves to walk away with their loot.
店裡鬆動的門鎖使小偷們能夠輕易地偷走贓物。

最 常考有關『back』片語整理

💡 **back down** 放棄；後退；屈服

Even cannons couldn't make the warriors back down.
連大砲都無法使戰士們撤退。

💡 **back of** 在…的後面；在…的背後

At the back of the teaching building, you will find a big square.
你能在教學大樓後面找到一個很大的廣場。

💡 **back out** 退出；撒手；食言

Before signing the contract, you are still allowed to back out.
簽定合約之前，你還是能退出。

💡 **back and forth** 來回；來回地；反覆地

Wilson rolled the basketball back and forth.
威爾遜來回滾動著籃球。

最 常考有關『be～for』片語整理

💡 **be bad for** 對…有害；對…不利

Driving is bad for the environment.
開車有害環境。

精準必考

be famous for 以…聞名

Hollywood is famous for movie making.
好萊塢因電影製作而聞名。

be hungry for 渴望得到

Albert is always hungry for new experiences.
亞伯特總是渴望獲得新體驗。

be known for 眾所周知

The population of the United States is known for its diversity in race.
美國的人口以其人種的多樣性而著名。

be sorry for 因…而抱歉

I'm terribly sorry for having given you so many suggestions.
我提出了這麼多的建議感到非常抱歉。

最 常考有關『be ~ from』片語整理

be separated from 與…分離

No child should ever be separated from his mother.
任何一個孩子都不應該與母親分開。

be tired from 因…而疲勞

You must be tired from the long flight. Please take a rest today.
長時間乘坐飛機，您一定很累，今天請好好休息吧。

be different from 不同於；與不同

American football, which is different from European football, is a very popular sport.
美式足球與歐式足球不同，是非常受歡迎的體育活動。

精準必考

最 常考有關『be ~ in』片語整理

💡 **be interested in** 對感興趣

He has always **been interested in** investing abroad.
他一直都對國外投資很感興趣。

💡 **be bound up in...** 熱衷於；忙於

Brown **was bound up in** work these days.
布朗這些日子以來一直忙於工作。

最 常考有關『be ~ of』片語整理

💡 **be aware of** 知道；預料到；意識到

We should **be aware of** the importance of learning English.
我們應該意識到學習英語的重要性。

💡 **be jealous of** 嫉妒

Bob **is jealous of** his colleague for getting that project.
鮑伯嫉妒那位得到了那個專案的同事。

💡 **be fond of** 喜愛

Jim **is fond of** antique cars; he spent much money on them.
吉姆對古董車很感興趣，他在這方面花了不少錢。

💡 **be proud of** 自豪；而以驕傲；高興

Peter **is proud of** receiving the prize from the boss.
彼得很榮幸能夠從老闆那裡得到獎勵。

💡 **be tired of** 厭倦

You may **be tired of** reading, but that is part of the learning process.
你或許會厭倦讀書，但那是學習中不可避免的環節。

💡 **be short of** 缺少；短缺；不夠；未達到

We **are** still **short of** one ingredient for this dish.
我們還缺少一樣製作這道菜餚的材料。

be capable of 有…能力的;可以…的

Jimmy is very capable of earning money.
吉米相當具有賺錢的能力。

be composed of 由…組成

The poem is composed of two parts.
這首詩由兩個部分組成。

be ashamed of 為…感到羞愧;感到羞恥

You should be ashamed of such behaviors.
你應該為這種行為感到羞恥。

As an adult, you should be ashamed of asking too much from your parents.
作為一個成年人,你應該為向父母索取太多東西而感到羞愧。

be characteristic of 特有的;獨特的

Buying unnecessary luxury items is the characteristic of some rich people.
購買不必要的奢侈品是某些富人的特色。

be made up of 由…組成

The human tissue is made up of cells.
人體組織是由細胞構成的。

最 常考有關『be ~ off』片語整理

be better off 更富有;更舒服;好轉

Grant is better off than his friends.
格蘭特比他的朋友們更富有。

be badly off 貧困的;近況不好的;缺乏的

The citizens were badly off due to the war.
因為戰爭的緣故,市民們都很貧困。

最 常考有關『be ～ to+原形動詞』片語整理

💡 **be bound to** 必定；一定

We **are bound to** finish the task in advance.
我們一定要提早完成任務。

💡 **be about to** 剛要；即將

I'**m about to** put an end to the job.
我馬上就要結束這項工作了。

最 常考有關『be ～ with』片語整理

💡 **be angry with** 對…發脾氣

She **was angry with** John.
她在生約翰的氣。

💡 **be busy with** 忙碌於

I will help with housework while you **are busy with** your paper.
你忙著寫論文的時候，我會幫忙做家事。

💡 **be concerned with** 關心；掛念；與…有關

A good leader **is** always **concerned with** every member.
好的領導者總是關心每一位成員。

💡 **be careful with** + 名詞 小心

William **was** very **careful with** the borrowed car.
威廉小心翼翼地照顧借來的車子。

最 常考有關『beyond ～』片語整理

💡 **beyond description** 難以言喻

The feeling of success is **beyond description**.
成功的感覺難以言喻。

🌱 **beyond all** 最重要地；超越其他部分

Beyond all other movies, "Spiderman" was this year's biggest hit.
「蜘蛛人」超越其他影片，成為今年最賣座的電影。

🌱 **beyond one's reach** 超出能力；超出範圍

Gates's success is beyond our reach.
蓋茨的成功是我們望塵莫及的。

最 常考有關『brush ~』片語整理

🌱 **brush aside** 漠視；不理；掃除

Brushing aside all difficulties, he finished the work in time.
不顧任何阻難，他按時完成了工作。

🌱 **brush off** 丟棄；脫落；拒絕

I invited Lorry to play football yesterday, but he brushed me off.
昨天我邀請羅睿踢足球，但是他拒絕了。

🌱 **brush up on** 重溫；（練習以）提高

He said he had to brush up on lessons before taking the final examination.
他說他得在期末考試之前先複習課程。

🌱 **brush up** 溫習

I'll have to brush up my English before going to New York on holiday.
去紐約渡假之前我需要重溫一下英語。

最 常考有關『by ~ 』片語整理

🌱 **by far** 多得多；目前為止

Lucy is by far the skinniest girl in class.
露西是目前班上最瘦的女孩。

● 片語／精準必考

※ by mail 通過郵寄；寫信

Sue sent me a new printer by mail.
蘇郵寄一台新印表機給我。

※ by turns 輪流

When George had a fever, he felt cold and hot by turns.
當喬治發燒的時候，他一陣子發冷，一陣子又發熱。

※ by degrees 漸漸地；逐漸地

The temperature is rising by degrees.
氣溫正逐漸上升。

※ by this time 到現在

His girlfriend will have finished her college education by this time next year.
他的女朋友在明年的這個時候就大學畢業了。

※ by and by 不久以後

Tom said he would return the money by and by, but he never did.
湯姆說他遲早會還錢，但是他始終沒有做到。

※ by chance 恰巧；偶然；運氣好

Tom came across his boss by chance.
湯姆恰巧遇到了他的老闆。

I overheard their talk by chance.
我偶然聽到他們的對話。

※ by all means 當然可以；一定；務必

Please by all means try to persuade him to come.
請務必盡力說服他來。

※ by any means 無論用任何方法

The company decided to beat its opponents by any means.
公司決定不惜一切代價擊敗對手。

最 常考有關『be ~ with』片語整理

be angry with 對…發脾氣

The teacher wasn't angry with John even though he didn't behave well.
雖然約翰不守規矩，但老師沒有生氣。

be done with 與…了結關係；完成；斷絕

Alice, come to my office when you are done with your work.
愛麗絲，事情完成後，請到我的辦公室來一下。

We are done with the job, so we can rest.
我們完成了工作，可以休息了。

be busy with 忙碌於

Peter was always busy with writing novels.
彼得總是忙於撰寫小說。

be familiar with 對…很熟悉

With the help of Mr. Lee, I am familiar with the new job.
在李先生的幫助下，我熟悉了這份新工作。

be popular with 受…歡迎

R&B music is very popular with youngsters nowadays.
時下的年輕人很喜歡聽節奏藍調。

be consistent with 與…一致的；始終如一的

The fact is consistent with what you have said.
事實與你所言相符。

be inconsistent with 與…不一致的；與…有落差

Such misdeed is inconsistent with our school's regulations.
這種惡劣的行徑有違學校規定。

片語／精準必考

最 常考有關『behind～』片語整理

behind schedule 延誤

I hope the plane is **behind schedule**, or else I will miss it.
我希望飛機會延誤，否則我就趕不上了。

behind the bushes 在草叢後面

The soldiers took cover **behind the bushes**.
士兵們隱蔽在草叢後面。

最 常考有關『better』片語整理

better than 好過；更好

Stationery sold in that shop is by far **better than** this one.
那家商店賣的文具比這家的好多了。

had better 最好；應該；必須

You**'d better** check the numbers before you leave the office.
你最好在離開辦公室之前核對一下數字。

much better 好的多；更好了

After hearing the good news, Allen felt **much better**.
聽到這則好消息後，艾倫的心情好轉了許多。

for the better 好轉；向好的方向發展

Lincoln moved to the seaside **for the better**.
為了讓生活更好，林肯搬到了海邊。

think better of 對…改變主意

I was going to buy a large house, but later **thought better of** it and bought a small one.
我本來決定要買一間大房子，但最後改變了主意買了一間小房子。

248

get the better of　戰勝；在…中占上風

This time, Sony got the better of Panasonic in the mobile phone war.
在這次的手機銷售大戰中，新力擊敗松下，占了上風。

最 常考有關『best』片語整理

try one's best　盡最大努力；盡力

Encouraged by the bonus, all employees are trying their best.
受到獎金的驅動，所有員工都盡力在工作。

make the best of　充分利用

Peter planned to get up early this morning, but laziness made the best of him.
彼得今天原本打算早起，但是懶惰戰勝了他。

最 常考有關『block』片語整理

block off　封鎖；封閉

The police blocked off the area to avoid the murderer from escaping.
警方封鎖了這片區域，以防止兇手逃脫。

block up　堵塞；擋住

The street is blocked up by heavy traffic.
街道被擁擠的交通給堵住了。

最 常考有關『break』片語整理

break away　脫離；逃脫

Can you break away from the bad habits?
你能夠脫離那些壞習慣嗎？

break down　發生故障；失敗；壞掉；損壞

We bought a new computer but it broke down today.
我們買了一台新電腦，但是今天壞掉了。

break into　強行闖入

The bandits tried to **break into** the bank, but they failed.
強盜試圖闖入銀行，但是他們失敗了。

break out　爆發；突然出現；突然發生；使逃脫；使逃走

Armed conflict is likely to **break out** between the two countries.
兩國之間可能發生武裝衝突。

Wars usually **break out** between countries whose interests collide.
戰爭往往在具有利益衝突的國家之間爆發。

break up　結束；終止；分手；打碎；分解

They decided to **break up** the marriage because their ideas were too different.
由於想法相距太遠，他們決定結束這場婚姻關係。

break through　突圍；有重要創見；突破

Although she tried hard, she still cannot **break through**.
雖然她努力嘗試，但還是無法取得突破。

break even　打平；不賠不賺

The business managed to **break even** during the first year.
公司在營運的第一年達到收支平衡。

break one's heart　使…心碎

Her puppy's death **broke her heart**.
小狗的去世讓她傷心欲絕。

break one's word　不信守諾言；失信

William never **breaks his word**.
威廉從不食言。

最常考有關『bring』片語整理

bring about　導致；引起；實現；造成

Will science **bring about** more happiness?
科學會為我們帶來更多幸福嗎？

bring down 使倒下；使下降；擊落

The soldier **brought down** many enemies.
那位士兵打倒了許多敵人。

bring forth 發表；產生；公布；提出

The manager asked me to **bring forth** my plan for discussion.
經理讓我把計畫提出來供大家討論。

bring into 使開始進入狀態

We must raise more money to **bring** the project **into** life.
我們必須募集到更多錢才能夠啟動計畫。

bring on 使發生；引起

Smoking on the bed may **bring on** fire.
在床上吸煙可能會引起火災。

bring out 出版；說明；闡明；襯托出；使顯出

Difficulties can **bring out** a person's best qualities.
困境可以幫助體現一個人的優秀品質。

bring up 教育；提出；培養

Being **brought up** in a small village, I have seen many animals.
由於在小村莊長大，我見過很多動物。

bring forward 提出；提議；提前（舉行）

You may **bring forward** your ideas while listening.
傾聽過程中你也可以提出自己的意見。

bring in 帶入；引入；引進；得到

The judge asked the guards to **bring in** the prisoner.
法官請守衛把囚犯帶進來。

精準必考

最 常考有關『burn』片語整理

💡 burn up 燒光；燒毀；燒起來

The fire burnt up the house within one hour.
火焰在一小時內燒毀了這座房子。

💡 burn down 把…燒成平地；燒光

But for the heavy rain, the house would have been burnt down.
如果沒有這場大雨，這間房子肯定已經燒毀了。

💡 burn the midnight oil 挑燈夜戰

The manager is a workaholic; he always burns the midnight oil.
經理總是熬夜工作，他是一名典型的工作狂。

最 常考有關『burst』片語整理

💡 burst into 闖入；爆發

The bandits burst into our house and told us to stand still.
強盜突然闖進家裡，叫我們站著不要動。

💡 burst into tears 大哭起來

I burst into tears when I was told that my dog had died.
當我得知我的狗死掉，我放聲大哭起來。

💡 burst into laughter 大笑起來

When he heard the news he burst into laughter.
聽到那個消息後，他忽然大笑起來。

💡 burst out 突然…起來；叫嚷

He burst out crying.
他突然放聲大哭。

💡 burst out laughing 大笑起來

Lucy burst out laughing at her colleague's story.
露西聽了同事的故事後大笑起來。

最 常考有關『by ~ of』片語整理

by way of 取道；經由；經過；當作；以…的方式

We traveled to France **by way of** London.
我們經由倫敦來到法國。

Tom got a promotion **by ways of** working hard.
湯姆通過努力工作獲得了晉升。

by courtesy of 承…的好意；由於…的作用

By courtesy of the judge, the two parties resolved their issues.
由於法官的影響，雙方得以解決了糾紛。

The shuttle to the train station is provided **by courtesy of** the government.
到火車站的接駁車是由政府所提供的。

by the name of 被稱為；名叫；以…為名；以…的名義

By a slip of tongue, Mary accidentally called Tom **by the name of** Tim.
瑪麗一不小心說錯話，把湯姆叫成了提姆。

Mr. Davis moved to another city, where he lived **by the name of** Mr. Smith.
戴維斯先生搬到了另一座城市，並在那裡以史密斯先生的名字生活。

最 常考有關『call』片語整理

call at 停靠（某地）；訪問（某地）

I am going to **call at** my grandparents tomorrow.
我明天要去拜訪爺爺和奶奶。

call forth 使產生；引起

Heavy rain always **calls forth** floods.
大雨總是會引起洪水。

call for 邀約；需要；要求；取

Remember to **call for** help when it is necessary.
必要時記得呼救。

精準必考

💬 **call in** 召來；召集；請來；來訪；收回

Please **call in** my daughters; I need to talk with them.
請把我的女兒們叫過來，我需要和她們談話。

💬 **call off** 取消

I **called off** the contract.
我取消了合約。

The football game was **called off** because of the heavy rain.
橄欖球賽因為大雨被取消。

💬 **call it a day** 結束一天的工作；下班

Let's **call it a day** and go home.
今天到此結束，我們回家去吧。

💬 **call attention to** 使注意

The war **called attention to** the public.
戰爭喚起了大眾的注意。

最 常考有關『carry』片語整理

💬 **carry out** 執行；實現；貫徹；完成

As the leader of the team, you should **carry out** your obligations.
作為團隊的領導者，你應當履行義務。

💬 **carry on** 繼續下去；繼續

No matter how hard it is, we will **carry on** for sure.
不管多麼艱難，我們一定都會繼續。

💬 **carry... through** 實踐；完成；使度過困難

We decided to **carry** the project **through**.
我們決定完成這項工程。

精準必考

最 常考有關『catch』片語整理

catch the attention 吸引注意力；引起關注

His unique voice has **caught the attention** of many customers.
他獨特的嗓音吸引了很多客人的注意。

catch on 理解；明白

I just can't **catch on** to your article.
我就是無法理解你這篇文章的意思。

catch a cold 感冒；著涼

Put on another coat or you will **catch a cold**.
多穿一件外套，否則你會感冒。

catch one's breath 喘氣；鬆口氣

Jenny ran to the company and tried to **catch her breath** in the elevator.
珍妮跑著到了公司，並試圖在電梯內喘口氣。

最 常考有關『check』片語整理

check in 辦理登記手續；報到；簽到

If you cannot **check in** at the office before eight, you will be punished.
如果你不能在八點之前到辦公室簽到，你就會受到懲罰。

check out 結帳離開；檢查；通過考核

Jack **checked out** my watch for me; it had stopped working.
傑克幫忙檢查了我的手錶，它已經壞了。

check on 核對；檢查；檢驗

Journalists need to **check on** the facts before writing the news.
在撰寫新聞之前，記者需要核對事實。

check up 檢查

I went to the hospital to have my teeth **checked up**.
我去醫院做牙齒檢查。

最 常考有關『clean』片語整理

clean up 清晰；清潔；清理

I plan to **clean up** the house before my mother comes.
我打算在我媽到達之前把房子打掃乾淨。

clean out 把…清理乾淨；把…打掃乾淨

Mom asked Mary to **clean out** the basement.
媽媽要求瑪麗清理地下室。

最 常考有關『close』片語整理

close down 關閉；歇業

Having found no solution to the pollution problem, the factory was forced to **close down** last week.
由於沒有辦法解決汙染問題，這間工廠於上週被迫關閉。

close in 包圍；圍住

They ran away when the enemy army began to **close in**.
敵軍開始進行包圍時，他們逃走了。

close to 靠近

Jim lives **close to** the company.
吉姆住得離公司很近。

最 常考有關『come』片語整理

come along 跟去；一道去；發生

Come along with us to the picnic.
跟我們一起去野餐。

come back 回來；想起來

As soon as his father **came back**, Tom took cover under the bed.
爸爸一回來，湯姆就藏到了床底下。

🌸 **come by** 得到；獲得；訪問；看望

Things that **come by** easily will not be cherished.
可以輕易得到的東西不會受到珍惜。

🌸 **come down** （物價）下跌；墜落；潦倒；流傳；傳下來

The light in the bathroom **came down** because it wasn't properly installed.
浴室的燈因為沒有安裝好而掉了下來。

🌸 **come from** 出生於；出身於；來自

The new president **came from** a famous university near to us.
新來的校長是從附近一所著名的大學調來的。

🌸 **come on** 走吧；趕快；發生；夠了

Come on, we can make it!
來吧，我們能夠做到！

🌸 **come over** 順便來訪

The boss would like to **come over** and see how the work is coming along.
老闆想要過來看看工作的進展如何。

🌸 **come out** 出現；浮現；顯露；出版；發表；結果是；被發現

Flowers **come out** in spring.
花朵在春天盛開。

The result for the experiment will **come out** as long as you keep trying.
只要你不斷實驗，結果一定會出現。

🌸 **come round** 甦醒；復原；順便來訪

They stayed by her bed, waiting for her to **come round**.
他們守在床邊，等待她甦醒過來。

最 常考有關『come to～』片語整理

🌸 **come to** 總數為；說到；涉及到

The time you have wasted on video games will **come to** a large sum.
你浪費在電動遊戲上的時間加起來將會非常多。

come to the conclusion 得出結論

We thought the new colleague was arrogant, but we've **come to the conclusion** that she is just shy.
剛開始我們以為新同事很傲慢,後來才得出結論她只是害羞罷了。

come to the rescue 前來救災；前來救援

Firefighters **came to the rescue**.
消防員前來救災了。

come to an end 結束

The sufferings of the people **came to an end** when the new king took control.
新國王繼位後,人民的苦難總算結束了。

最 常考有關『come into ~』片語整理

come into being 產生；建立

These mountains **came into being** when two giant land masses collided with each other.
當兩大陸塊彼此相撞時,這些山就誕生了。

come into one's mind 在某人的腦海中浮現

An idea **came into my mind** when I saw her.
當我看到她時,一個想法浮現在我腦海中。

最 常考有關『come up ~』片語整理

come up 發生；被提到；升起；想到

When I was doing my homework, many questions **came up** and I needed to ask my friends for help.
我做作業時碰到了許多問題,使我必須向朋友尋求幫助。

come up to 達到

Customers complained that our products did not **come up to** their expectations.
客戶抱怨我們的產品沒有達到他們預期的標準。

🌼 **come up with** 提供；提出；發明

After the meeting, we **came up with** a plan.
會議之後，我們想出了一個計畫。

🌼 **come up against** 偶然遇到；突然遇到

When they were about to finish the task, they **came up against** a series of new problems.
正當他們快要完成任務的時候，又遇到了一系列新問題。

最 常考有關『confidence』片語整理

🌼 **gain confidence** 得到信心

I am **gaining confidence** in myself.
我對自己越來越有信心。

🌼 **have confidence** 有信心

What you need is to **have confidence** in yourself, and to believe that you will win the match.
你所需要的僅僅是對自己有信心，並相信自己會贏得比賽。

🌼 **(cf) be confident that** 對…有信心；有把握

I **am confident that** he will come.
我有把握他會來。

🌼 **(cf) confide in** 對…信任；信賴

Do you **confide in** her drawing ability?
你對她的繪畫能力有信心嗎？

最 常考有關『convenient』片語整理

🌼 **convenient to** 對…方便；合適

The shuttle bus is **convenient to** all the workers in the company.
對公司的全體員工來說，有接駁車很方便。

精準必考

convenient for 對…（來說）方便

Metro is **convenient for** the citizens.
捷運對於市民來說很方便。

最 常考有關『count』片語整理

count on 依靠；指望；信賴

John wants to **count on** Jack for his help.
約翰指望傑克能夠幫忙。

count up 算出…的總數；共計

Count up your points and tell the teacher your total score.
計算一下你的得分，然後告訴老師你的總分數。

count for much 意義重大

The contract signed last month doesn't **count for much**.
上個月所簽訂的合約意義不大。

最 常考有關『cut』片語整理

cut across 打斷；抄近路

We can get to school earlier if we **cut across** this field.
如果我們從運動場抄近路過去，我們就可以早點到學校。

cut back 消減；減縮；減少

The company is starting to **cut back** on staff.
公司開始精簡人員了。

cut down 砍倒；減少

Jack's pocket money has been **cut down** by his parents because he overspent.
因為傑克亂花錢，所以他的父母減少了他的零用錢。

cut in 插話

Excuse me, may I **cut in**?
抱歉，我能插句話嗎？

🌸 cut into 侵犯；打斷

Mary always **cuts into** people's conversation.
瑪麗老是打斷別人的談話。

🌸 cut off 切斷；阻斷

The high tower **cut off** the princess' communication with the outside world.
高聳的塔樓阻斷了公主與外界之間的聯繫。

🌸 cut out 停止；切除；刪除

The electricity in this building was **cut out** because bills were not paid.
這棟大樓因為沒有支付電費而被斷電了。

🌸 cut through 割破；切…

The knife **cut through** his skin and into his flesh.
刀子割破了他的皮膚，傷到了肌肉。

🌸 cut up 切開

Tom **cut up** the watermelon.
湯姆把西瓜切開。

🌸 cut (one) short 插嘴；打斷

If you **cut** the boss **short** while he is talking, you will be in trouble.
如果你在老闆講話時打斷他的話，你會惹上麻煩的。

最 常考有關『difficult』片語整理

🌸 has / have a difficult time 有困難做某事

Our class is **having a difficult time** adjusting to our new teacher.
我們班很不能夠適應新老師

🌸 There is no difficulty (in) + 動名詞 做某事沒有困難

There is no difficulty in doing one good deed, but to do it throughout your life is not easy.
做一件好事並不困難，但要做一輩子的好事可就不容易了。

difficult to 難以

College graduates find it **difficult to** get a job.
大學畢業生覺得找工作很困難。

最 常考有關『down ~』片語整理

down and out 窮困潦倒

Her father has been **down and out** ever since the factory closed.
自從工廠關閉後,她的父親一直處於貧困潦倒的狀態。

down the road / street 沿路;沿街

If you think you'll need more money, there's an ATM **down the street** on the left side of the road.
如果你覺得還需要更多錢的話,沿這條路下去的街道左邊就有一台自動櫃員機。

最 常考有關『~ down』片語整理

beat down (陽光)強烈照射;殺價

The sun **beat down** on his neck and shoulders.
強烈的陽光照射在他的脖子和肩膀上。

boil down 歸結;煮濃

The failure of the project **boiled down** the lack of funds.
計畫的失敗歸結於缺乏資金。

break down 壞掉;損壞;崩潰;故障

Jim's car **broke down** on the way to work.
吉姆的汽車在上班途中拋錨了。

calm down 冷靜

Tom is too angry to utter a word; he needs some time to **calm down**.
湯姆氣得說不出話來,他需要一點時間冷靜。

jot down 迅速抄下；快速地寫

The supervisor talked so fast that the employees could only **jot down** a few points.
主管說話太快了，職員們只能快速記下幾個重點。

knock down 拆卸；擊倒

Kevin was **knocked down** by a car.
凱文被車撞倒了。

put down 放下；記下；鎮壓；貶低

When reading an interesting book, you will find it difficult to **put** it **down**.
閱讀有趣的書籍時，你會發現自己很難放下書本。

walk down the street 沿街散步

I met my old friend when I was **walking down the street**.
我在街上走的時候遇到了一位老朋友。

ups and downs 盛衰；起伏

White witnessed the **ups and downs** of the firm.
懷特見證了公司的興衰。

最 常考有關『draw ~』片語整理

draw forth 引出；帶動

My boss always said facing difficulties could **draw forth** a person's best qualities.
老闆常說面對困境可引出一個人最好的品質。

draw one's attention 引人注意

Lily likes to **draw the boss's attention** by speaking up during the meeting.
莉莉為了吸引老闆的注意力，喜歡在會議上大聲發言。

draw / come to a close 臨終；接近尾聲

As the class **drew to a close**, the teacher assigned some homework.
隨著課程接近尾聲，老師為我們分派了一些作業。

精準必考

● 片語／精準必考

最 常考有關『even』片語整理

even though 即使；雖然

Even though Wilson exercises every day, he still can not become as strong as Tom.
雖然威爾遜每天都運動，但依然無法像湯姆那麼強壯。

even if 即使；雖然

Even if Tom comes to the party, he would still be unhappy.
即使湯姆來參加派對，他也不會開心

最 常考有關『face』片語整理

face to face 面對面

It's a face to face interview, which means that you will have to talk to the manager directly.
這是場面對面的面試，這意味著你必須和經理直接交談。

face with 面對

It is difficult for John to face with the fact that his company is in debt.
公司負債的事實讓約翰很難面對。

long face 臭臉

She always pulls the long face when she is unhappy about something.
每當她不開心時總會擺出一張臭臉。

straight face 一本正經

The director always keeps a straight face.
主管老是擺出一本正經的臉。

save one's face 顧全面子

To save Tom's face, the boss allowed him to resign on his own.
為了顧及湯姆的面子，老闆允許他自己辭職。

精準必考

最 常考有關『favor』片語整理

do + 某人 + a favor 幫…忙

The engineer did me a favor by improving the old machine.
那位工程師改造舊機器，幫了我大忙。

in favor of 支持

Jane said she was in favor of giving lessons on a daily basis.
珍說她偏好每日都上課。

最 常考有關『for』片語整理

for sale 出售；待售

The company's headquarter has been moved abroad, leaving an empty office building here for sale.
這家公司的總部已經遷移至國外，留下這棟待售的閒置辦公大樓。

for certain 確定；確信

Tom knows for certain that the work can be finished by ten.
湯姆確信十點前就能完成工作。

for a while 暫時；一段時間

May I use your mouse for a while?
你的滑鼠可以借我用一下嗎？

for all I know 就我所知

For all I know, AAA company will win the bid.
據我所知，AAA公司將會贏得競標。

for the better 好轉；向好的方向發展

Sometimes changes are for the better.
有時候改變是為了讓情況變得更好。

for that matter 關於那件事

For that matter, Mary has not got a clue yet.
關於那件事，瑪麗還沒有什麼頭緒。

精準必考

☀ **for ... sake** 為了…的緣故

For safety's **sake**, no one should stay inside the dangerous building.
為了安全起見，大家都不應該繼續待在危樓裡面。

☀ **for the sake of** 為了…（之故）

For the sake of other readers, please be quiet in the library.
為了其他讀者，在圖書館內請保持安靜。

最 常考有關『～for』片語整理

☀ **apply for** 申請；請求

Mike, majoring in Physics, is **applying for** a PhD program at Cambridge University.
邁克主修物理，他正在申請劍橋大學的博士課程。

☀ **blame for** 責備；怪

Mr. Johnson always **blames** Tom **for** being late.
強森先生總是批評湯姆遲到的事情。

☀ **pay for** 為付出代價；支付

Every employee has to **pay for** the compulsory insurance.
每個雇員都得給付強制性保險。

☀ **stand for** 象徵；支持；代表；意味

Dictatorship **stands for** the denial of individual freedom.
獨裁意味著否定個人自由。

☀ **cry out for** 迫切需要；呼喊

The little boy is **crying out for** his mother.
那個小男孩哭著呼喊媽媽。

☀ **have an eye for** 對…有鑑賞能力；有辨識能力

Everyone says that the boss **has an eye for** people with great abilities.
大家都說老闆有辦法辨識出那些有能力的人。

精準必考

🗨 **make way for** 為…開路；為…讓路

Young people should make way for old people.
年輕人應該為老年人讓路。

🌼 **be good for** 有利於；有益

Exercising is a good way to kill time because it is not only good for our health but also quite interesting.
運動是打發時間的好方法，因為它不僅有益健康，還很有趣。

🗨 **be bad for** 對…有害；不利於

Fried chicken, though delicious, is high in cholesterol and bad for our health.
雖然炸雞美味，但膽固醇很高，對健康不利。

🌼 **give one credit for** 獎賞；鼓勵；歸功於

Emily was given a lot of credit for having done a good job.
艾蜜莉因為表現良好而受到了很多鼓勵。

🗨 **as / so far as... be concerned** 就…而言

As far as I am concerned, I like apples better than oranges.
就我個人來說，比起橘子我更喜歡蘋果。

🌼 **as for** 至於；就…而言

As for Mary, writing novels is a great pleasure.
對於瑪麗而言，撰寫小說是件樂事。

最 常考有關『from』片語整理

🌼 **from beginning to end** 自始至終

Betty enjoyed the movie from beginning to end.
貝蒂自始至終都很享受這部電影。

🌼 **from west to east** 自西向東

He traveled Europe from west to east.
他自西向東遊遍了歐洲。

❂ from one's heart 發自內心

We should always congratulate the winner **from our heart** even if we lose.
即使失敗我們也應該發自內心恭喜勝利者。

最 常考有關『～from』片語整理

❂ aside from 除…之外（還有）

Aside from reading, he also spends time writing every day.
除了閱讀之外，他還每天花時間寫作。

❂ ban from 禁止

This kind of medicine has been **banned from** being sold.
這種藥已被禁止銷售。

❂ borrow from 從…借

John **borrowed** one million dollars **from** the bank.
約翰向銀行借了一百萬美元。

❂ graduate from 畢業於

He is one of the brightest students who have **graduated from** Oxford University.
他是牛津大學的畢業生裡最聰明的之一。

❂ originate from 發源於；源自

Jazz, a form of music, **originated from** the New Orleans music scene.
爵士是一種音樂形式，它起源於新奧爾良樂壇。

❂ refrain from 抑制；克制；忍住

Staff should be **refrained from** smoking during working hours.
員工在工作時段應該被禁止吸煙。

❂ run away from 逃離；逃走

Tina regrets having **run away from** home; now she misses her parents.
蒂娜後悔離家出走了，現在她很想念父母。

suffer from 患…病；受…之苦

Sometimes I still suffer from these weaknesses.
有時候我還是會因為這些弱點吃苦。

withdraw from 退出

John decided to withdraw from the working unit.
約翰決定退出工作單位。

be made from 由…製成

This table is made from new materials.
這張桌子是由新材料製成的。

receive ... from ... 從…收到…

Phillip received a present from his boss yesterday.
昨天菲力浦從老闆那裡得到了一份禮物。

far from 遠離；很遠

We are far from success, and we have just got started.
我們才剛剛開始，距離成功還很遙遠。

最 常考有關『get』片語整理

get away 逃掉；逃跑

The thief failed to get away, and will be face with six months in prison.
小偷逃脫失敗，且將面臨六個月的牢獄生活。

get back 回來；收回

If you are interested in our project, you can get back in touch with us.
如果您對我們的項目有興趣，可以再回來聯絡我們。

get married 結婚

I think they will let us know when they get married.
我想，他們結婚的時候會告訴我們的。

get around 迴避；流傳

As soon as he made the decision, words **got around**.
他剛下決定，謠言就開始四處傳開了。

get stuck 被堵住；卡住

The bracelet **got stuck** on her arm.
那只手鐲卡在她的手臂上了。

get through 度過

The company pulled together to **get through** the crisis.
整個公司團結一心，度過難關。

get to 開始；到達；接觸

I'm lost; could you please tell me how I can **get to** Holiday Inn?
我迷路了，您能不能告訴我該怎麼去假日酒店?

get in touch with 和⋯聯絡

A client named John was trying to contact you today; you'd better **get in touch with** him right now.
一位名為約翰的客戶今天想和你聯絡，你最好現在就去聯繫他。

get on one's nerves 使某人煩惱；惹人討厭

A new colleague **got on my nerves** when he kept asking me questions.
當新同事不斷提問時，我感到非常厭煩。

最 常考有關『get ~ of』片語整理

get hold of 拿到；掌握；找到；抓住

The captain **got hold of** the steer to change direction.
船長抓住了方向盤來改變航向。

get out of 脫離；離開；洩漏

I have had enough of your nonsense, so **get out of** my office or I'll call the police.
我已經受夠了你的胡言亂語，你再不離開我的辦公室，我就打電話報警。

get rid of 消滅；擺脫

It's hard to get rid of insects.
要擺脫蟲子不容易。

get a sight of 看見

Having reached the peak, John wanted to get a sight of the rising sun.
到達山頂後，約翰想要看看山上的日出。

get into the habit of 染上⋯的習慣

We should get into the habit of keeping good hours.
我們應該養成早睡早起的習慣。

get to the bottom of 追根究底

We must get to the bottom of this case.
對於這個案件，我們必須追根究底。

最 常考有關『give』片語整理

give up 放棄

Having found the opportunity, the manager won't give it up.
既然找到這個機會，經理就不會放棄它。

give out 分發

The student will be handing out fliers as the waiter gives out tasting samples.
當服務員分發品嚐樣品時，學生將分發傳單。

give in 讓步；屈服；妥協；投降

Must the company give in to the employees?
難道公司一定得屈服於員工嗎？

give rise to 惹起；引發

Conflicts may give rise to fights.
衝突可能會引起打架。

精準必考

🌟 give way to 讓步；代替

The park **gave way to** a skyscraper.
公園被摩天大樓給代替了。

🌟 give + 人 + a pay raise 把某人加薪

Judging by his overall performance, we need to **give him a pay raise**.
根據他的綜合表現來判斷，我們必須為他加薪。

🌟 give the floor 發言

After the boss finished speaking, he decided to **give the floor** to a manager.
老闆發言完畢後，決定將發言權交給一位經理。

🌟 given to 熱衷於…的

John is **given to** traveling abroad.
約翰熱衷於出國旅行。

People **given to** impulse cannot become good decision-makers.
容易衝動的人不會成為好的決策者。

最 常考有關『give a～』片語整理

🌟 give a speech 作演講

Jason doesn't like to **give a speech**.
傑森不喜歡演講。

🌟 give a pat on the back 給予鼓勵

I **gave** John **a pat on the back** because I knew he tried his best.
我鼓勵了約翰，因為我知道他盡力了。

最 常考有關『go』片語整理

🌟 go across 穿越

John **went across** a desert last month.
上個月約翰橫越了一座沙漠。

💡 **go after** 追求；設法得到

He left his wallet on the table, so I went after him.
他把錢包忘在桌子上了，所以我追去找他。

💡 **go ahead** 請；進行；說吧；先走

Please go ahead and start eating.
請開始用餐吧。

💡 **go abroad** 出國

Jenny will go abroad.
珍妮將出國。

💡 **go bad** 變壞；（食物）壞掉

The meal will go bad if we leave it overnight.
這頓飯隔夜就會壞掉。

💡 **go by** 走過；經過

I will go by the supermarket on my way home.
我回家的途中會經過超市。

💡 **go nuts** 狂熱；著迷；發瘋

My colleagues went nuts on Saturday night.
我的同事們週六那晚玩瘋了。

💡 **go off** 離開；開火；響起；中斷；變質

Lily and her husband went off to Hawaii.
莉莉和他的丈夫前去夏威夷了。

The lights suddenly went off as we were watching TV.
我們正在看電視的時候，燈突然全滅了。

💡 **go out** 出去；熄滅；過時

Some people choose to go out on weekends, while others enjoy staying at home.
一些人選擇週末外出，另一些人則喜歡待在家裡。

💡 **go over** 溫習；複習；重溫；檢查

It is important to go over what one has learned after class.
課後溫習所學過的知識是非常重要的。

精準必考

273

go up 上漲；上升

Share price **went up** by 24 points today.
今日股票上漲了二十四點。

Jim's body temperature has **gone up**; he must be sent to the hospital.
吉姆的體溫上升了，得送他去醫院。

go on doing something 繼續做某事

If you **go on gambling** like this, you will lose all your property as well as family.
如果你再繼續這樣賭博，你將會失去所有財產和家人。

go on the stage 登台（演出）

It would be embarrassing if I had to **go on the stage** and sing to the entire school.
如果我必須上台當著全校的面唱歌的話，我會覺得很尷尬。

go in for 喜歡；愛好；參加；從事

Not only boys but also girls **go in for** basketball.
不僅是男孩，女孩們也喜歡打籃球。

最 常考有關『go on a ~』片語整理

go on a strike 罷工

If the workers **go on a strike**, the company won't be able to operate.
如果工人們發動罷工，公司將無法運行。

go on a picnic 去野餐

We will **go on a picnic** this weekend.
我們這個週末要去野餐。

最 常考有關『go out of』片語整理

go out of 離開

Conceiving a new plan, William **went out of** the office.
威廉一邊構想新計畫，一邊走出辦公室。

go out of one's way 特地

Jenny **went out of her way** to help her good friend.
珍妮特地去幫助她的好朋友。

最 常考有關『hear』片語整理

hear from 從…得到消息（來信、電話）

Tom has been waiting to **hear from** his girlfriend, but the phone never rang.
湯姆一直在等女朋友的電話，但她從未打過來。

hear of 聽說過；聽聞

I'm glad to **hear of** your success.
聽到你成功的消息，我很高興。

hear about 聽說；得知

They must have **heard about** something.
他們一定有聽到什麼事。

最 常考有關『hand』片語整理

hand over 託付；把…交出來

The boss can't find anyone to **hand over** the job to.
老闆找不到適合託付這份工作的人。

Many salesmen prefer to receive money before they **hand over** the merchandise.
很多推銷員喜歡先收錢，後送交商品。

hand in 上交；遞交；繳交

Hand in the test paper along with the answer card.
請把考卷和答題卡一起遞交上來。

hand out 分發

We ran from dormitory to dormitory to **hand out** the newspapers edited by ourselves.
我們一個一個寢室的分發我們自己編輯的報紙。

hands off 不許觸及；不許干涉

The teacher told the children to keep their **hands off** dirty things.
老師告訴孩子們不要去碰髒東西。

in hand 在手中；在手邊

With authority **in hand**, the director can make decisions on his own.
掌握權力後，主管現在可以獨自做決定了。

at hand 在附近；在手邊

The salesman had a notebook **at hand** to record his customers' opinions.
推銷員的手邊有本專門用來記錄顧客意見的筆記簿。

give one a helping hand 給予某人幫助；向某人伸出援手

I am glad to have **given the new colleague a helping hand**.
我很高興能幫助新同事。

give + 人 + **a hand** 幫助某人

Would you **give me a hand** in moving the boxes outside?
你能幫我把這些箱子搬出去嗎？

join hands with 與…聯合；與…團結

They promised to **join hands with** each other on business.
他們許諾要攜手作生意。

bad hand at 不擅長

His **bad hand at** the investment cost him a lot.
他對於投資的不擅長使他損失慘重。

big hand 熱烈鼓掌（＝applause）

The board of directors gave a **big hand** to chairman's speech.
董事會成員對主席的演講報以熱烈的掌聲。

clean hands 無罪；清白的

The chairman claimed he had **clean hands** at the board meeting.
主席在董事會上自稱清白。

🌱 **on the other hand** 另一方面

We need to boost our sales; on the other hand, we also need to lower our cost.
我們需要提升業績，另一方面，我們也必須降低成本。

🌱 **gain the upper hand** 占上風

Mary gained the upper hand at the very beginning of the competition.
瑪麗在比賽剛開始時就占了上風。

最 常考有關『hardly』片語整理

🌱 **hardly any** 幾乎沒有

After the concert, hardly any of the fans left the hall.
演唱會結束後，幾乎沒有歌迷離去。

🌱 **hardly ever** 很少有

Mary hardly ever goes swimming during winter because she fears of getting sick.
因為害怕生病，瑪麗很少在冬天游泳。

最 常考有關『here』片語整理

🌱 **here and there** 到處；各地

Signs of prosperity are shown here and there in the city.
這座城市到處都是繁榮的景象。

🌱 **here today and gone tomorrow** 短暫；曇花一現

The success of the firm was here today and gone tomorrow.
這家公司的成功僅是曇花一現。

最 常考有關『in all』片語整理

🌱 **in all** 總共；總計；總的來說

There are seven rooms on the first floor and four on the second floor, so there are eleven rooms in all.
一樓有七間房間，二樓有四間房間，所以一共是十一間房間。

in all ages　各個時期；各種年齡

The employees of this workshop are in all ages.
這個工作坊內有各個年齡層的員工。

in all directions　各個方向

When the bell rang, students ran away in all directions.
鈴聲一響，學生們便朝各個方向跑開了。

最常考有關『in ~』片語整理

in advance　提前；事先

We should make another plan in advance if, by any chance, the first plan doesn't work.
我們應該事先擬定另一個計畫，以防第一個計畫無效。

in concert　一齊；一致

We decided to study for the exam in concert.
我們決定一同學習，準備考試。

in demand　受歡迎的；非常需要的

The book Harry Potter is very popular and is always in demand.
《哈利‧波特》這本書非常地受歡迎且需求量大。

in effect　生效

The medicine is in effect but the patient still needs to be under close watch.
藥物已經生效了，但是這名病患還需要持續的觀察。

in half　一半

The angry director tore the document in half.
生氣的主管把文件撕成了兩半。

in mind　在心裡；頭腦裡；想到

Jerry already has a method in mind on how to cope with his manager.
傑瑞腦海裡已經想好該怎麼對付他的經理了。

精準必考

in need 需要

As the saying goes, a friend **in need** is a friend indeed.
俗話說，患難之中見真情。

in short 總之；簡而言之

In short, the task is important and we must be well prepared.
總而言之，這項任務非常重要，我們必須做好充足的準備。

in bulk 大批；大量

I am used to washing clothes **in bulk**.
我慣於清洗成批的衣服。

in part 部分地；在某種程度上

The flood was due **in part** to unusual weather conditions.
這起水災部分原因是由於天氣失常而造成的。

in pieces 呈碎片狀

The angry customer tore the contract **in pieces**.
憤怒的顧客把合約撕成了碎片。

in point 中肯的；相關的；恰當的

The story was used as a case **in point** to help the audience comprehend.
這個故事被拿來作為例子，以幫助觀眾理解。

最 常考有關『in a～』片語整理

in a fury 暴怒；狂怒

The director left the office **in a fury**.
導演盛怒的離開了辦公室。

in a hurry 匆忙；急忙

Mary rushed out **in a hurry** to give Alice an umbrella when it started to rain.
天空開始下起雨時，瑪麗急忙跑出去送傘給愛麗絲。

精準必考

◉ 片語／精準必考

💡 in a word 簡言之；簡潔的

In a word, Mary did a very good job with this program.
總之，瑪麗把這個節目做得相當好。

💡 in a few words 總而言之；三言兩語

Jane, a strong minded girl, expressed her ambition in a few words.
珍，一個有主見的女孩，僅僅用了幾個詞就表達了她的企圖心。

最 常考有關『in the ~』片語整理

💡 in the details 詳細地

The teacher explained the subject in the details so that students could understand.
老師詳細的解釋了這個科目，好讓學生們能夠理解。

💡 in the end 最後；終究

All rivers in the end flow to the sea.
條條江河終歸大海。

The conflict was eventually settled in the end.
爭端最後終於被解決了。

💡 in the future 在將來；以後

Have you considered improving your work in the future?
你以後有打算改善你的工作品質嗎？

💡 in the sky 在天空；傳播中

What is it flying in the sky?
那個在天上飛行的東西是什麼？

💡 in the world 世界上

There are only a few people in the world that we can trust.
世界上只有少數人是我們能夠信任的。

💡 in the meantime 同時（= meanwhile）

In the meantime, we should prepare for an alternative plan.
於此同時，我們應該準備替換方案。

精準必考

in the mood for 有情緒做

With so much work to do, I am not in the mood for shopping lately.
最近有那麼多工作要做，我沒有心情去購物。

in the years to come 在將來的幾年

The economy is expected to come out of the recession in the years to come.
經濟預期將在未來幾年走出衰退。

最 常考有關『in the ~ of』片語整理

in the face of 在…面前；面對

In the face of financial crisis, the company quickly took actions.
公司面對金融危機迅速行動起來。

in the field of 在…領域；在…方面

Mike's invention broke new ground in the field of LCD.
邁克的發明為液晶面板領域開創了新的局面。

in the habit of 有…的習慣

Tom is in the habit of sleeping in class.
湯姆有上課睡覺的習慣。

in the hope of 希望

Jack worked hard in the hope of winning the heart of a cute girl.
傑克非常努力，希望能夠贏得一位可愛女孩的芳心。

in the name of 以…的名義

The messenger announced the new law in the name of the king.
信使以國王的名義宣布了新法令。

in the wake of 緊隨…之後

In the wake of the tornado, people gathered to pray.
龍捲風過境後，人們聚集在一起禱告。

精準必考

◑ 片語／精準必考

�', in the course of 在…期間；在…過程中

Eva left her seat several times **in the course of** the meal.
用餐期間，伊娃離開了座位好幾次。

🌀 in the absence of 不在；缺乏

The athletes exercised passionately **in the absence of** supervision.
運動員在無人看管的情況下熱情的練習著。

🌀 in the front of 在…前部；前面

In the front of the picture is the figure of a man.
這張照片的前面是有一位男士的身影。

🌀 (cf) in front of 在…面前

There is a skyscraper **in front of** my department.
我的公寓前面有座摩天大樓。

最 常考有關『in ~ of』片語整理

🌀 in aid of 為援助…

Funds were raised **in aid of** the flood victims.
籌募款項是為了援助水災災民。

🌀 in charge of 負責；主管；管理

The manager is putting Paris **in charge of** this case.
經理要讓帕里絲負責這件案子。

🌀 in command of 控制住；統領

The respected general is **in command of** the army.
那位受人尊敬的將領現在是軍隊的統帥。

🌀 in celebration of 慶祝

A grand party is held **in celebration of** my nephew's graduation.
為了慶祝我的外甥畢業，我們舉行了盛大的派對。

精準必考

in consideration of　考慮到

In consideration of the lack of demands, they reduced production.
考慮到缺乏需求，他們便減低了生產量。

in commemoration of　紀念；慶祝

Millions of people gathered in commemoration of the 30th anniversary of the end of WWII.
數百萬人聚集慶祝二次世界大戰結束三十週年。

in defense of　防禦；保衛；防護

In times of crisis, 50 million young people joined the army in defense of the country.
危機來臨的時刻，五千萬名青年加入了軍隊保衛國家。

in favor of　喜歡；支持

The company's leaders are in favor of promoting the new product in China.
公司的領導階層贊成在中國推廣新產品。

Koreans tend to be in favor of domestically manufactured cars.
韓國人傾向支持國產汽車。

in possession of　據有；持有

John is in possession of eighty percent of the company's share.
約翰持有這家公司百分之八十的股份。

in support of　為了支持…

In support of his opinion, Jerry brought out a new piece of evidence.
為了支持自己的看法，傑瑞提出了一件新證據。

最 常考有關『in ~ (of)』片語整理

in danger　在危險中

Love was one of the factors that made him act like a hero when she was in danger.
當她身處危險，愛是使他表現得宛如英雄的因素之一。

精準必考

💬 **in danger of** 危險；處於危險中

After the earthquake, some buildings are in danger of collapsing.
地震過後，部分建築有倒塌的危險。

💡 **in case** 如果；假如；以防萬一

Please call me in case you get into trouble.
如果遇到困難，請打電話給我。

💡 **in case of** 以防；萬一

The wall was built along the river in case of floods.
河邊沿岸築起了防護牆以防洪水。

💬 **in case of emergency** 如有緊急情況

In case of emergency, please call 119.
如有緊急情況，請撥打119。

💡 **in case of fire** 萬一發生火災

In case of fire, stay calm and leave the building as soon as you can.
萬一發生火災時，盡量保持冷靜並迅速離開建築物。

最 常考有關『in ~ with』片語整理

💡 **in line with** 符合；與…成一直線

I'm sure what we have delivered is in line with what you have ordered.
我確定我們發送的貨物和您所訂購的物品一致。

💡 **in contact with** 與…有聯繫；有接觸

John is frequently in contact with his customers.
約翰和顧客保持頻繁的聯繫。

💬 **in collaboration with** 與…合作；與…勾結

In collaboration with the famous artist, the product is sold well.
與知名藝術家合作推出的產品賣得很好。

💬 **in connection with** 與…有關

The operation is **in connection with** the military.
這個行動與軍方有關。

最 常考有關『〜in』片語整理

💬 **join in** 加入；參加；與…一起

Thousands of people **joined in** the campaign.
數千人參加了活動。

💬 **succeed in** ＋ 動名詞　成功做…；做成

Scientists **succeeded in** cloning sheeps.
科學家成功複製了綿羊。

最 常考有關『keep』片語整理

💬 **keep cool** 保持鎮靜

The employees couldn't **keep cool** about not having gotten a pay raise.
員工因為沒有得到加薪而無法冷靜。

💬 **keep on** 愛好；繼續；不斷

He did the work so well that his boss **kept on** praising him.
他工作做得相當出色，老闆對他讚不絕口。

💬 **keep track of** 記錄；保管

The supervisor told everyone to **keep track of** the files.
主管叫大家把檔案保管好。

💬 **keep off** 避開；擋住

Keep your hands **off** the museum collections.
請勿碰觸博物館內的收藏品。

💬 **keep quiet** 保持安靜

Would you please **keep quiet** while we are working?
你能否在我們工作的時候保持安靜？

精準必考

✿ **keep healthy** 維持健康

Jogging everyday is considered a good way to **keep healthy**.
每天慢跑被認為是維持健康的好辦法。

✿ **keep on** ＋ 動名詞　繼續做某事

Jim will be fired if he **keeps on coming** to work late.
如果吉姆上班繼續遲到，他就要被開除了。

✿ **keep an eye on** 看守；注意

John, will you **keep an eye on** my briefcase for a while?
約翰，你可不可以幫我看管一下公事包？

✿ **keep in mind** 牢記；謹記

Mary **kept** Tom's advice **in mind**.
瑪麗謹記湯姆給她的建議。

最 常考有關『keep one's ~』片語整理

✿ **keep one's word** 遵守諾言

You must always **keep your word** when doing business or you will fail.
做生意時你一定要遵守諾言，否則你就會失敗。

✿ **keep one's temper** 保持鎮靜；忍住脾氣

A good supervisor should always **keep his temper** under control.
一個好主管應該能夠掌控自己的脾氣。

最 常考有關『keep the ~』片語整理

✿ **keep the promise** 信守諾言

You should be ashamed of yourself for not **keeping the promise**.
你應該為沒有信守諾言而感到羞恥。

✿ **keep the ball rolling** 繼續進行

The boss was happy about the work, so he told everyone to **keep the ball rolling**.
老闆對工作成果很滿意，所以鼓勵大家繼續努力。

精準必考

最 常考有關『keep ~ with』片語整理

keep company with 與…結交

Keep company with the wise and you will become wise.
與智者結伴，你也將變得有智慧。

keep up with 跟上；追上；趕上

In order to sell more products to customers, our designs should keep up with the trend.
為了向消費者推銷更多產品，我們的設計應該跟上潮流。

keep pace with 跟上

We should try our best to keep pace with the schedule.
我們必須盡力讓我們的步調與工作計畫一致。

keep in touch with 和…聯絡

Keep in touch with your friends working in Oracle. They may teach you how to work in big foreign companies.
和你在甲骨文公司工作的朋友保持聯繫吧，他們或許能教你如何在大型外國企業裡面工作。

keep in step with 與…步調一致

A good supervisor should always keep in step with the times.
一個好主管應該跟上時代的步伐。

最 常考有關『kind』片語整理

kinds of 各種各樣的；不同種類的

The assignment for science class was to bring three kinds of insects to class.
科學課的作業是帶三種昆蟲來上課。

a kind of 一種

A new kind of technology is needed to resolve the pollution problem.
我們需要研發一種新技術來解決汙染問題。

● 片語／精準必考

💡 like to + 原形動詞　喜歡；願意

Many Americans like to spend their holidays exploring the beautiful countryside.
許多美國人喜歡去美麗的鄉下渡假。

💡 would like to + 原形動詞　想要；願意

I'd like to take a good rest.
我想好好休息。

💡 feel like + 動名詞　想要；想做

I feel like trying some because the cake looks so good.
我想要嚐嚐看蛋糕，因為它看起來很好吃。

💡 look like　看起來像；似乎；顯得

It looks like we will be getting off work soon; our boss is leaving.
看來我們馬上就能夠下班了，因為老闆正準備離開。

💡 lose face　丟臉

The stupid mistake made Jenny lose face.
那個愚蠢的錯誤讓珍妮很丟臉。

💡 lose ground　輸；退卻

We worked hard on the project and did not lose ground to the opponents.
我們很努力做那項企劃案，因此沒有輸給對手。

💡 lose sight of　看不見

We lost sight of the mountain at night.
我們晚上看不見山。

💡 lose track of　失去紀錄；忘了

Jenny looked at her watch so she won't lose track of time.
珍妮看了一下手錶，以免忘記時間。

lose a chance 失去機會

Lucy had lost her chance of getting the good job.
露西失去了獲得那份好工作的機會。

lose one's way 迷路

The lambs followed the sheep so they won't lose their way.
小羊跟隨著大綿羊，以防迷路。

最 常考有關『look』片語整理

look back 回想

I looked back on my schooldays with terror.
回想起學校裡的日子，我感到很恐懼。

look back on 回顧

Jenny looked back on her career with great satisfaction.
珍妮回顧職業生涯，感到心滿意足。

look into 研究；調查

Have you looked into the sales?
你有深入調查銷售情況嗎？

look for 尋找

Since we don't have enough money to pay for this apartment, I think we'd better look for a smaller one.
既然我們的錢不夠買這套公寓，我想我們還是去找間小一點的公寓吧。

look out for 小心

Look out for the glass on the floor!
小心地上的玻璃！

look down on 輕視；瞧不起；看不起

The manager looked down on Tom because of his poor working ability.
經理因為湯姆的工作能力差而看不起他。

精準必考

● 片語／精準必考

※ **look up to** 尊敬；景仰

I **look up to** my grandfather.
我很尊敬祖父。

※ **take on a new look** 煥然一新

Our country has **taken on a new look** every since the new laws are enforced.
自新法律實施後，我們國家的樣貌煥然一新。

※ **have a look at** 看一下

What kind of camera do you want? May I **have a look at** that black one? Sure!
您想要哪種相機？我能看看那個黑色的嗎？當然！

最 常考有關『make』片語整理

※ **make amends** 賠罪；賠償

You must **make amends** for the chairs you broke, which are quite expensive.
你必須賠償你弄壞的椅子，它們十分昂貴。

※ **make…angry** 使…生氣；憤怒

Lily's always being late **made** her boss and colleagues very **angry**.
莉莉經常性的遲到讓老闆與同事們很生氣。

※ **make clear** 說明；解釋；弄清楚

It has been **made clear** that traffic regulations cannot be broken.
已經說得很清楚了，不能違反交通規則。

※ **make faces** 做鬼臉

The monkeys **made faces** at the tourists.
猴子朝著遊客們做鬼臉。

※ **make it** 成功；趕上

Mary called in to say that she won't **make it** tonight.
瑪麗打電話來說她今晚來不了了。

精準必考

make peace　和好

Walt and Mary **made peace** with each other, because they were tired of the conflicts.
華特和瑪麗厭倦了衝突，最後和好了。

make sure　確定；設法確保

Make sure you close the curtains before you go to bed.
睡覺前記得一定要拉上窗簾。

make one's way　前往；前進；成功

The Greens **made their way** to the store to buy groceries.
格林斯一家前往商場購買雜物。

make way for　為…開路；為…讓路

We always **make way for** the boss.
我們總是會為老闆讓路。

make ends meet　應付開支；量入為出

Being out of work and having two young children, Tom and Mary found it difficult to **make ends meet**.
湯姆和瑪麗發現，在既失業又要養活兩個小孩的情況之下很難維持生計。

make many attempts　多次嘗試

Anna had **made many attempts** to swim across that river, but failed.
安娜多次嘗試游過那條河，但是都失敗了。

最 常考有關『make a ～』片語整理

make a living　謀生；維生

Many people **make a living** by carrying merchandise from place to place.
很多人靠在不同地方之間運輸商品來謀生。

make a noise　吵鬧；發出聲音

The aged computer **made a noise** on startup.
老電腦開機時發出了一陣聲響。

● 片語／精準必考

💡 make a mess 弄亂；搞砸

The spilled coke made a mess on my drawings.
打翻的可樂把我畫的圖潑得亂七八糟。

💡 make a boast of 吹牛；吹噓

Jenny likes to make a boast of her achievements.
珍妮喜歡吹噓自己的成就。

💡 make a plan for 為…作計畫

We are trying to make a plan for the coming holidays.
我們正試著為即將來臨的假日作計畫。

💡 make a point of 刻意強調

Tom made a point of giving his thanks to the boss.
湯姆特意向老闆致謝。

💡 make a scene 把事情鬧大；大吵大鬧

Don't make a scene on the street.
不要在街上大吵大鬧。

💡 make a promise 答應；承諾

Don't make a promise unless you can keep it.
不要做出無法兌現的承諾。

💡 make a difference 產生影響；改變

I want to make a difference to my company.
我想要對公司作出影響。

💡 make a decision 做出決定

As the coach of the team, you must make a decision for them.
作為球隊教練，你必須為了隊員們做出決定。

💡 make a mistake 犯錯誤；做錯

He is not a freshman, but he is always making stupid mistakes.
他不再是一名大一新生了，但卻老是犯下愚蠢的錯誤。

精準必考

💡 **make a fool of** 愚弄；使出洋相

I **made a fool of** myself at the meeting.
我在會議上出了洋相。

最 常考有關『make up～』片語整理

💡 **make up** 構成；占；編造；彌補

Lily's beauty can't **make up** for her stupidity.
莉莉的美麗無法彌補她的愚蠢。

💡 **make up for the lost time** 彌補損失的時間

The production line workers worked too slowly, so they were told to **make up for the lost time**.
生產線上的工人動作太慢了，因此他們被要求彌補損失的時間。

最 常考有關『make use of』片語整理

💡 **make use of** 善加利用

We have to **make use of** everything available in order to finish the job on time.
我們必須善加利用手邊的資源以按時完成工作。

💡 **make full use of** 充分運用…

All I need is a group of investment experts. I promise to **make full use of** them.
我需要的只是一組投資專家，我保證我會充分運用他們的才能。

💡 **make full use of time** 充分利用時間

Tom is still not clear about how to **make full use of time**.
湯姆還是不太明白該怎樣充分利用時間。

精準必考

片語／精準必考

最 常考有關『money』片語整理

pocket money 零用錢

Giving children a lot of **pocket money** is not recommended.
給小孩子大量零用錢是不被建議的。

hush money 遮羞費；封口費

The criminal paid the witness with some **hush money**.
那名罪犯給了目擊者一筆封口費。

raise money 募款

We are **raising money** for the Red Cross.
我們在為紅十字會募捐。

最 常考有關『move ~』片語整理

move on 繼續；前進

We will **move on** to the next item tomorrow.
明天我們將進入下一個項目。

move in 搬進來

A new neighbor is going to **move in** this month.
一個新鄰居這個月會搬進來。

move out of 搬出

For the child's sake, we'd better **move out of** this noisy neighborhood as soon as possible.
為了孩子著想，我們最好儘快搬出這個吵雜的城區。

最 常考有關『no ~』片語整理

no point 沒理由；毫無意義；無濟於事

Alice had already done the survey, so there is **no point** in doing it again.
愛麗絲已經做過問卷調查了，再做一次是沒有意義的。

no wonder　難怪

No wonder Jeff was promoted as the manager; he works so hard!
難怪傑夫會被提升為經理，他工作得真努力！

no such thing　沒有這樣的事；不存在的

There is no such thing as the purple monster!
紫色怪物並不存在！

no matter what happens　無論發生什麼事

No matter what happens, we won't give up.
無論發生什麼事，我們都不會放棄。

最 常考有關『not ~ 』片語整理

not to mention　不用說

My roommate refused to pay for water, not to mention rent!
我的室友拒絕支付水費，更不用提房租了！

not a bit　一點也不

The iPhone seems not a bit expensive to Apple supporters.
對於蘋果支持者而言，蘋果手機一點也不顯得昂貴。

no / not at all　根本不；一點也不

When we were discussing our vacation plans, Lily showed no interest at all.
當我們討論旅遊計畫時，莉莉顯得毫無興趣。

not say much for　對…評價不高

I won't say much for the new restaurant.
我對於新開的餐廳沒什麼正面的評價.

not only　不僅；不止是

Not only did we lose our money, we also came close to losing our lives.
我們不僅失去了錢財，還差點沒命。

⟩ 片語／精準必考

☀ not until 直到…才…

Not until the old man got lung cancer did he quit smoking.
那位老先生直到得了肺癌才開始戒煙。

最 常考有關『nothing~』片語整理

☀ nothing but 不過只是；都是

He has **nothing but** a couple of coins left in his pocket.
他的口袋裡只剩下幾個硬幣。

☀ has/have nothing to do with 和…無關

Tom explained by saying that he **had nothing to do with** the accident.
湯姆解釋說他和這件意外一點關係都沒有。

最 常考有關『of~』片語整理

☀ of all things 在所有事情當中

When buying a car, quality is the most important **of all things**.
購買車輛時，品質是最重要的考量。

☀ of course 當然；自然

Of course he doesn't understand you; he doesn't even speak Chinese.
他當然聽不懂你在說什麼，因為他連中文都不會講。

☀ (cf) in the course of 在…期間；在…過程中

They learned how to fish **in the course of** summer camp.
他們在夏令營中學會了釣魚的方法。

最 常考有關『~of』片語整理

☀ conceive of 想像；想到；考慮

College students cannot **conceive of** studying without computers.
大學生無法想像沒有電腦該怎麼學習。

精準必考

🌱 **dream of** 嚮往；夢見；夢想

Google is one of the companies many people **dream of** working in.
谷歌是很多人夢想能夠進去工作的公司之一。

🌱 **deprive of** 失去；剝奪

The employee was **deprived of** the right to work here.
那位員工被剝奪了繼續在這裡工作的權利。

最 常考有關『～off』片語整理

🌱 **brush off** 打發掉；無視；拒絕

I told her that I could lend her money, but she **brushed** me **off**.
我告訴她我可以借錢給她，但是她拒絕我。

🌱 **buy off** 收買（某人）

We heard that the new manager **bought off** our boss to get the position.
聽說新的經理為了得到這個職位事先收買了老闆。

🌱 **call off** 取消；把⋯叫開

The manager had to **call off** the deal because the contract had problems.
由於合約內容有問題，經理只好取消交易。

🌱 **cut off** 阻斷

The road was **cut off** and the troop couldn't back off.
因為路被阻斷，軍隊無法後退。

🌱 **dash off** 迅速離去；匆忙地把⋯寫好；匆忙地把⋯畫好

Jack **dashed off** a note before leaving.
傑克在離開前快速留下了一張便條。

🌱 **laugh off** 一笑置之

He decided to **laugh off** the fact that he was fired.
他決定對自己被解雇的事情一笑置之。

片語／精準必考

ring off 掛斷電話

It is polite to wait for the elders to **ring off** first.
讓前輩先掛斷電話是有禮貌的行為。

take off 脫掉；起飛；離去

Mary **took off** at once after receiving her mother's call.
接到母親的電話後，瑪麗立刻離開了。

be better off 更富有；更舒服；好轉

Winning the lottery definitely made Mr. Green **better off**.
彩票中獎後，格林先生絕對過的比以前更富裕了。

最 常考有關『on～』片語整理

on average 平均；通常

On average, Bobby works more than twelve hours per day.
鮑比平均每天工作超過十二個小時。

Watching movies in the city is very expensive; it costs over 100 dollars **on average**.
在城市裡看電影非常昂貴，平均花費超過一百美元。

on an average 平均；一般

On an average, they sold more cars in May than February.
以平均銷售量來說，他們五月份賣出的車比二月份多。

on board 在船（車、飛機等）上

The food **on board** is free of charge.
飛機上的食品是免費供應的。

on cue 恰好在這時候

Professor White walked in **on cue** when the bell rang and told us not to come the next day.
鈴聲剛剛響起，懷特教授就走了進來，並告訴我們明天不用來上課了。

精準必考

298

on duty 值日；值班

A policeman is not allowed to smoke on duty.
警察值班時不被允許吸煙。

on fire 著火

Woken by the heat, he found his bed on fire.
被熱醒後，他發現自己的床著火了。

on foot 走路

Tim rather goes to work on foot than to take a bus.
提姆寧願走路上班，也不願意乘坐公共汽車。

on guard 站崗；警惕

The sentry was on guard when the commander entered.
指揮官進來時，哨兵正在值班。

on holiday 休假

You shouldn't have woken our boss this morning. He is on holiday.
你今早不該把老闆叫醒的，他正在休假。

on occasion 偶爾

Employees in the office went out for dinner on occasion.
辦公室的員工偶爾到外面聚餐。

on vacation 在渡假中

My secretary was on vacation last week, so her work was delayed.
我的祕書上個星期放假，所以她的工作拖延了。

on behalf of 代表；為了

Will you attend the meeting on behalf of our firm?
你願意代表我們公司去參加那場會議嗎？

On behalf of all the workers, I welcome you to our plant.
我代表全體工人歡迎您來我們工廠參觀。

💡 **on all sides** 到處地；四面八方的

The enemy is being surrounded **on all sides**.
敵人被四面包圍。

Spectators are **on all sides** of the hall of the opening ceremony.
開幕式上，大廳四周都是觀眾。

💡 **on one's side** 支持某人

I will be **on your side** if you act according to what my boss told you.
如果你按照我們老闆的話行事，我會支持你。

最 常考有關『～on』片語整理

💡 **base on** 以為根據；基礎

When writing your report, you must **base** your point of view **on** actual studies.
撰寫報告的時候，你的觀點必須以實際研究作為基礎。

💡 **bear on** 與…有關；對…有影響

One's health has much **bearing on** one's life style.
一個人的健康與他的生活方式非常有關。

💡 **comment on** 評論；發表意見

The chief manager of Jack's company refused to **comment on** the scandal.
傑克公司的總經理對這則醜聞不予置評。

💡 **dwell on** 沉思默想；思考

Johnson loves to **dwell on** things and he never gets tired of it.
強森喜歡思考事情，且從不感到厭倦。

💡 **feed on** 以…為食

Bats **feed on** small insects and uses supersonic waves to prey.
蝙蝠利用超聲波捕捉小昆蟲來作主食。

💡 **insist on** 堅決要求；堅持；強調

I **insist on** not accepting Mary as a member because she has a bad temper.
我堅持不同意瑪麗入會，因為她脾氣不好。

move on to 移到

Susan **moved on to** the next page of the novel.
蘇珊繼續閱讀下一頁的小說。

settle on 決定；選定

I can't **settle on** where to spend the holiday.
我無法決定該去哪裡渡假。

最 常考有關『on the ~』片語整理

on the spot 當場

The clerk was fired **on the spot**.
那個職員被當場解雇。

on the way 在途中

No wonder Mr. Lyan was late; his car broke down **on the way**.
難怪萊恩先生會遲到，他的車在路上拋錨了。

on the way home 在回家途中

She stopped at the supermarket **on the way home** to buy some printing materials.
她在回家途中順便去超市購買列印材料。

on the safe side 安全起見

To be **on the safe side**, the store was closed during the turmoil.
為了安全起見，商店在動亂期間停止營業。

on the ground 當場；在地上；實地

Those who spit **on the ground** will be despised by others.
隨地吐痰的人會被他人鄙視。

精準必考

最 常考有關『on the ~ of』片語整理

on the brink of 瀕臨；處於…的邊緣

She was **on the brink of** resigning after her manager announced the company's latest employee regulation.
經理宣布了公司最新的員工條例後，她處在辭職的邊緣。

on the edge of 在…的邊緣

Margaret was sitting nervously **on the edge of** her chair.
瑪格麗特忐忑不安地坐在椅子的邊緣。

最 常考有關『~ out』片語整理

break out 突發；爆發

The war **broke out** in 2003 and greatly damaged the economy.
戰爭於2003年爆發，經濟遭受重創。

bring out 出版；說明；闡明；襯托出

The dress really **brings out** the color of your eyes.
這件洋裝確實地襯托了妳眼睛的顏色。

carry out 執行；實現

Let's **carry out** the plan before our competitors figure out our strategy.
在競爭者發現我們的戰略之前，執行計畫吧。

cross out 劃掉

My boss **crossed out** the wrong numbers from the report.
老闆劃掉報告裡面錯誤的數字。

dash out 衝出

Everyone **dashed out** of the burning restaurant.
大家都從起火的餐廳內奪門而出。

give out 分發；散發；用完

A delivering system has been established to give out food.
分發食物的傳輸系統已經建立完成。

make out 辨認；理解；填寫；說明

Can you make out the names listed on the paper?
你能夠辨認出這張紙上的名字嗎？

rule out 否決；排除

The manager ruled out my proposal this morning.
經理今早否決了我的提案。

sell out 售完；賣光

All the down jackets were sold out in the extremely cold winter.
在這個異常寒冷的冬季，所有羽絨夾克都銷售一空。

spread out 散布；散開

I spread out the jam on the bread.
我把麵包上的果醬塗開。

squeeze out 擠出

She squeezed out some toothpaste onto her toothbrush.
她把一些牙膏擠到了牙刷上。

wear out 穿壞；使精疲力盡

Children wear out their shoes very quickly.
孩子們很快就能把鞋穿壞。

be tired out 累壞

The students were tired out after hiking.
遠足結束後學生們都筋疲力盡了。

After jogging for an hour, Tom was tired out.
慢跑一小時後，湯姆筋疲力盡。

精準必考

最 常考有關『out of ~』片語整理

💡 out of breath　上氣不接下氣；喘不過氣

By the time Jim finished the marathon he was completely out of breath.
吉姆跑完馬拉松後完全喘不過氣來。

💡 out of blue　未預料到；突如其來

Enterprises often have to deal with problems that are out of blue.
企業經常要處理突如其來的狀況。

💡 out of date　過時的

Many machines in the workshop are out of date.
工作坊裡的許多機器都是過時的。

💡 out of danger　脫離危險

The operation was successful; the patient is now out of danger.
手術很成功，病患現在脫離了危險。

💡 out of fashion　退流行

This dress is out of fashion now.
這件洋裝現在退流行了。

💡 out of one's mind　忘卻；發狂；心不在焉；失去理智

Mary is a weirdo; everyone thinks she's out of her mind.
瑪麗是個古怪的人，大家都認為她瘋了。

This old man seems to be out of his mind.
這位老人看起來失去了理智。

💡 out of order　壞了；無法正常運作

This device is completely out of order.
這台儀器徹底壞了。

💡 out of reach　無法取得

Tom had to use a ladder to pick the apples because they were out of reach.
因為搆不著，湯姆只好靠梯子來摘蘋果。

out of one's reach 搆不著

The alert squirrel climbed up to the top of a tree and was out of my reach.
那隻警惕的松鼠跑到了樹頂上，讓我搆不著牠。

out of stock （商品）賣完

Please notify our boss that the computers are out of stock.
請通知老闆，電腦已經沒有現貨了。

out of use 作廢；不再使用；淘汰了的

Many out of used Russian weapons were sold to India.
許多已淘汰掉的俄羅斯武器被賣到了印度。

out of work 失業；沒工作

It is unbelievable that an expert like uncle Bush would be out of work one day.
連像布希叔叔那樣的專家也有失業的一天，真是難以致信。

out of touch with 不接觸；不聯繫

Satellite phones can prevent climbers from being out of touch with the outside world.
衛星電話可以防止登山者與外界失去聯絡。

最 常考有關『out of the ~』片語整理

out of the blue 未預料到；突如其來

The news of Mary's marriage came nowhere out of the blue.
瑪麗即將結婚的消息來得很突然。

out of the way 讓避

Tom drove all the jellyfishes out of the way.
湯姆把所有水母都趕開了。

out of the question 不可能；沒得商量

We can go to Taipei for Christmas, but going to Hawaii is out of the question.
我們可以去台北過聖誕節，但我們絕不可能去夏威夷。

◐ 片語／精準必考

🤍 out of the ordinary 不尋常；特別

Has anything **out of the ordinary** happened since I've been away?
我不在的時候有沒有發生不尋常的事情？

最 常考有關『pay～』片語整理

🤍 pay off 償清；奏效

Did your bold plan **pay off**?
你大膽的計畫成功了嗎？

🤍 pay for 為付出代價；支付；賠償

We **paid** two hundred dollars per month **for** the machine.
為了這台機器，我們每月支付兩百美元。

🤍 pay a visit to 參觀

Peter **paid a visit to** the company.
彼得參觀了那家公司。

🤍 pay attention to 注意

The supervisor told the employees to **pay attention to** their attitude.
主管告訴員工要注意自己的態度。

最 常考有關『plan～』片語整理

🤍 plan on 打算；計畫

Is Jasmine still **planning on** getting her master's abroad?
賈斯敏還在計畫出國讀碩士嗎？

🤍 plan to 計畫；打算做某事

Believe it or not, the company is **planning to** add a new RD department.
信不信由你，公司正計畫新增一個研發部門。

最 常考有關『play~』片語整理

play a trick on 捉弄

My friends played a trick on me on Halloween.
萬聖節那天我被朋友們捉弄了。

play the piano 彈鋼琴

My younger sister is very artistic. She can dance, sing, and play the piano.
我的妹妹很有藝術天份,她會跳舞、唱歌,還會彈鋼琴。

play the role of 扮演…角色;擔任…的角色

Tom was asked to play the role of the villain.
湯姆被要求扮演戲劇中壞人的角色。

最 常考有關『point』片語整理

point out 指出

We have to point out that your computer is apt to break down.
我們必須指出你的電腦很容易壞。

in point 中肯的;相關的;恰當的

To give a case in point is a good way to introduce new ideas.
舉個中肯的例子是介紹新概念的好方法。

see the point 領會其意義;瞭解重點

I don't see the point of the boss's remark.
我不明白老闆那番言論的重點。

beside the point 離題;無關緊要的

The manager asked Mary to ignore details that are beside the point.
經理叫瑪麗忽略那些無關緊要的細節。

⬤ 片語／精準必考

最 常考有關『poor ~』片語整理

💡 **poor chance** 機會不大

They have a poor chance of winning the bid.
他們贏得競標的機會不大。

💡 **poor in spirit** 精神不好

Jeff was poor in spirit after the night shift.
傑夫值過晚班後精神不佳。

最 常考有關『put ~』片語整理

💡 **put away** 存起來；收拾起來

I have finally put away enough money for a trip to Egypt.
我終於存到了去埃及的旅行費。

💡 **put down** 鎮壓；記下；登記；寫下來

The riot was put down by the troops.
暴亂被軍隊鎮壓了。

💡 **put through** 使經歷；完成

The project has been put through successfully.
那項計畫已經大功告成。

💡 **put out** 撲滅；關熄

The huge fire was not put out due to strong wind.
因為強風的影響，大火尚未被撲滅。

💡 **put forth** 呈現；提出

The coach told the players to put forth their efforts in order to win.
教練告訴球員們，表現出最佳的實力並以此獲勝。

💡 **put into use** 使用

Another robot has been put into use recently.
近來又有一個機器人開始被投入使用。

精準必考

be put into practice 實施

The new rules will **be put into practice** starting from July 1st.
新規範將於七月一日起開始實施。

put one's mind on 專心於

Putting your mind on work will help you perform better.
專心工作會讓你有更好的表現。

最 常考有關『raise～』片語整理

raise a question 提出問題

The boss **raised a question** for discussion.
老闆提出了一個需要討論的問題。

raise one's voice 提高音量

It is considered impolite to **raise one's voice** in the office.
在辦公室大聲講話是不禮貌的。

最 常考有關『run～』片語整理

run for 競選

Bob intends to **run for** mayor after two years.
鮑伯想在兩年後競選市長。

run into 陷入；撞到；遇見

I **ran into** an old friend on my way to your house.
我在來你家的路上遇到了一個老朋友。

最 常考有關『second～』片語整理

second nature 後天養成的習慣；第二天性

Tom is a very good actor. Acting is like the **second nature** to him.
湯姆是一位非常優秀的演員。演戲就像他的第二天性。

second to none 不亞於人；無人能出其右

The handcraft of Swiss watches is second to none.
瑞士手錶的工藝無人能及。

on second thought 再度考慮後；深思

On second thought, the boss changed his mind.
再度考慮後，老闆改變了主意。

a second language 第二語言

In general, students who learnt English as a second language don't get a chance to speak it at home.
通常，以英語作為第二語言的學生在家裡都沒有講英語的機會。

最 常考有關『secret』片語整理

open secret 公開的祕密

It's an open secret that Tom and Mary are engaged.
湯姆和瑪麗訂婚之事是個公開的祕密。

business secret 商業機密

We should be cautious not to disclose business secrets to our rivals.
我們要小心謹慎，不能把商業機密洩露給競爭對手。

in secret 保密

The two companies made a deal in secret.
兩家公司偷偷達成了協議。

keep secret 保密

Letters with important information should be kept secret.
包含重要資訊的信件應該保持機密。

make no secret of 毫不隱瞞

Tom makes no secret of the fact that he is gay.
湯姆對他是同性戀的事情毫不隱瞞。

最 常考有關『sense』片語整理

make sense 符合邏輯；講得通；有意義

What you just said did not make sense at all.
你剛說的話一點也不符合邏輯。

in a sense 在某種意義上；某種層面上

In a sense, the chairman has no actual authority.
從某種意義上來說，這個主席並沒有實際的權力。

moral sense 道德感

The businessman has lost his moral sense.
這名商人已經失去了道德感。

common sense 常識

It is common sense that water will become vapor when the temperature is high enough.
溫度夠高時，水就會變為蒸氣，這是一種常識。

a sense of humor 幽默感

She is a person with a sense of humor; people always enjoy hanging out with her.
她是個有幽默感的人，人們總是喜歡和她在一起。

最 常考有關『set』片語整理

set about 出發；著手

She set about the report once she was available.
一有時間她便開始著手寫報告。

set off 出發

In order to arrive there on time, we had better set off early tomorrow morning.
為了準時到那裡，明天一早我們最好就出發。

💬 **set out** 出航；出發

The rock climbing expedition **set out** from base camp early this morning.
攀岩探險隊一大早就從大本營出發了。

💬 **set sail** 起航

The liner **set sail** for New York at 8:30.
輪船八點半起航開往紐約。

💬 **set up** 建立；創立

James **set up** his own company when he was 17 years old.
詹姆斯在十七歲那年就成立了自己的公司。

💬 **set an example** 樹立模範；以身作則

Serena **set an example** to us by working hard.
薩蓮娜通過努力工作，為我們樹立了榜樣。

最 常考有關『so』片語整理

💬 **so far** 目前

So far, our sales are terrible.
目前，我們的銷量差極了。

💬 **not so much as** 甚至沒有

Ann won't do **so much as** cleaning her own room.
安連清理自己的房間都不願意。

💬 **so as to** 以便

Tom quickly finished supper **so as to** get to the theater on time.
湯姆匆忙吃完了晚飯，以確保能夠準時到達電影院。

最 常考有關『stand』片語整理

💬 **stand at** 躊躇；達到；站立

Tom **stood at** the table, waiting for the guests to come.
湯姆站在桌旁，等候客人到來。

精準必考

🌱 **stand by** 在一旁；袖手旁觀

No matter what happens, I will always **stand by** your side.
不論未來發生什麼事，我都會永遠站在你這邊。

🌳 **stand for** 代表；象徵

The popular word "DINK" **stands for** "double income no kids".
流行用語「頂克」的意思是指「夫妻皆有收入，但是沒有孩子」。

💡 **stand a chance** 有機會；有…的希望

The company didn't **stand a chance** of winning the bid against its opponents.
這家公司沒有可以擊敗對手獲得競標的機會。

最 常考有關『start』片語整理

🌸 **start a fire** 放火；生火

Tom mixed the two substances together, which immediately **started a fire**.
湯姆把兩種物質混合起來，結果立刻就起火了。

🌱 **start to** + 原形動詞 開始；著手

Realizing how serious the problem was, he **started to** worry.
意識到問題的嚴重性後，他開始擔心了。

🌱 **start** + 動名詞 開始；著手

He walked into the office, sat on the chair and **started** working.
他走進辦公室，坐在椅子上然後開始工作。

最 常考有關『step』片語整理

🌸 **step inside** 走進裡面

Steve fell fast asleep right after **stepping inside** the house.
史蒂夫剛邁入家門就呼呼大睡。

○ 片語／精準必考

💡 **step out of** 從…出來

As they **stepped out of** the plane in Honolulu, the tourists were given leis.
在檀香山一踏出飛機，遊客們就被獻上了花環。

最 常考有關『surprise』片語整理

💡 **take ~ by surprise** 奇襲；使吃驚

The company **took** everyone **by surprise** with its growing profit.
這家公司利潤的增加使所有人感到吃驚。

💡 **to one's surprise** 出乎…意料

To our surprise, the slowest employee finally caught up with the others.
出乎我們的意料，動作最慢的那名員工最後終於趕上了大家的進度。

最 常考有關『take』片語整理

💡 **take advice** 採取建議

Jim was so stubborn that he never **took advice** from others.
吉姆固執到從不接受別人的建議。

It's important to **take advice** from the consultant company.
聽從顧問公司的建議是很重要的。

💡 **take apart** 剖析；拆開

I know how to repair the speakers without **taking** the radio **apart**.
我知道如何在不拆卸收音機的情況下維修喇叭。

💡 **take away** 帶走

The old machine has been **taken away**.
那台舊機器已經被帶走了。

💡 **take care** 當心；注意

We must **take care** so that no one overhears our conversation.
我們要謹慎些，不讓任何人聽見我們的談話。

精準必考

take off 出發;起飛;發射;脫掉

The spectators were eager to see the rocket take off into space.
觀眾迫不及待地要看火箭發射到太空中。

take cover 躲避

It was snowing heavily and we took cover in the garage.
我們躲到車庫,避開外面的大雪。

take pains 盡力去做

Kathy took great pains in decorating her new house.
凱西花費了很大的力氣裝修新房子。

take place 發生

I had to alter my plan because some changes took place.
由於情況有變,我只好改變原訂計畫。

take risks 冒險

To innovate sometimes means to take risks.
改革創新有時候意味著冒險。

take up 拿起;占據;開始從事

Last year's research on mobile phones took up all my energy.
去年那個關於手機的研究耗費了我所有的精力。

take somebody's breath away 使羨慕不已;使目瞪口呆

The flowers took my breath away.
那些花美得幾乎讓我窒息。

take some time to do 花費時間做某事

It took a short time for Lucy to manage the company.
露西花了很短的時間就成功管理了這家公司。

take it or leave it 要麼接受要麼放棄;不容討價還價

It is the only food I could find in our fridge; take it or leave it.
這是我在冰箱裡唯一能找到的食物,取捨請自便。

take ~ by surprise 奇襲；使吃驚

The gift from John **took** Mary **by surprise**, and she couldn't wait to open it.
約翰送的禮物讓瑪麗十分驚訝，她迫不及待地想打開這份驚喜。

take great pains 花大力氣；煞費苦心

Samuel **took great pains** to design a new model for laptop computers.
薩穆爾嘔心瀝血地為筆記型電腦設計了新機種。

take ... for granted 習以為常；視為理所當然

The way that Mike **took** everything **for granted** enraged others.
邁克把每件事情都視為理所當然的行為激怒了他人。

最 常考有關『take a ~』片語整理

take a ride 乘車；乘坐遊樂設施

Tom and Jim came to the amusement park to **take a ride** on the roller coaster.
湯姆和吉姆為了乘坐雲霄飛車而來到了遊樂園。

take a step 採取步驟

The manager taught the employees how to **take a step** in the right direction.
經理教導員工如何向正確的方向前進。

take a (one's) seat 就座；坐下

After all the interviewees **took a seat**, group interview began.
每位面試者都就座後，群體面試便開始了。

take a favorable turn 好轉

The firm's condition finally **took a favorable turn**.
公司的情況終於有所好轉。

After some unfortunate years, Tom's life finally **took a favorable turn**.
過了幾年悲慘的日子，湯姆的生活終於好轉起來了。

take a day off 休假一日

You'd better **take a day off** to go to the beach.
你最好休假一天，去海邊玩玩。

🌱 **take a chance** 冒險；投機；試運氣

He decided to take a chance on the investment.
他決定冒險投資。

🌱 **(cf) stand a chance of** 有…的希望；有…的可能

The basketball players did not stand a chance of winning the competition.
這些籃球隊員完全沒有機會贏得比賽。

最 常考有關『take ~ in』片語整理

🌱 **take pride in** 以…為驕傲；以…為榮

Employees of Sona used to take pride in their company.
索納公司的員工曾經以他們的公司為榮。

🌱 **take part in** 參加

The boss agreed to take part in the meeting next week.
老闆同意參加下週舉行的會議。

🌱 **take pleasure in** 享受其中的樂趣

Jane takes pleasure in her work as a cook.
珍享受當廚師的樂趣。

最 常考有關『take ~ of』片語整理

🌱 **take care of** 注意；處理；負責；照顧；撫養

Being well taken cared of, the baby is very strong.
在受到良好的照顧之下，孩子長得很健壯。

🌱 **take charge of** 負責

I took charge of the team after the captain had left.
隊長離開後，由我接管球隊。

🌱 **take hold of** 抓住；握住

We should take hold of every business opportunity.
我們應該抓住每一個商業機會。

● 片語／精準必考

常考有關『throw』片語整理

💬 **throw up** 嘔吐；拋起

I don't feel like eating anything. I feel like **throwing up**.
我什麼也不想吃，我想吐。

💬 **throw out** 扔出；突出；扔掉

The old business books will be **thrown out** and new ones will be printed.
那些舊的商業書籍將會被丟棄，新的書籍將會被發行。

💬 **throw a party** 舉辦派對

The students always **throw a party** on Christmas Eve.
學生們總會在聖誕節前夕開派對。

💬 **throw oneself into** 熱心從事；投身於

Frank **threw himself into** revitalizing the company's sales and successfully gained support from others.
弗蘭克投身於重振公司的銷售業績，並且成功獲得了其他人的支持。

💬 **throw ... at** + 某人 朝某人丟東西

I have always wanted to **throw** something **at** him.
我早就想拿東西丟他了。

Kids are told not to **throw** things **at** others.
小孩子被教導不可以朝別人扔東西。

💬 **throw ... away** 丟掉⋯

Throw it **away**.
把它丟掉。

常考有關『to ~』片語整理

💬 **to begin with** 首先

To begin with, I will explain the framework of the plan.
首先，我會解釋一下這個計畫的框架。

精準必考

🌱 to tell the truth　說實話

To tell the truth, the phone you have bought is overpriced.
說實話，你買的那部電話實在太貴了。

最 常考有關『to one's ~』片語整理

🌱 to one's face　當面

The boss told Bob to his face that he was fired.
老闆當面告訴鮑勃他被解雇了。

🌱 to one's surprise　令人吃驚的是

Much to our surprise, Anna, who is only twenty-two, got married last month.
令我們驚訝的是，才二十二歲的安娜上個月結婚了。

最 常考有關『to + 原形動詞』片語整理

🌱 begin to　開始；開始做某事

Becoming aware of the importance of environment protection, we began to develop the technology on recycling.
意識到環境保護的重要性後，我們開始發展回收利用的技術。

🌱 decide to　決定

Acting on my advice, Jack decided to study harder.
根據我的提議，傑克決定更加努力學習。

🌱 intend to　想做；打算

The puppy was so cute that Jane intended to buy it.
小狗是那麼的可愛，以致於珍想要買下牠。

🌱 manage to　達成；設法

I can manage to finish the job before deadline.
我可以在截止日期前完成工作。

◐ 片語／精準必考

💬 **prepare to** 為準備；做準備

You must **prepare to** deal with the customers' tall order.
你必須準備好應對顧客不合理的要求。

💬 **advise ~ to** 規勸；建議某人做某事；勸告

I **advised** you **to** study everyday.
我勸你每天都要研讀功課。

💬 **be about to** 剛要；即將；打算

It is said that the vice president **is about to** resign.
據說副董事長將要辭職。

💬 **be ready to** 準備好做⋯

These new comers **are** not yet **ready to** handle such difficult cases.
這些新來的人還不能夠處理這麼麻煩的案件。

💬 **tell** + 某人 + **to** + 做某事　告訴某人做某事

She **told** him not **to** call her anymore, but he called anyway.
她叫他不要再打電話給她，但他還是打了。

最 常考有關『to + 名詞』片語整理

💬 **to the day** 恰好；一天不差

We joined the Youth Club one year **to the day**.
我們恰好一年前加入了青年俱樂部。

💬 **to the core** 透頂的；十足的

These pears are delicious **to the core**.
這些梨子好吃至極。

💬 **to one's taste** 合某人的胃口

This beverage answered **to the customers' taste**.
這款飲料很符合顧客的胃口。

💬 **much to one's taste** 很合某人的胃口

The design is **much to teenagers' taste**.
這個設計相當符合青少年的胃口。

💬 **to some degree** 稍稍；多少；到某程度

To some degree, the chairman is not in actual control of the enterprise.
就某種程度來說，主席並沒有真正的掌控這家企業。

最 常考有關『~ to + 名詞／代名詞』片語整理

🌱 **amount to** 合計；總共達到；等於

The total sales of the company didn't **amount to** more than a few million dollars.
這家公司的總銷售額並沒有超過幾百萬美元。

🌱 **cling to** 堅持

He still **clings to** the wrong ideas no matter what we tell him.
不管我們怎麼說，他始終堅持那些錯誤的觀念。

🌱 **consent to** 同意；贊成；答應

The boss **consented to** giving her a promotion.
老闆答應幫她升職。

🌱 **due to** 由於

The sports meeting was called off **due to** the storm.
運動會因為暴風雨而取消了。

🌱 **listen to** 聽講；聽；聽別人說

My brother likes to **listen to** deafening rock music.
我弟弟喜歡聽震耳欲聾的搖滾樂。

💬 **next to** 幾乎；緊挨著；差不多

Let's put these materials **next to** the computer.
讓我們把這些材料放在電腦旁邊吧。

owe to 歸功於；靠

I **owe** it **to** the director who recently promoted me.
我還欠最近提拔我的主管一份人情。

stick to 堅守

All along the firm has **stuck to** the principle that customers are gods.
這家公司一直堅守顧客是上帝的原則。

turn to 求助於；翻到；轉到

You'd better **turn to** the police for help.
你最好還是請警察幫忙處理。

be loyal to 對…忠實

Every soldier should **be loyal to** his motherland.
每一位士兵都應該對祖國忠心。

be helpful to 對…有幫助；對…有益

Thank you for your kindness. You have **been** very **helpful to** me.
感謝您的仁慈，您對我的幫助很大。

最 常考有關『try ~』片語整理

try out 試驗；測試

Jane decided to **try out** the DVD player before buying it.
珍決定在購買前先測試一下這台DVD播放機。

try one's best 盡最大努力；盡力

We will **try our best** to meet the deadline.
我們會竭盡全力趕上交期。

try to 設法；試著

Tom **tried to** make the baby laugh by making faces.
湯姆試圖用做鬼臉來逗嬰兒笑。

精準必考

最 常考有關『turn』片語整理

turn against 敵對；反感

The clerk's rude and unpleasant manners caused the others to **turn against** him.
這個職員粗魯且討人厭的舉止讓其他人開始敵視他。

turn down 關小；減低

Mary **turned** the TV **down** as Tom started his work.
湯姆開始工作後，瑪麗便調低了電視音量。

turn in 歸還；上交；繳交

We were asked to **turn in** the essay by this Friday.
我們被要求在這週五前上交文章。

turn off 關掉

I told you that you should **turn off** the computer after finishing your work.
我告訴過你工作完成之後應該關掉電腦。

turn on 打開

Could you ask your secretary to **turn on** central heating?
你能請你的祕書打開中央供熱系統嗎？

turn out 證明是；結果是；生產；翻轉

Though Mary worked hard on the program, it **turned out** to be not satisfactory.
雖然瑪麗很努力的做這個項目，但結果並不令人滿意。

turn to 求助於；轉向；變成

Nobody knows the word; I had to **turn to** the dictionary for help.
沒有人認得這個單字，我只好求助於辭典。

turn a deaf ear to 充耳不聞

Teenagers often **turn a deaf ear to** their parents' words.
青少年總是對父母的囑咐充耳不聞。

精準必考

最 常考有關『under ～』片語整理

👅 under no circumstance 在任何情況下都不；無論如何都不

Tom is monitored and under no circumstance can he leave the house.
湯姆受到監視，他在任何情況下都不被允許離開房子。

👅 under any circumstances 在任何情況之下

The boss won't change his mind under any circumstances.
老闆在任何情況下都不會改變意見。

👅 under the circumstance 在這種情況下；既然如此

Under the circumstance, we may say that we have made the right choice.
在這種情況之下，我們可以說之前的決策是正確的。

👅 under the command of 在…指揮下

The clerks cleaned the office under the command of the manager.
職員們在經理的指揮下打掃辦公室。

最 常考有關『～up』片語整理第一組

👅 back up 支持

Will you back me up on my sales plan, John?
約翰，你會支援我的銷售計畫嗎？

👅 brush up 溫習

I have to brush up on math tonight, as there is an exam tomorrow.
我今晚得溫習數學，因為明天有考試。

👅 clean up 打掃…

It's your turn to clean up the classroom.
輪到你們打掃教室了。

👅 cover up 掩飾；蓋住；掩蓋

Every thief thinks he can cover up his crime.
每個小偷都以為自己能夠掩蓋犯罪行徑。

dig up 挖掘

Newspapers love to **dig up** scandals.
報紙喜歡揭發醜聞。

end up 下場

Dan loves gambling and may **end up** in debt.
丹熱愛賭博，下場可能會是負債累累。

fix up 修理

The wrecked car was sent to the car repair factory to be **fixed up**.
撞壞的車子被送去修車廠進行維修。

make up 彌補；化妝；編造

Tom said he would try hard to **make** it **up** for his mistakes.
湯姆答應要盡力彌補自己犯的錯。

mess up 搞砸

Tom's mistake **messed up** the plan.
湯姆的失誤搞砸了計畫。

最 常考有關『～up』片語整理第二組

pop up 突然出現；突如其來

The supervisor often **pops up** out of nowhere.
主管常常會不知從哪突然跳出來。

speak up 提高說話的音量

The boss asked Jack to **speak up**.
老闆叫傑克說話大聲點。

speed up 加速；加快

How should I **speed up** the reaction?
我應該怎麼加快反應的速度呢？

精準必考

⊙ 片語／精準必考

💡 **stay up** 不睡；晚睡；熬夜；站立

We are not allowed to **stay up** even on weekends.
即使在週末我們也不被允許晚睡。

💡 **stand up** 站起來

When the new director showed up, everyone **stood up** all at once.
當新主管出現時，所有人都一起站了起來。

💡 **turn up** 出現；發現；發生

Since she hasn't **turned up** yet, I think we'd better go.
既然她到現在還沒有出現，我覺得我們還是先出發吧。

💡 **use up** 用光

The floating capital is getting **used up**.
流動資金快被用光了。

💡 **wrap up** 包裝

Dick **wrapped up** his stuff and left the office.
迪克包起他的東西，離開了辦公室。

最 常考有關『～ up with 』片語整理

💡 **catch up with** 趕上

Tom is **catching up with** Jerry in the relay race.
接力比賽中，湯姆正追趕上傑瑞。

💡 **come up with** 提供；提出；想出；發明

I can't **come up with** any ideas.
我想不到任何主意。

💡 **be bound up with** 與…有密切關係

One's outcome **is bound up with** one's efforts.
一個人的成果與其付出的努力有很大關聯。

精準必考

最 常考有關『～with』片語整理

coincide with 與…一致；符合

His tastes and habits **coincide with** those of his older brother.
他的品味和習慣都與他哥哥的一致。

comply with 遵守；照做

If you don't **comply with** the rules, you will get punished.
如果你不遵守規矩，你會遭到懲罰。

continue with 繼續做

Would you please **continue with** your work and allow me to leave?
請您繼續工作，並允許我離開，好嗎？

deal with 處理；應付；涉及

After a period of time, we will continue to **deal with** that project.
一段時間之後，我們將繼續處理那項工程。

dance with 與…跳舞

As the concert began, the audience cheered and **danced with** exhilaration.
音樂會一開始，觀眾們高興地開始歡呼和跳躍。

fight with 吵架

The two sisters are constantly **fighting with** each other.
那對姊妹經常吵架。

grapple with 與…搏鬥；努力克服

We **grappled with** the problem for a long time before we found a solution.
找到解決方法之前，我們和這個問題搏鬥了好久。

quarrel with 與…爭吵

Grandpa Lee **quarreled with** the two boys who broke his window.
李爺爺和那兩個打破他家窗戶的男孩吵了一架。

● 片語／精準必考

🗣 reason with 和⋯理論

I realized it was useless to **reason with** Tom.
我發現和湯姆理論毫無意義。

🗣 start with 從⋯開始

Let's **start with** the leading issue on social welfare.
讓我們從社會福利的主要問題開始進行討論。

🗣 be satisfied with 滿意

Not **satisfied with** the salary, Lily made the decision to resign.
因為對薪水不滿意，莉莉決定辭職。

🗣 something wrong with 有問題；出毛病；不對頭

There is **something wrong with** your company's marketing strategy.
你們公司的行銷策略有點問題。

最 常考有關『~up with』片語整理

🗣 come up with 提供；提出；想出

How do they **come up with** ideas for the new inventions?
他們是如何想到新發明點子的？

🗣 catch up with 趕上

In order to **catch up with** others, Jack worked very hard.
為了趕上大家，傑克非常努力地工作。

🗣 keep up with 追上；趕上

I found it hard to **keep up with** my associates when I first started working.
剛開始工作的時候，我覺得很難趕上同事們的步調。

🗣 make up with 和⋯和好

After the argument, Tom and Mary decided to **make up with** each other.
吵完架以後，湯姆和瑪麗決定和好。

精準必考

put up with 忍受

Ann is an annoying person that can be very hard to put up with.
安是個煩人的人，讓人難以忍受。

be fed up with 受夠了

The worker was fed up with his boss and quit his job.
員工受夠了他的老闆，終於辭職了。

be bound up with 與…有密切關係

His wealth is tightly bound up with the stock price.
他的財產和股價緊密相連。

最 常考有關『work~』片語整理

work abroad 在國外工作

He's working abroad.
他在國外工作。

work hard 努力工作

You have to work harder to catch up with Peter.
為了趕上彼得，你必須加倍努力工作。

work out 實現；解決；算出；健身；結果

It seems incredible for them to have worked out the problem in two days.
他們僅用了兩天就解決了問題，這顯得很不可思議。

最 常考有關『talk~』片語整理

talk with 與…交談；談論

It is a tradition of the company for the CEO to have a face to face talk with every new employee.
總裁與每位新進的員工面對面交談，這是公司的傳統。

精準必考

💡 **talk about** 談論某事；談話

Having a lot in common, we had many things to **talk about**.
因為有許多共同之處，我們有很多事情可以聊。

💡 **talk over** 討論

I need to **talk** it **over** with my son first to see if he wants to play basketball.
我必須先跟兒子討論看看他是否想打籃球。

💡 **talk back at** 和…頂嘴

She regrets having **talked back at** her mother. Now she is being grounded for a month.
她後悔和她母親頂嘴，如今她被禁足一個月。

💡 **talk of** 談論；議論；說到

Talking of fantasy novels, have you read "Twilight"?
說到奇幻小說，你有沒有看過《暮光之城》？

💡 **talk to** 和…說話

Ennis and Jack share an office room but they hardly **talk to** each other.
恩尼斯和傑克共用一個辦公室，但他們幾乎不和對方講話。

Don't **talk to** him anymore because he is a mean person.
不要再和他說話了，他是個小人。

國家圖書館出版品預行編目資料

圖解商業英文單字片語／李冠潔著.--初版.--
臺北市：書泉,2014.03
　面；　公分
ISBN 978-986-121-897-7（平裝）
1.商業英文　2.詞彙　3.慣用語
805.12　　　　　　　　　103000915

3AN5

圖解商業英文單字片語

作　　　者 — 李冠潔(96.5)

發 行 人 — 楊榮川

總 編 輯 — 王翠華

主　　編 — 朱曉蘋

責任編輯 — 吳雨潔

封面設計 — 吳佳臻

出 版 者 — 書泉出版社

地　　　址：106台北市大安區和平東路二段339號4樓

電　　　話：(02)2705-5066　　傳　　真：(02)2706-6100

網　　　址：http://www.wunan.com.tw

電子郵件：shuchuan@shuchuan.com.tw

劃撥帳號：01303853

戶　　　名：書泉出版社

經 銷 商：朝日文化

進退貨地址：新北市中和區橋安街15巷1號7樓

TEL：(02)2249-7714　　FAX：(02)2249-8715

法律顧問　林勝安律師事務所　林勝安律師

出版日期　2014年3月初版一刷

定　　　價　新臺幣390元